Our
Place on
the Island

Also by Erika Montgomery

A Summer to Remember

Our Place on the Island

A Novel

Erika Montgomery

ST. MARTIN'S GRIFFIN
NEW YORK

First published in the United States by St. Martin's Griffin, an imprint of St. Martin's Publishing Group

OUR PLACE ON THE ISLAND. Copyright © 2023 by Erika Montgomery Marks. All rights reserved. Printed in the United States of America. For information, address St. Martin's Publishing Group, 120 Broadway, New York, NY 10271.

www.stmartins.com

Designed by Meryl Sussman Levavi

Library of Congress Cataloging-in-Publication Data

Names: Montgomery, Erika, author.
Title: Our place on the island : a novel / Erika Montgomery.
Description: First edition. | New York : St. Martin's Griffin, 2023.
Identifiers: LCCN 2022060138 | ISBN 9781250783790 (trade paperback) | ISBN 9781250274113 (ebook)
Subjects: LCSH: Martha's Vineyard (Mass.)—Fiction. | LCGFT: Domestic fiction. | Romance fiction. | Novels.
Classification: LCC PS3613.O54856 O67 2023 | DDC 813/.6—dc23/eng/20230113
LC record available at https://lccn.loc.gov/2022060138

Our books may be purchased in bulk for promotional, educational, or business use. Please contact your local bookseller or the Macmillan Corporate and Premium Sales Department at 1-800-221-7945, extension 5442, or by email at MacmillanSpecialMarkets@macmillan.com.

First Edition: 2023

1 3 5 7 9 10 8 6 4 2

Again, always, for Ian, Evie, and Murray

The Baltimore Sun
June 2, 1999

RESTAURANT REVIEW

Not since hotspot À La Carte opened in 1992 has a restaurant appeared on the Baltimore food scene with such well-deserved fanfare as Piquant.

From start to finish, dining at Piquant is more than a meal—it's an event. No wonder twenty-nine-year-old owner Mickey Campbell was just picked as one of *BON APPÉTIT*'s Ones To Watch in the new century. After four years running the kitchen at the Boathouse, Campbell decided to trade her *TOQUE BLANCHE* for an owner's hat, and the result is a perfect fit.

Head chef Wes Isaac, formerly of Dish and whose smoldering good looks could as easily find him on a movie screen as in a kitchen, is the perfect partner for Campbell's dramatic culinary vision. No stranger to bold flavors, his daring menu—which includes a three-chile ceviche, and a smoked sea bass over wasabi angel hair—will heat up even the coolest palate.

Housed in an old bank building, Piquant's décor, like the restaurant's innovative dishes, is a blending of both old and new elements. Vivid Alexander Calder–inspired mobiles spin above original upholstered booths where customers once viewed their safety deposit boxes. The teller window now serves as the restaurant's bar, where head bartender Lucas Conway serves up signature cocktails like the Smoke Screen, a devilish concoction of mezcal and mesquite. Even the original vault door has been preserved; you'll find the restaurant's lively kitchen just beyond it.

And if you don't have room for dessert, don't worry. The expert waitstaff will gladly send you home with your meal's closer packaged in—what else?—a mini safe. (And trust me, their bourbon butterscotch tart is a valuable you'll want to keep locked up just for yourself.)

1

"No walls."

When Mickey Campbell led the first contractor through the old bank building two years ago—even before he plucked the flat pencil from his back pocket and drew with it in the dust-speckled air to show her where he planned to start framing up first—she told him firmly that she didn't want walls in her restaurant.

"But people like walls," he told her. "People need walls. Especially when they're eating." Then he shot her a smile that was nearly all gums. "Trust me. You're going to want walls."

But Mickey didn't trust him—and she didn't hire him. Instead, she found a ponytailed preservation contractor who loved her vision of turning an old bank into an upscale restaurant, and who was as excited as she was to keep the historic fabric in place. A contractor who, with the exception of the bathrooms, didn't erect a single new wall.

But tonight, trying to stay out of sight in the restaurant's office on the second-floor mezzanine, Mickey would give her right arm for just one wall.

The review from the *Sun* sits in the middle of her desk. She's picked it up a dozen times in the last two hours, scanned every glowing word to memory, and she still can't

believe it's real. A restaurant owner could go her whole career and never earn a review half this good. Before opening
Piquant, Mickey was a head chef for four years. She knows
this is true.

She also knows that she should be downstairs celebrating
her success with the rest of her hardworking staff, winding her
way through the collection of two- and four-tops, stopping to
make sure her guests are enjoying their meals, checking the
pass and the bar for what's selling, all the things she does every
night at Piquant.

Instead, she's up here alone and about to jump out of her
skin, nursing a flat Diet Coke in her bare feet, her red leather
pumps cast off into the corner while below her the restaurant
roars with life. It's a soundtrack she knows well: The cheerful
hustle of her beloved servers, expertly zigzagging through the
sea of tables like synchronized swimmers. The clatter of plates
picked up and set down. The clink of ice and the thump of
popped corks as Lucas and his barbacks cruise the gleaming
counter where bank customers used to fill out their deposit
slips.

And, of course, just beyond the old vault door, the restaurant's beating heart: Wes's kitchen, her boyfriend's com-
manding voice rising above the din of the hiss and sizzle of
garlic in a hot pan, the even chop of a blade mincing herbs,
the chime of finished plates landing in the pass. Coming up
the ranks, from runner to prep to sous, Mickey had worked
for chefs who treated their kitchens like libraries, hushing
anyone who dared to raise their voice. She endured the tombs
of their cooking temples and vowed that when she finally had
her own restaurant, she would insist on noise. Lots of it.

Her naivete infuriates her now. That she really believed

ensuring a lively kitchen would be all it took to keep a restaurant in the black.

She gathers the clutter of past-due notices into a pile and shoves them inside her desk. Not so unlike the way she used to cram dirty clothes and magazines from her bedroom floor into her closet when her friends came over after school. If only she could clean up this mess so easily.

She's always known the chance of financial failure for new restaurants is high, that almost sixty percent of them close their first year, and of those that do survive, only twenty percent will still be around in five years. It was Wes who reminded her of the odds within fifteen minutes of their first meeting years earlier, when Mickey had asked him to join her for a cup of coffee at the café down the street from Dish, where he was head chef and creating quite a stir in the industry, quickly becoming known as one of the most innovative—not to mention attractive—young chefs in Baltimore.

When she began thinking seriously about opening her own restaurant, Mickey made a wish list of chefs she wanted running her kitchen, and Wes Isaac was at the top. When he seemed uneasy about signing on with someone who had never owned a restaurant before, Mickey told him what she lacked in experience she made up for in passion and nerve, which piqued his interest enough to grant her a second meeting, then a third. Back and forth they went, phone calls and more after-hours coffee conversations, until, four weeks later, Wes showed up at her doorstep with a bottle of single malt and a shake to seal their agreement. When his hand closed around hers, Mickey felt the electricity of attraction sizzle up her arm, but both agreed they couldn't muddy their partnership with romance—a vow they maintained, miraculously, for almost two months. Until one night in the restaurant's half-finished kitchen, tucked in with takeout and going over possible menus, they stopped to compare kitchen scars. Within minutes, they were like grizzled swordfishermen, hands thrust out over the gleaming stainless countertop, palms up like they were having their life lines read. Wes tried to impress with a brick-oven burn on his wrist, and Mickey matched it with a half-moon on her middle finger from a paring knife that earned her four stitches. He displayed a healed gash on the side of his hand from a Santoku blade, and she raised him the ghost of a blister from a kitchen torch, their bodies leaning closer with each reveal. When she bared a scar on the meat of her thumb, he traced the faint pink thread so slowly that she puddled like an undercooked pot de crème. After they christened the mezzanine (and the floor behind the not-yet-stocked bar) they swore over the rest of their Chinese food that they wouldn't—couldn't—act on their feelings again. But not twenty-four hours later, they were tumbling into her unmade futon. From that night on, they were inseparable—partners in the kitchen as well as the bedroom. A team.

Mickey swigs her soda, regret sizzling as she swallows. If they're such a team, then why has she waited so long to tell him her poor management skills have sent their restaurant into debt?

She picks up the review and scans it again, determined not to let the distraction of tonight's celebration allow her any more excuses. Enough is enough. She has vowed to tell Wes how dangerously behind they are, and she will, dammit.

"So this is where the great Mickey Campbell is hiding from her fans."

Nina, Piquant's front of house manager, appears at the top of the stairs. Her frizzy blond head is peeking around the giant bouquet of pink and peach roses she's holding, the flowers bursting from a flared frosted vase.

Mickey manages a tired smile. "Very funny," she says. "And I'm not hiding."

"Good. Because someone who gets a big, sloppy kiss from the career-make-or-break queen Janine Cowell shouldn't be hiding." Nina sets the arrangement down on Mickey's desk and wipes her palms on her black leather miniskirt. "They're from Duncan. Card's inside."

Mickey's old boss at the Top Shelf, where she got her first job in a kitchen after culinary school. She leans over and buries her nose in the cloud of blooms for a sugary whiff.

"Jeffrey and Lee are waiting at the bar. They want to buy you a celebratory bottle of Dom."

Mickey appreciates the offer from her and Wes's dear friends, but the last thing her frayed nerves need right now is a glass—let alone a bottle—of champagne.

"And Wes wanted me to tell you he'll be up in ten," Nina says, then squares Mickey with a hard stare. "You're going to come clean with him, right?" After Nina accidentally picked up a voice mail from a disgruntled vendor two weeks ago, Mickey had no choice but to confess their financial woes.

Mickey bobs her head calmly, even as her heart races. "Tonight," she says. "I promise."

"Good—because he's still asking me why we stopped hiring new servers and I can't keep lying to him."

"That makes two of us," Mickey mutters, tossing the review back onto her desk with an exasperated sigh.

Nina turns to go. "Oh, and your mother's holding on line two."

Mickey looks over at the blinking console, torn. She doesn't want to be on the phone when Wes comes up, but it's not like her mother to try her at work. If Hedy is calling, there's a good reason.

Mickey picks up. "Hi, Mom."

"I hear congratulations are in order. That lovely manager of yours told me the big news. Four stars! Didn't I feel like a terrible mother not knowing?"

Glancing down, Mickey spots a past-due notice she missed in her earlier sweep and stuffs it into her desk with the others, bumping the drawer closed with her hip. "You couldn't have known, Mom. The review only just came out."

The line goes quiet. "Sweetheart, are you okay? You sound rattled."

"I'm just tired, that's all."

"I know the difference between tired and rattled, Michelle."

Of course, she did. Mickey might have been able to fool her mother when it came to the difference between a bisque and a soup, but on the subject of distinguishing emotions, Hedy Campbell was an expert. An unexpected skill of almost thirty years selling real estate, she claimed.

"I have some news . . ." Her mother pulls in a breath and blows it out dramatically, the sort of exhale that could signal excitement or dread. "Cora's engaged."

Mickey blinks at the bouquet. "Engaged?" She repeats the word as if there's a chance her mother has misused it. Or maybe Mickey has heard wrong. Yes, surely she's heard wrong. Because if her widowed, seventy-two-year-old grandmother— the woman whose passion for food and cooking made Mickey want to be a chef in the first place—if that woman had fallen in love, Mickey would know.

"I don't understand . . ." Mickey reaches behind, wanting

to be sure her chair is close enough to catch her. "Grams is getting married?"

"Remarried, if you want to be technical about it."

Mickey drops into her seat. "To who?"

"To Max Dempsey."

The name is vaguely familiar. "You don't mean the guy who fixes things around the house for her?"

"That's exactly who I mean."

"They're in love?"

"That's usually why people get married, Michelle."

Mickey scans the top of her desk, trying to take this in. "But—but when?"

"When, what?"

"When did they fall in love?"

"I don't have an exact date. You'll have to ask your grandmother."

A pencil sits on the edge of the desk. Mickey grabs it and turns it nervously in her fingers. "But it hasn't been that long since . . ."

"Three years. I can't believe it, either."

Mickey's face flushes with shock but her mother's math is right. The last time she was on Martha's Vineyard was for her grandfather's funeral, just two months before Mickey put down the deposit on the old bank, and the realization startles her almost as much as the news of her grandmother getting married again. How was it possible? Three years away from Beech House is the longest she's ever been gone.

"I wouldn't have bothered you at work, honey, but the thing is . . ." Another deep breath in and out. "They want to have the wedding at Beech House as soon as possible."

"How soon is soon?"

Mickey recognizes the familiar whistling sound that follows: her mother nervously pulling air between her teeth. "This Saturday."

Six days from now? Mickey looks down at the pencil in her hand, wishing suddenly it were a cigarette. She wants to ask why the rush, then lets the question wither in her throat, feeling badly for it: At their ages, who would want to wait?

"I know it's last-minute," her mother says, "but it would mean so much if you could come."

"Of course I want to come, but—"

Movement flashes and Mickey looks up, her breath catching at the sight of Wes standing there.

He swings his side towel over his shoulder and leans easily against the file cabinet, his dark eyes holding hers, and a familiar pulse of longing circles her stomach.

"Michelle? Honey, are you still there?"

Mickey breaks from his gaze and taps the end of her pencil purposefully on a stack of kitchen-supply catalogs. "I'm not sure I can get away just now, Mom."

"I know things are busy . . ." This time her mother's sigh is pure exasperation. Or maybe surrender. Mickey can't decide. "Just say you'll think about it, okay? Oh, and your grandmother wants you to know you can bring a date."

Mickey glances reflexively over at Wes, his wavy, dark hair—the only untidy thing in his kitchen—looking especially thick tonight. He folds his arms patiently over his whites and smiles at her. She's been so anxious to introduce him to her family, and the thought of him in a coat and tie is making her heart race . . .

She clears her throat pointedly. "I'll call you later, okay, Mom?"

"Okay, honey. Love you."

"Love you, too."

Hanging up, Mickey leaves her hand on the phone, needing an extra second, an extra breath, before she rises.

Wes nods to the review on her desk. "I think the *Sun* likes us."

"They like us," Mickey says. "But they love *you*."

He stretches his mouth into a crooked grin. "Is that why you're hiding up here? Because you're jealous?"

"Why does everyone think I'm hiding?" Mickey tosses the pencil back onto her desk and pushes her hair behind her ears. "And I'm not jealous," she says. "I just came up to . . . you know . . ." She gestures lamely at the cluttered surface. "*Organize*."

"Organize later, Beautiful," Wes says. "There are about a hundred people downstairs waiting to buy you a drink."

"So I heard." Perspiration prickles the back of her neck. She spins her long strawberry-blond hair into a twist and holds it up, wanting to get air on her damp skin. Why can she never remember to keep a clip in her drawer?

He pushes off the file cabinet and comes around the desk. "You tell your mom about the review?"

"Nina did before I could." Mickey lets the heavy coil of hair drop to her shoulders again, a deep sigh releasing with it. The mention of Piquant's manager reminds her, giving her a perfect opener—*And speaking of things I need to tell people*—but the words stick in her throat. As much as Mickey vowed to confess their money troubles to him tonight, this news of Cora getting married in six days might mean having to table the truth for a while longer.

"Mick . . ." Wes narrows his gaze. His voice drops an octave. "Is everything okay?"

She picks up the pencil again and resumes a steady

drumbeat against her fingertips. "My grandmother's getting married."

"I didn't know she had a boyfriend."

"Neither did I."

"But I thought you guys were close."

"We are," she says, feeling suddenly as if she's on some kind of trial, the urge to defend herself overwhelming. "I've just been so busy. First trying to get the restaurant open and then trying to make it work." She's tapping the pencil faster now, the reality of all she's put aside to get Piquant off the ground hitting her at once, and that it might be for nothing. "I can't just pick up and run off like I used to, and I didn't exactly think Grams would go and get engaged—"

"Hey . . ." Wes eases the pencil from her hand and pulls her into his arms. Mickey falls against his chest and pulls in a hard breath. "So when's the wedding?" he asks.

"This Saturday."

"Wow."

"I know."

"You told her you'll be there, right?"

"Actually . . . I haven't decided yet."

Wes leans back abruptly, narrowing his dark eyes on her. "Mick. As long as we've been together, I know exactly two things about your life growing up: your grandmother and that house." Mickey wrinkles her lips in a sheepish smile— he's not exaggerating. "You have to be there."

She spreads her hands over his chest and slides her fingers through the two rows of buttons that march up the front of his jacket. "Grams says I can bring a date . . ."

But when she looks up again, Wes's dark eyes are strained, lines of worry carved deep in his heavy brow. "You know I'd go with you in a heartbeat, but that's going to be tough to swing on short notice. There's no way I can get Pete up to speed in time to take over the kitchen for me."

Even as disappointment blooms in her chest, Mickey manages to rearrange her lips into a stoic smile. Bringing Wes to Beech House, to the place where she first learned to love cooking, has been a dream of hers since the first time they cooked together. But even if Wes doesn't know the danger they're in financially, he's right: His brilliant dishes are the reason people are filling their seats—having him gone for even a few days would be disastrous.

Still tears prickle behind her eyes as she worries the curved edge of his collar, not yet daring to meet his gaze.

"Next time, okay?" Wes tips her face up to his, his dark eyes holding hers. "I promise."

Even as he kisses her deeply, her body softening under his mouth like butter left out, a knot of dread cinches in Mickey's stomach, the possibility that after Wes learns she may have mismanaged them into bankruptcy, there won't be a next time.

"I should get back downstairs," he says, pulling away. "Just don't stay up here all night, okay?" Wes raps his knuckles for emphasis on the desk as he rounds it. "By the way . . ." Almost to the stairs, he slows, pivots back. "I thought we were paid up with Sullivan."

Their seafood vendor. *Shit.*

Dread sprints across her scalp. Mickey swallows, praying her voice won't crack. "Why?"

"They never made today's delivery. We had to eighty-six the prawns. You might want to call them."

She manages an agreeable nod, waiting until he's down the stairs before she falls into her chair and drops her forehead into her hands.

Almost fifteen years working in restaurants and Mickey knows all the ways to cut corners: Smaller buns so guests don't notice that you've shaved an ounce or two off their lamb burgers. Up-charging the cheap wine. Replacing twelve-inch plates with eleven-inch ones. Putting fewer berries on the spinach salad. But their money troubles are way past that. And even if the alterations might save them a few bucks, she would never stoop to tricks.

Her gaze drifts back to the phone and her mother's news, and the thought of returning to the warm hug of Beech House fills her tangled heart with calm.

Maybe getting away for a few days wouldn't be such a bad thing?

After all, hadn't the Vineyard and the sanctuary of Beech House always been that for her all those summers growing up—escape? A place to call home when life with Hedy was always up in the air, her mother constantly moving them from apartment to apartment?

Maybe the security of home is just what Mickey needs right now.

Leaning back, she closes her eyes, letting the possibility grow real, and images of Beech House take shape: Rambling rooms fragrant with the smell of the sea, wood floors gritty with beach sand, doorknobs and drawer pulls sticky with watermelon juice and slick with suntan lotion. A kitchen bright with sunlight, bouquets of just-picked herbs fanned out on the counter. Mickey's grandmother Cora pulling down pots and drawing out ingredients from the pantry and the fridge, and setting them down on her beloved kitchen island. Sticks of butter to soften, heads of garlic to roast. Cora's cookbook—pages splattered with oil and floured fingerprints—spread open to a new recipe, the day's treasure map to undiscovered flavors . . .

Longing swells behind Mickey's ribs. If only she could be that girl again, hiding in the warm, fragrant bubble of Beech House's kitchen, where there was no problem that couldn't be washed down with a slice of lemon meringue pie, or, as she grew older, a foamy pitcher of lobster daiquiris.

One upon a time, Beech House was the one place heartbreak and hurt couldn't stick. Water to the world's oil—the two refusing to mix. All these years later, does she dare to think its healing magic might still work?

One thing is certain: She's been gone too long.

Hauling herself up, Mickey reaches across the minefield of bad news and frees the phone from the console.

Her mother picks up on the first ring.

2

MARTHA'S VINEYARD

The sunburned man next to Mickey on the ferry's upper deck wears a watch, and she sneaks a peek. Six-fifty. She meant to get on the road earlier—hoped to—but there had been fires to put out at the restaurant, last-minute calls to make, just desperate plugs in a cracked dam that she hopes will hold for the few days she's gone. Now it will be sunset when the ship finally floats into the harbor, and Mickey finds the low light unsettling. It feels strange to be arriving this late in the day to the Vineyard—as if the whole world has woken up on time and she forgot to set her alarm.

Around her, people line the railing, trying to talk over the roar of the ferry's engines below, women using both hands to hold back their wind-whipped hair, desperate to keep it from lashing their own faces or those of their companions. Children scramble over the benches, determined to test every seat. Mickey smiles, watching them. She, too, used to spend the whole ride on top—no matter the weather, no matter the season—wanting to witness every moment of her arrival, the long-awaited passage from the mainland to the island; a trip across a frothy, green-blue highway that signaled more than just going back to Beech House: It was going back to the place she always considered home.

This trip, however, she can't seem to stay in one place for too long. As many times as she's given herself permission to leave her troubles in Baltimore and allow herself the chance to escape for a few days on the island, Mickey's still spent the hour ride across Vineyard Sound in constant motion, sitting in the cabin, climbing the stairs, or anxiously circling the deck.

And suddenly, she sees the smattering of sailboats, their bare masts like toothpicks from afar, finally visible, and she pulls in a sharp breath, excitement and trepidation flooding her lungs. Here on the ferry she has fought to find comfort in the familiar—the prickly feel of old metal when she squeezes the railing; the cold, salty spray of the wake when she looks over the side—but she can't pretend there won't be changes when she docks. Her grandfather gone. Her grandmother getting married to a man Mickey doesn't know. A man other than her grandfather will be standing in the kitchen when Mickey walks into Beech House this time. A man who will be reaching for her grandmother's hand, who will be climbing the stairs with her at night.

A man, Mickey thinks with a fresh pulse of concern, who might even be there to greet her at the pier.

She needs to start preparing her heart.

The engines quiet as the ship crawls to the dock, and it still strikes her as strange that she's not at the front of the line anymore to disembark when she makes her way to the stairs with the rest of the throng. That she's not eight, dashing around passengers, slippery as an eel, leaving her mother in her wake, yelling for Mickey not to clock anyone with her overstuffed bag as she runs, the soles of her plastic flip-flops resembling Clydesdale hooves as she races down the metal gangplank.

The pier is washed in a silvery pink, the dock crowded with people waving and shouting as they all descend. A quick scan and Mickey sees her mother, Hedy Campbell's copper-colored hair, cut in a chic bob, flame-like in the low light, waving as she steps out of the pack, effortlessly stylish as always in a coral satin shell and white linen pants. Mickey picks up her pace down the gangplank to reach her and lunges in for a long squeeze, pulling in a soft, citrusy breath of her mother's orange-blossom perfume.

When they part, Hedy takes both of her hands. "You look beautiful. And tired." Her mother studies her intently with narrowed eyes, her bronze eyelashes barely fluttering. "You're still not smoking, right?"

Mickey recalls the cigarette she bummed off Lucas on the loading dock a few weeks back after an exhausting night. "Next question."

"Then how about that charming boyfriend of yours?"

"Wes doesn't smoke, Mom."

Her mother's right brow arches. "Cute." She cups Mickey's cheek and sighs. "I saw his picture in *Food and Wine*. No wonder you're rattled."

Mickey leans into her mother's warm palm and smiles. "You have no idea."

* * *

Hedy points them to her silver rental in the crowded lot, clicking the key remote to send the trunk up as they arrive.

Mickey drops her duffel inside and taps it closed. "You didn't have to pick me up, Mom. I could have gotten a cab."

"And risk having the paparazzi tackle you for your picture?" Hedy says as they climb in, and Mickey rolls her eyes. "I'm not kidding." Her mother turns in her seat, eyes huge. "You're a big deal here, kiddo. Prepare yourself. Tiffany framed your *Bon Appétit* article. I saw it when I picked up clam strips yesterday. Right over the order window," she says, starting up the car. "I told her you're coming in tonight. She said she'd swing by tomorrow to check in."

Hedy steers them into the queue of cars waiting to enter the line of stop-and-go traffic on Main Street and Mickey sends her window down, eager to replace the powdery smell of warm upholstery with the malty smell of fried clams drifting over from the seafood shacks that line the pier. She toes off her sandals and presses her bare feet into the rubber mat—the discarding of her shoes upon arrival to the Vineyard as ritualistic as someone changing their watch after an overseas flight: She's on island time now.

"I wondered if they would come with you," Mickey says.

"Your grandmother wanted to get everything ready for you, and Max is staying at his brother's in Edgartown. He wanted us to have the first night to ourselves, just the three of us."

Nice of him, Mickey thinks.

Her mother glances over. "I know it wasn't an easy time to get away."

"Grams is getting married. It's a big deal."

"A very big deal, apparently."

"How big?"

Her mother's glossed lips are a tight line. "She's invited seventy-five people."

Mickey blinks at the dashboard, stunned by the number. "I just assumed it would be something . . ."

"Smaller? Well, that makes two of us." Hedy loosens her fingers on the steering wheel, flexing them nervously before resuming her grip.

Nearing an intersection, the light changes to red and traffic comes to a stop. In front of them, a station wagon with New Jersey plates carries a lopsided stack of luggage on its roof rack. A golden retriever circles the back seat.

"When did you get here?" Mickey asks.

"Yesterday."

"And you and Grams are already fighting?"

Hedy shoots her a chastising look, but her indignation is short-lived. Mickey has witnessed nearly thirty years of her mother and grandmother's prickly relationship. "I'm trying my best, Michelle. It's not exactly a walk in the park, you know. You know how emotional she can be—now imagine your grandmother as a bride."

A group of girls in Black Dog Bakery Café T-shirts, arms linked, dash in front of their stopped car, sending the retriever howling.

The light changes and traffic rolls forward.

"In Grams's defense," Mickey says, "I think every bride must get emotional at some point."

Mickey waits for her mother to weigh in on her theory, but Hedy just glances in her rearview and accelerates. Her mother speaks so rarely of her marriage to Mickey's father, Grant—a union that Mickey knows was made official sooner than planned when Hedy got pregnant, and lasted barely long enough for Mickey to be born before it was dissolved.

Her mother snaps on her blinker and swings them around the station wagon. "We were all disappointed Wes couldn't join you. But I understand. That's how it is when it's your own business and things are hot. You don't dare let them cool."

Mickey shifts in her seat, desperate to change the subject. "Do you like him?"

"I wouldn't know. You refuse to let me meet him."

She rolls her head toward her mother. "I was talking about Max, Mom," she says dryly. "But duly noted."

A satisfied smile tugs at the corners of her mother's mouth.

"So do you?" Mickey asks.

Hedy's shoulders rise and fall. "Max is hard not to like." Her mother says it as if she's actually tried.

They near a sedan going at least ten miles slower, Mickey bets, based on the speed with which her mother gains on the car's bumper. Hedy pumps the brakes but continues to keep a close pursuit. Since when is her mother a tailgater?

Mickey leans back. "Is Max an islander?"

"I really don't know that much about him. Just that he's been on the Vineyard off and on for as long as your grandmother has."

"So Grams has known him a while then?"

"They didn't travel in the same circles—it wasn't like that."

Of course not. Even when she was young, Mickey understood the social order of the island, what it took to be part of the club. And not just the one that sat on the edge of the bluff surrounded by tennis courts and golf links.

"Apparently he was the one who redid the kitchen," Hedy says.

Mickey twists in her seat, this news almost as shattering as the news of Cora's engagement. "Max built the island?"

Everything Mickey learned about cooking at Beech House, she learned standing—first on a step stool, then on her own feet—at that island. More than just a work station, the island was the beating heart of Beech House's kitchen. Customized with special drawers and shelves, it was her grandmother's pride and joy, and as central to the home's operations as the captain's bridge on a ship.

A thought sparks. "Then you must have met him at some point growing up," Mickey says.

Without signaling, Hedy passes the sedan, cutting it close enough that the car in the oncoming lane blares an angry horn before her mother can swerve them back into the lane.

Mickey looks over at her. "Someone's in a hurry."

"You know I don't like being on the road at this hour. All the deer."

"So did you?"

Her mother drums her fingers on the wheel. "Did I what?"

"Ever meet Max when you were younger?"

"If I did, I don't remember."

Mickey wants to press for more information but lets the subject fall away as Hedy steers them around a baby-blue VW bug. There will be time later. For now she just wants to sink into the warm bath of the view and let the comforting embrace of memories take hold. They pass the Vineyard Basket, the grocery store that Mickey used to bike to for last-minute ingredients. The market is shuttered this late, the parking lot empty, but in her mind, Mickey can still see the interior clearly: the baking aisle that always smelled deliciously smoky, where she used to memorize all the herbs in their glass jars; the teeming baskets of freshly baked bread, rounds of sourdough and boules, narrow baguettes standing like swords.

The round sign for Oyster Point glistens in the path of the car's headlights, and her mother pumps the brakes to turn them onto the rutted dirt, the Point's gatehouse appearing in the cone of light, the squat shingled building set in the wedge where the road splits into two drives. More dirt drives disappear into the trees, their shingled cottages hidden behind the thick curtains of pines, and Mickey feels a flush of anticipation when the even purr of the dirt road turns into the crackle of crushed oyster shells under the tires. As they come down the driveway, the silhouette of the carriage house is the first structure Mickey sees in the milky dark, then, briefly, the giant leafy dome of the home's namesake weeping beech in the distance.

When her mother pulls in and cuts the engine, Mickey is struck by the silence. She remembers all the summers they would arrive to a flurry of sound and activity—screen doors and car trunks banged shut, calls for dibs on bedrooms or a race down to the water. Only at night, when the glorious universe of day-chaos finally sank into the hush of darkness and the house slept, could the whoosh of the curling surf below the bluff be heard.

Now Mickey detects the deep breathing of the sea so clearly, it startles her.

"God," she whispers. "It's so quiet."

Stepping out, she feels a flutter of nerves, stranger and more unfamiliar than any silence. When has she ever been nervous about walking into Beech House?

"Enjoy it while you can," her mother says, exiting too. "In a few days, there'll be so many people here you won't be able to hear yourself think." She swings an arm around Mickey's waist and steers them into the cone of floodlights. "You know Beech House can never stay quiet for long."

* * *

Which is exactly what Mickey always loved about it. The noise. The motion. The constant clap of a screen door— someone coming, someone going—the promise of a surprise guest, an impromptu bonfire on the beach, the arrival of greasy take-out bags from Chowder's, heavy with clam strips and onion rings so big that Mickey would slide her hand through them and stack them over her wrists like bracelets, jangling them to make her grandmother laugh.

The formal entrance is at the center of the house's facade, down a winding brick path, but instead, Mickey heads for the dented screen door and the familiar rectangle of amber light behind it, as she always did growing up, choosing the side door because it was the one that would get her to the kitchen fastest.

Stepping inside, Mickey sees the row of hooks where baseball caps and rain slickers dangled and catches the faint, familiar smell of the warm, damp, and peppery old wood of the entry. Where once a tower of shoes—discarded sandals and laceless sneakers—covered the sand-soaked straw mats, only a few pairs occupy the straw mats now, matched and tidy, and Mickey feels irrationally giddy when she toes off her sandals and adds them to the collection. On the bench are a stack of wrapped packages and a few glittering gift bags, bursting with tissue and tendrils of curling ribbon.

Through the mudroom and at the kitchen's threshold, Mickey's feet finally slow, as if her body wants to give her raw heart a minute to catch up, or maybe even a head start, but it's too late.

Cora is already there waiting, arms outstretched. "Hello, darling girl."

Her grandmother's hazel eyes flicker with affection first, then her lips, stained with the faintest blush of pink, stretch into a tender smile. Her enviably high cheekbones—which Hedy inherited but apparently skipped every third generation, Mickey was crushed to learn—are even more pronounced with old age. Her long, frizzy hair, once as copper as Mickey's mother's, is threaded with equal parts silver and red and sits in a whirl atop her head, tied off at the very top with a tiny knot, a hairstyle that Mickey has always and fondly thought resembles a steamed bun.

Maybe it's where Cora is standing, directly under the sink light, or maybe it's just that Mickey's eyes are still adjusting to the brightness after riding in the dark, but her grandmother is glowing. And suddenly, whatever worries Mickey has arrived with slide off with her dropped duffel, to be unpacked later.

She crosses to the island and buries her face in her grandmother's shoulder, not even aware that tears have leaked out until she leans back and Cora brushes them away with her fingertips.

"Sweetie, everyone knows you're supposed to wait until the wedding to start crying."

"Yeah, well . . ." Mickey lets out a little chuckle. "I always forget that part."

Cora appraises her with narrowed eyes. "You're too skinny. I thought chefs were supposed to like to eat."

"I've put on five pounds since Christmas, Grams."

"Then you've gotten taller."

Mickey laughs. "Sure, that must be it."

Her grandmother links her arm through Mickey's and guides them down the counter.

"How was the trip? Are you starving? You're starving," Cora decides, before Mickey can answer. "Let me whip you up an eggplant parmesan sandwich."

Only her grandmother—and maybe Julia Child—would

think an eggplant parmesan sandwich was something pulled together as easily as a PB and J.

"Or how about something cold?" Cora motions to the fridge. "Your mother made a pitcher of lobster daiquiris."

Just the name and Mickey feels her limbs lighten. All the afternoons she'd rush into the kitchen to find a waiting stack of watermelon wedges and piles of glossy peach slices. No one could be sure who came up with the recipe, only that lobster daiquiris—coined for their color but the name always raising a questioning eyebrow from uninitiated guests—were legion at Beech House. As much as Mickey would love nothing more than to draw down a milk-glass tumbler from the cabinet and tuck in with a tall, frosty pour, she doesn't dare.

"I'm so tired, Grams," she says. "One sip would put me out for the night."

"Probably wise . . ." Cora slides a disparaging frown at Hedy. "The way your mother makes them, a few splashes could strip off marine paint."

"Blame Dad." Hedy raises her hands, offering an un-apologetic shrug. "I make them the way he taught me."

Cora presses a hand to Mickey's cheek, her palm warm and velvety soft. "Your bed's all made up in the Hollandaise Room."

Beech House has seven bedrooms—three on the kitchen-wing side and four in the main house—and Cora named every one after a classic cooking sauce. Hollandaise, in honor of the silky egg-yolk-and-butter mixture that was poured over so many Beech House brunches' crabs Benedict, has always been Mickey's favorite. Its sheers and window trim are as bright and lemony as the sauce itself. She can't wait to peel back the faded yellow chenille bedspread and sink into the room's creaky old twin.

Turning to the fridge, Mickey flushes with appreciation
to see a gallery of her magazine articles and newspaper clippings. *Food and Wine. Bon Appétit.* The *Gourmet* feature
with the photo of her and Wes in Piquant's kitchen. Reflexively, her gaze shifts to the wall clock, and longing thrums.
Eight o'clock. Wes will be in the weeds right now. As much
as she wants to hear his voice, to let him know she's arrived
safely, she doesn't want to bother him during dinner rush.

"These are just xeroxes." Her grandmother points to
the articles. "I keep the originals in a scrapbook," she says.
"And I bought up all the copies of *Gourmet* from the drug-
store. I hand them out like Halloween candy."

"You think she's joking," Hedy says, reaching into a
cabinet for a glass. "I caught her leaving one behind at the
stationery store yesterday."

"You don't need to do that, Grams . . ."

"Why shouldn't we all be proud of you?"

Does her grandmother want a list of reasons? Because
Mickey could give her one.

"Max and I are already planning a trip to Baltimore in
the fall and I told him not to be shocked if I apply for a job
in your kitchen."

Even as Mickey laughs, her chest feels tight with worry.
Having her grandmother eat at her restaurant is all she's ever
wanted. Now she just has to keep Piquant in business long
enough to get her there.

Among the articles, Mickey spots a familiar picture of
her grandfather Harry taken on the porch a few years before
he died, held up with a lighthouse magnet. Then another
photo beside it, of a man in a thick sweater with wavy white
hair and a broad grin.

Mickey leans in. "Is this Max?"

Cora nods. "Handsome devil, isn't he? Everyone used to say he looked like Burt Lancaster."

Hedy holds her glass under the tap. "I think that might be before her time, Mom."

"Mom said he was the one who built the island," Mickey says.

"Max built the whole kitchen, actually."

"The sign, too?" Mickey asks.

Her grandmother's gaze drifts fondly around the room, catching briefly on the hand-carved sign that hangs above the sink, set into the wooden arch that hides the fluorescent tube: CORA'S KITCHEN.

"The sign, too," Cora says.

"Then how did we never know about him?"

Her grandmother shrugs. "You never asked."

"Well, I'm asking now."

Cora laughs. "I thought you were tired?"

"I must be getting my second wind." Mickey looks at the fridge and grins. "Maybe I'll have a daiquiri after all."

3

Cora stared down into the machine and watched the tangle of sheets she'd just stripped from their bed swirl in the soapy whirl, relief washing over as she envisioned the constellation of red dots being thrashed from the cotton with every frothy spin.

She was grateful Harry hadn't seen the telltale spots when he'd risen that morning, that it had been too early, still too dark. Because if he had seen the proof of another lost month, Cora's husband would have woken her, would have configured his lips into one of the soothing smiles he'd become expert at, would have placed his hands on her shoulders and kept them there with just enough pressure, as if she were an untethered balloon in danger of floating away.

She'd have to tell him when he got back that afternoon, of course. Or maybe she would wait a bit longer, out of kindness, or cowardice—Cora could never be sure which. He'd been in such a good mood that morning when he'd rolled over and kissed her on the shoulder, anticipating a perfect day for a sail on the new boat belonging to one of his friends, and already gone by the time she stepped into the bathroom and found her underpants soaked.

Cora closed the washing machine's metal lid and wiped her hands briskly on the sides of her house dress.

But why shouldn't her husband be in a good mood? After all, this was going to be a summer for celebrations and fresh starts, or so she'd been told. For many of the families who owned cottages on Oyster Point, this would be the first summer since the war that they could gather again. A significance, Harry had said, that Cora couldn't entirely appreciate, since this would be her first time to the Vineyard, despite having been Mrs. Harry Campbell for almost two years. Beech House, named for the massive weeping beech tree that stood sentry in the front, had been in the Campbell family since 1902 and, according to Harry, had never seen a summer empty before the war.

But settling in wouldn't be as easy as flinging up sashes and pulling sheets off furniture. The property, once in the hands of Harry's parents, was now theirs, and Cora's husband, newly promoted to partner at the bank, was determined to update Beech House in every possible way, just as so many were doing to their cottages up and down Oyster Point this summer. A long list of renovations and repairs had been drawn up that spring and sent on ahead to the island so that by the time she and Harry arrived in June, the most disruptive of the projects—otherwise known as the ones that might impair entertaining—would be complete. A new roof, repairs to the stretches of rotted woodwork on the veranda, new pavers on the patio, fresh coats of paint on the trim. But when they'd pulled into the driveway three days earlier, the lawn was still covered with tools and lumber, the driveway a crush of trucks and wagons. Still Harry assured her they would have privacy—though Cora wasn't entirely sure how much they could really expect. Just a few minutes earlier, passing the great room's picture window on her way to the laundry room, her arms full of the balled-up sheets, she let out a startled shriek at the unexpected sight of a man pressed against the glass, glazing a new pane.

It was a big house, one of the largest on the Point, rambling but warm thanks to wood-paneled walls and upholstered window seats. Covered in the same weathered gray shingles as all the others that sat high above the shore, its roofline was a whimsical collection of gables and dormers. The first time Cora had stepped inside, following Harry through the side door into the home's kitchen, the smell of undisturbed dust had been so choking, her eyes had watered. She'd rushed to the closest window, and as soon as she threw up the sash, soft sea air had rushed in. Every window she opened after that gave the same delighted cry, unsealing loudly with a sucking sound, like a pair of parted lips, as if the house had been holding its breath in their absence.

A knock sounded from several rooms away and Cora stilled. At least she thought it was a knock. It was hard to be sure over the clatter of the washing machine.

She snapped off the cylinder's power, the churning water calming, plunging the room into silence, and the knock repeated, clearer now, louder.

Maybe one of the workmen with a question? Had to be—she wasn't expecting company. Not in a house dress, and certainly not with her unwashed red hair scooped up in a crocheted snood. She walked briskly down the hallway, slowed at the bottom of the stairs where she'd left her slippers, and pushed her feet into them as she hurried through the living room for the kitchen. There was nothing she could do to improve her hair or her dress, but at least her feet would be covered.

Through the kitchen, Cora saw the outline of a woman on the other side of the screen door, her silhouette drawn against the glare of sunlight, and Cora crossed to let her in.

The woman waved through the mesh. "Good morning!"

Cora pressed open the screen. The visitor wore a floral dress, her dark hair lifted in two perfect victory rolls. She stood in white suede summer wedges, making her a few inches taller than Cora.

"You must be Cora," the woman said cheerfully. "I'm Lois. Lois Welch?" She blinked expectantly, as if giving Cora a chance at recognition, though none came. "Ours is the house with mint trim? You can see it from the beach."

"Oh. Right." Cora nodded agreeably, even though she hadn't been that far down the beach yet. It seemed easier to pretend. Learning her way around Harry's friends and family these past few years, Cora found it often was.

She smiled and stepped back. "Come in."

Lois followed her into the kitchen. "I hope I'm not catching you at a bad time? I probably should have rung first."

"You wouldn't have gotten through if you did. They've been having trouble with the line."

"All the construction, I'll bet. It's bound to happen." Lois Welch's dark eyes darted around the room, her thick lashes fluttering appraisingly. Cora wondered if the woman brushed Vaseline on them. "Is Harry here?"

"He's on the water. One of his friends bought a new sailboat. I can't recall who."

"Probably Dennis." Lois offered a dismissive wave, her gaze still sweeping the space. "He's notoriously impulsive. He buys boats the way we buy lipsticks at the counter."

Cora couldn't recall the last time she'd bought a lipstick, let alone more than one tube at once.

Perspiration bubbled at her hairline. A fan whirred on the counter, its blades spinning furiously but too far away to bring much relief.

"I have lemonade, if you'd like a glass."

"That would be lovely," Lois said, already sliding herself into the banquette on the water-facing side of the room. Halfway in, the hem of her skirt caught as she shifted, becoming taut across her abdomen, revealing a small rise. Feeling a flicker of unease, Cora turned to find glasses, reaching up to the open shelving that served as the kitchen's only storage. She looked forward to getting proper cabinets and countertops installed when the men came to work inside.

"I'm sorry for the heat," Cora said. "I've got the stove on. Lemon meringue." But as she poured, Cora marveled at Lois Welch's smooth forehead and temples, the skin without the shine of perspiration. How did she manage to stay so fresh?

"I wondered what that marvelous smell was," Lois said.

Outside, a saw whirred to life. The gunfire of hammering resumed somewhere on the roof.

Lois glanced in the direction of the window. "Harry certainly isn't wasting any time, is he?"

"He hoped they would have made more progress before we arrived." Cora set down their lemonades on napkins and offered a sheepish smile. "I'm afraid I haven't figured out where the coasters are yet."

"You're lucky that he wants to make changes," Lois said as Cora slid onto the other side of the bench. "Ned's mother insists on spending July with us, so I so much as move an ashtray to a different room and I don't hear the end of it." Lois reached for her glass. Her nails were perfectly shaped and painted the same shade of coral as her lips. How Cora would have loved having manicured nails, but her fingers were always either stained with some sort of berry juice or chapped from constant washing, never mind the collection of cooking scars she'd amassed over the years, burns or knife cuts. Keeping nails polished was impossible. Had Lois taken note? Fearful, Cora took her hands from her glass and lowered them to her lap to hide them in the folds of her skirt.

"When did you arrive?" Lois asked.

"Tuesday."

"And Harry's already abandoned you?"

Cora bristled at the suggestion, then rearranged her tight lips into a smile. Harry always said she was too sensitive, too quick to feel affronted. Surely Lois Welch didn't mean anything by it.

"I don't mind. I can take care of myself." Cora glanced up at the bread box on the sideboard, remembering the leftovers she'd put away. "I have raspberry muffins."

"Thank you, but I don't dare." Lois leaned back to rub her abdomen. "It's all I can do to keep liquids down. I could eat anything I wanted with Timmy, but this one is determined to starve me, the little stinker." Lois lifted the sweating glass to reveal a ghostly ring of moisture on the napkin. "So who did Harry get?"

Cora blinked at her, lost. "Excuse me?"

"To do the work on the house."

"Oh." Looking to the window, Cora was relieved to see one of the trucks parked close, the passenger door in view, the name in block letters. "Dempsey Brothers Construction," she reported.

Lois frowned, just enough to carve a pair of creases between her tall brows. "I'm not familiar with them."

"They came from over in Edgartown, I think."

"Down-island. You say they came from down-island. Where we are is up-island." Lois smiled. "It's confusing, I know, but don't worry. You'll get the hang of it."

It was hardly geometry. But still Cora felt a pang of doubt shudder behind her ribs. Just a few days in Oyster Point and it was clear there was already a great deal she would have to get the hang of.

"I love your snood, by the way."

"Oh, thank you," Cora said, reaching back to give the crocheted net a fond tap. "It's an old habit from the restaurant when I'm in a rush. Harry hates when I wear it." Which was why, in the spirit of fresh starts, as this summer promised, Cora had recently started wearing her red hair in a more modern fashion, abandoning her tried-and-true chignon for a more stylish side part, brushing the top flat but allowing the fluffy curls at the bottom to wreath her neck, but this morning, rushed and rattled, she hadn't bothered.

Lois cocked her head. "Did you say restaurant?"

Cora nodded. "Marigold's. It was my uncle's. I worked there while he was deployed. It was just down the street from the bank." She smiled. "That's where Harry and I met. He used to come in for a slice of my lemon meringue pie."

"Sounds exhausting," Lois said, screwing up her face. "And hot, too, I'll bet."

"I didn't mind," Cora said, smoothing the edges of her napkin where they had curled from the moisture. "Honestly, I miss the work. They practically had to change the locks to keep me from coming in after my uncle Theo got back from the war and didn't need me anymore."

"I couldn't stand filling in at Ned's business. I make a much better hostess than a bookkeeper." Lois set down her glass. "Speaking of which, Neddy and I are having a little get-together at the house Sunday night. Cocktails, hors d'oeuvres. Nothing too fancy. Just a way to break the seal on summer, so to speak. I hope you and Harry can make it?"

"I don't see why we couldn't," Cora said.

Lois shifted to scan the room again. "So what are your plans for in here? Surely you'll put in an electric stove? You really should. They're marvelous. I've got one on order for the cottage."

Cottage. Harry had used the same word to refer to Beech House, a term Cora found perplexing for so large a home.

"I'd like to keep the stove, actually," Cora said. "It's so much better to cook on gas. Better control." Cooking at the restaurant had taught her that.

But Lois looked at her as if she'd sprouted horns for a long moment before she resurrected her smile. "You must be anxious for them to start work."

"It won't be for another week, Harry says. Apparently, the youngest of the three brothers is the one who does the fine carpentry, and he's finishing up a job somewhere on the island." Cora wrapped her fingers around her glass, grateful for the prickle of cold against her damp palms. "I don't mind the wait. It all feels very rushed to me. Like we're on some kind of deadline."

Lois sighed. "Construction always feels that way."

Cora forced a polite smile. Lois couldn't know, of course. Cora wasn't just talking about the pace of the repairs.

Another sip and Lois reached for the edge of the table. "I won't keep you," she said, already sliding out the other side of the bench. "It's going to be such an exciting summer. A new beginning for us all. It really is so wonderful to have everyone back on the Point."

Cora may have been new to the island's inner circle, but she was still able to appreciate the Point's feverish excitement. Every time she had put her hand down somewhere—on a tabletop or gripping a bannister—she swore she could feel a pulse thumping under her palm, like the whole of the island was one giant beating heart.

At the screen door, Lois turned back. "I do hope you and Harry will join us Sunday," she said. "I know everyone is looking forward to seeing him after so long. And meeting you, too, of course."

Cora nodded. "We wouldn't miss it."

* * *

It was almost six by the time Harry returned, his face still flushed with sun and exertion as he regaled Cora with all the details of the sail while she set out their dinner of breaded chicken, garlic potatoes, and sautéed peas. The workmen had packed up hours earlier, leaving the house to be theirs alone again. Instead of the groan and growl of tools, the sizzle of crickets was the only sound to come in through the screens as they ate.

"I met Lois Welch today," Cora said as she guided peas onto her fork with the edge of her knife.

Harry lowered his utensils and blinked at her, looking panicked. "Lois came over?"

"Don't look so worried," she said. "I don't think I embarrassed myself too terribly without you."

"I didn't mean that, darling," he said, resuming his eating, whatever flicker of unease she'd seen washed from his features. "I didn't think they were coming until after the Fourth, that's all."

"They're having a party Sunday and she invited us."

"That was nice of them." Harry sawed spiritedly at his meat. "Chicken is delicious tonight, darling."

Cora smiled, flushing with pride. "It's the fresh pecorino. Gives it that little bite."

"So what did you think of her?"

"Lois? She's very nice," Cora said, trying to settle on the right words. "Very . . . very on top of it all."

"Well, that's Lois. Was Ned with her?"

"No, just her."

Harry speared a bite of chicken. "How about Timmy? He must be, what, four or five now?"

"They have another on the way," Cora said.

"Really? How wonderful."

"I'm afraid we don't."

Harry's lips closed around his fork and froze, staring at her for a strained moment before he swallowed, too soon, Cora suspected, because he winced briefly, as if the chicken was still too big to go down, and she felt a flicker of remorse. It hadn't been the gentlest way to tell him. In previous months, she'd always delivered the news over dessert. Cushioning the sour with something sweet. It had been why she'd made the lemon meringue in the first place. His favorite. But tonight, she'd felt the need to be direct. Clinical, even.

"Why didn't you tell me first thing?" His eyes pooled with hurt—not for the news but for her waiting to deliver it—and Cora felt another pang of guilt.

"Because you were like a spun top," she said gently. "I didn't want to spoil your wonderful day."

He sat back in his chair and set his hands on the tops of his thighs, taking her in for a long moment before he expelled a resigned breath. "Well, it's to be expected, sweetheart. All the activity of getting here. The packing and unpacking . . .

It wasn't reasonable to think everything would fall in to place as easily as the construction schedule."

Excuses. They had a whole catalog of them by now. Most days Cora was grateful for them, but today, his justifications felt false. Even his encouraging smile seemed forced. Cora wondered when his frustration would start to show in earnest. Another month? Another year? It was to be expected. All of their friends—not just those who also summered here on the Point, but their friends back in Boston—nearly all of them had children now. Even her dearest friend, Lizzie, who had married the same month as Cora, was expecting a baby soon.

"I thought I could bring one of my strawberry mint pies," Cora said later that night as they sat out on the veranda, finding an area free from the clutter of the workmen's tools, just big enough for two chairs.

"Perfect. See?" Harry flashed her an encouraging wink over his magazine. "Three days here and you're already in the swing."

Cora smiled appreciatively back down at her book, but she wouldn't go that far.

4

1999

According to the gallery of portraits that cover Beech House's Wedding Wall, there have been nearly twenty nuptials at Beech House over the years. The first, in 1904, was the union of Landon Campbell and his bride, Josephine, who, family lore had it, wanted so desperately to wear a modest blouse and skirt for her wedding—and not the weighty, rib-crushing gown of her future mother-in-law—that she intentionally spilled a glass of raspberry cordial on the dress the morning of the ceremony. The other nearly twenty nuptials, commemorated in an impressive grid of frames that hang above the sideboard in the great room, are time capsules of the fluctuating and often fraught century that followed. Some unions proved lasting, like Henry and Dorothy, who, Mickey has learned, just celebrated their seventieth anniversary the month before in Miami. Others, less so, like Violet and Christopher Campbell, who barely made it through their honeymoon before calling it quits—a prediction easily made after one glance at their equally glum faces in the portrait. A few were considered downright scandalous, such as sixty-year-old Margaret Campbell, who exchanged vows with a forty-one year-old grocer named Rudolph; their rightful spot on the wall was under family debate for months before the portrait was finally slid over its nail. Some unions, of course, didn't even last long enough to find their portraits in a frame, let alone hung on the wall. Like any exhibit, the collection is fluid, in constant rotation. When a couple part ways, their wedding photo parts with the wall. (It was, after all, a Wedding Wall, not a Divorce Wall, as repeatedly defended by one Campbell curator.) Although there were exceptions to that rule, too: Frances and Robert Campbell, having divorced and remarried, were not only added to the collection after their second ceremony but their original wedding photo was also restored to the wall (albeit in a lower row).

Growing up, Mickey memorized every photograph. Each year she would imagine her own wedding portrait there, mooning over the wall as a young girl with her best friend, Tiffany, predicting their respective grooms depending on which boy they had a crush on that particular summer. While most of the portraits featured family members, blood wasn't a hard-and-fast rule, since Beech House had hosted several weddings of close family friends over the years as well. So when Tiffany asked Mickey's grandfather for permission to marry Danny Bartlett at Beech House, she and Mickey realized that Tiffany, not Mickey, would be the first of the two of them to grace the wall. Entirely uncomfortable with that fact, Tiffany even suggested they hold off on hanging their wedding photo for a bit, sure that Mickey would follow soon with her own wedding. But when Mickey's journey through culinary school proved too consuming for romance, Tiffany and Danny's photo went up, taking its rightful place beside the 1969 snapshot of family friends Franklin and Ivy Dettmer, passionate scuba divers who married in matching white wetsuits.

Walking past the collection this morning, barefoot and dressed in a ribbed tank and drawstring shorts, Mickey

slows reflexively, her gaze dancing along the various portraits, smiling as if greeting old friends who have been waiting for her at the bar. The sun is high enough that it spears
the great room's wide stone fireplace, varnishing the edge of
the oak mantel, signaling midmorning. She didn't mean to
sleep so late, and would have slept even later if not for the
beep of a delivery truck backing up, especially loud because
her room faces the driveway, and then the faraway ringing
of the kitchen phone. By the time she called Wes, he had
already left for the restaurant, his machine clicking on after
three rings. She left a disjointed, rambling message, feeling
uncharacteristically inarticulate, frazzled, and tentative, as
if she were calling him for the first time and not the four
hundredth, as if they'd only just met and not been sharing a
kitchen, a bed—a whole world—for almost two years now.
Calling the restaurant immediately after had been equally
discouraging. Pete, his sous chef, answered and then disappeared for several minutes while he tried to find Wes, only
to come back to report that Wes hadn't yet arrived but that
he'd relay the message when he did.

Almost to the kitchen doorway, Mickey can already hear
the wonderful clatter of mixing bowls. The nutty smell of
coffee is rich enough to overtake the briny scent of low tide
that blows through the screens, a combination that has always lifted her spirits, even before Mickey was old enough
to start drinking coffee.

"The star chef wakes!" Her grandmother, and the intricate web of wrinkles that pleat her eyes and smile, is lowering the standing mixer onto the island. "I thought I was
going to have to start pounding out 'Chopsticks' on the baby
grand like the old days."

Mickey laughs as she moves to the cabinet and draws down a mug. "Mom's not up yet?"

"You think I dare poke the bear?"

"Wise," Mickey says, pulling out the carafe and tipping it, relishing the comforting crackle of the coffee filling her mug. She glances out the window at the view of the lawn, where a white sailcloth tent has appeared. "I see the tent fairies came in the night."

Her grandmother smiles. "The forecast is for clear skies but you can't be too careful."

"Does this mean you hired a band?"

"Didn't have to. Max's nephew is a DJ. And my dear friend Vincent offered to tickle the ivories for us, too. He performs every summer at Tanglewood. He's quite good. We'll roll the piano on to the porch."

Mickey has so many memories of her grandfather sitting on that creaky piano bench at evening's end, a sweaty cocktail glass leaving water marks on the lid, Harry Campbell's worn loafer thumping over the pedals; how he was always trying to teach Mickey "Für Elise" when all she wanted to learn was the theme from *Ice Castles*. The recollection, warm and inviting, is still bittersweet. As she sips her coffee, Mickey can't decide whether to find the symmetry of having her grandfather's piano used for her grandmother's ceremony to another man comforting or upsetting.

"So what are we cooking?" Mickey asks as she turns to join her grandmother at the island, where flour, salt, olive oil, and a carton of eggs are set out.

"I thought I'd break us back in with something simple," Cora says, rubbing her hands together. "Crab ravioli."

Fresh pasta? Mickey laughs. "Something simple, huh?"

"You come back here as a big shot in the culinary world—what did you think I'd have us make? Boxed brownies?" Cora points an empty measuring spoon at the pantry. "Go suit up."

With an obedient nod, Mickey makes her way across the kitchen. For her tenth birthday, Cora bought them matching aprons in heavyweight cotton (*Professional grade, sweetheart. The kind real chefs use!*) red-and-white striped, with two deep pockets running around the skirt. Never mind pencil notches on walls; it was the rising hem of Mickey's apron, climbing from below her knee, that was used to measure her growth summer after summer. The last time Mickey tied it on had been for Tiffany's wedding. She had offered to make her friend's wedding cake. The apron had grazed mid-thigh.

Mickey opens the pantry door, and the dry smell of old shelf paper pricks her nose before an unfamiliar wave of bright blue swings into view. "You got us new aprons?"

"I thought it was time," Cora says. "You can take it home with you."

Mickey sends her grandmother a quizzical look, as if Cora has suggested she leave with something nailed down; the sink, maybe, or the island itself. Unthinkable. Her apron always stays here.

Mickey swings the ties around her waist and knots them, giving her hands a quick rinse under the tap.

"Dough first, then we'll make the filling while it chills," Cora says, handing Mickey a clean towel to dry with. "Please say you brought a copy of your most recent menu for my collection."

The reminder sparks a fresh pang of dread, but Mickey buries it with her measuring cup in the island's flour drawer and pulls up a rounded scoop, reminding herself once again that she's come here to forget whatever problems she's made in Baltimore. Her grandmother has waited years to share in the joy of her restaurant—they both have—so what's the harm in indulging that celebration for a few days?

"I couldn't stop making that lemon pesto you had on your last one," Cora says, handing Mickey a butter knife to scrape the flour level. "I didn't have the same luck with the shrimp and coconut soup, though. I couldn't get the right balance in the flavors—all I could taste was the coriander. What's your secret?"

"You'd have to ask Wes. That's his recipe."

"I thought you came up with them together?"

"We used to. In the beginning." Mickey can't remember the last time she and Wes collaborated on a recipe, and a sudden flutter of longing blooms behind her chest.

Cora arches a brow. "Seems like the whole point of a chef opening a restaurant is to come up with the dishes," she says.

"Except I'm not the chef anymore, Grams. I'm the owner." When she meets her grandmother's eyes, Mickey hopes to find agreement in them, but they continue to flash with doubt.

Cora tugs the mixer's paddle from the drawer. "Well, back here, you're the chef," her grandmother says firmly, handing it to Mickey. "Now mix."

Mickey starts on the eggs, sending the mixer into motion after each one until the dough is combined. The fresh, powdery smell rises, sweet and warm. Why was it that everything smelled better at Beech House?

She turns off the mixer and reaches in to snap the paddle free.

"Aren't you forgetting something?"

Mickey turns to find Cora holding out the olive oil and Mickey groans, prickling with shame as she swirls a generous drizzle over the dough; a rookie mistake. Where is her head?

But her grandmother's smile is absolving. "It's harder than you expected, isn't it?"

"I can't remember the last time I made pasta dough," Mickey says, watching the threads of oil folded in, turning the dough glossy. "I'm just out of practice."

"I was talking about running a restaurant, sweetheart."

Mickey meets her grandmother's pressing gaze, the urge to confess just how much harder it is pushing up her throat, but she forces the truth down and manages a stoic smile instead.

Cora sprinkles flour over the island's butcher-block top and spreads it into a wide circle with her palm. "I remember your uncle Theo used to tell me that if I really loved to cook, I should never open a restaurant."

Mickey scoops out the ball of dough and sets it on the floured surface. "Did he stop loving to cook?"

"Of course not. He would only say that when a customer would complain—which was rare. Sure, some nights he slathered a bun with peanut butter and called it dinner when he was too tired, but he never fell out of love with cooking."

Mickey smiles, thinking of how she and Wes often make boxed mac and cheese when they come home late from the restaurant, tired but ravenous. How they won't even bother with bowls, just eat it straight out of the pot, and how it is always her favorite part of the day. That her fine flavor palate be damned—somehow it always tastes like the best macaroni and cheese she's ever eaten.

She kneads the dough, pushing it out and rolling it back

in, the rhythm returning to her hands without thinking, the silky feel of the dough so satisfying. "You know, Granddad said the same thing to me when I told him I was going to culinary school. But I told him he didn't need to be jealous. That I'd still cook for him."

Cora's voice quiets. "I know this feels strange, sweetheart. Back here without him. It's still hard for me some days. But Max is a wonderful man. You'll see."

Mickey takes her hands off the dough and runs them thoughtfully over the edge of the butcher block, letting her fingers linger on the seam where the old block was joined with the new frame. "All the years I've stood at this island, the hundreds of recipes we've made together here, and I never knew how it came to be built. Or by who."

Her grandmother pulls a roll of plastic wrap from one of the island's drawers and tears off a long sheet. "Have you called that handsome chef of yours this morning?"

"I couldn't reach him. I was hoping that was him calling earlier."

Cora shakes her head as she rolls the dough into the plastic and wraps it snugly. "That was Max's son, Tom. He'll be here soon."

Will that mean her mother has a stepbrother? Mickey wonders. Or maybe there's an age limit on that? It's a funny thought.

Cora gives the wrapped dough a final pat, then carries the ball to the fridge. "We'll let this chill for an hour."

The crackle of tires sails in through the screen above the sink. Mickey turns for the window just as a red minivan pulls into the mushroom of shade under the beech, the curls of the white logo that dance up one side still familiar: Chowder's Clam Shack.

"And perfect timing, too," her grandmother says, her face breaking into a smile. "You have a visitor."

* * *

To look at them working at the order window at Edgartown's landmark clam shack, a person might have thought Mickey Campbell and Tiffany Bartlett weren't just best friends, but twins. After all, they were the same age (fifteen), they wore the same tops (red polos with CHOWDER'S stitched in white below their popped collars), and they even pulled their hair back into the same low ponytails. For nine weeks that summer, and six summers after that one, burning their fingertips and palms carrying steaming paper baskets of freshly fried clam strips, growing hoarse from having to yell orders over the roar of the kitchen's turbine-like hanging fans, they became a dynamite team. While Tiffany ran the order window like a drill sergeant, Mickey advised customers on flavors and condiment pairings. During their breaks, they would climb onto the picnic table behind the shack and map out their futures while they sucked down fountain drinks and, later, a shared cigarette; they planned the boys they would marry and, more important, the restaurants they would open—though Tiffany was perennially skeptical. "You have to be the chef, not the owner," Tiffany would say. Mickey would balk: "Why can't I be the owner?" Tiffany would level her with a nonplussed stare. "Mick, come on. All you care about is what goes into that fry mix. You can't make change to save your life. Why do you think Buzz never lets you split the tip jar?"

As Mickey pushes through the screen door and hurries across the lawn, she wonders if Tiffany remembers those conversations. Her old friend looks amazing, but then, she always did. No one could ever believe someone with Tiffany's

willowy figure and porcelain skin spent her days eating—
never mind breathing—fried food. Her blond hair, a few
shades darker than when they were younger, is still pulled
back in its thick, loose ponytail. Like Mickey, the feathered
bangs have long grown out. Mickey remembers how they
used to reunite, when she would return every summer and
they'd barely take a breath, wanting to catch up on everything in the first five minutes, as if they were playing a game
of Perfection and had to get all their news in before the timer
ran out.

Tiffany leans back and takes in Mickey's apron. "Look
at you! Barely here a day and she's already got you cooking."

"Some things never change."

"Because I couldn't arrive empty-handed." Tiffany holds
out the grease-speckled bag. "Welcome home."

"You goddess." Mickey takes it and peeks in, moaning
as she inhales a warm, oily breath before seeing the little
blooms of fried clams at the bottom. "Come on inside," she
says, already steering them to the house. "There's coffee."

"Can't," says Tiffany. "I have to get back."

"You and Danny are coming to the wedding, right?"

"Of course. We wouldn't miss it."

"Then give me the quick version for now." Mickey squares
Tiffany with a serious look. "How are you? How's Danny?
How's business?"

"Never mind boring old us." Tiffany snorts and swats
the air. "Let's talk about you, Miss One to Watch! And how
about that *Gourmet* spread. Speaking of which . . ." Her
friend scans the house. "Is Mr. Wonderful here? Your mom
said he might come."

Mickey shakes her head. "Wes stayed with the restaurant."

"Too bad. But things are good?"

"Things are great. Things are, you know . . ." Mickey shrugs. "Busy."

It's the short answer, the simple one, and Mickey forces herself to give it, because even just a few minutes back in Tiffany's company and she feels the reflexive need to confess to her. About Wes, about her troubles at Piquant. But it's like a loose thread on a knitted sweater. One tug and the whole weave of problems she's left in her wake in Baltimore will unravel. Too many to cover standing in the driveway when Tiffany has left the van door open.

"Max wants to throw a clambake tomorrow. Please say you guys can come?"

"Tomorrow might be tough for Danny. The contractors are supposed to come around for the—" Tiffany stops abruptly and looks back at the van.

Mickey tries to catch Tiffany's roving gaze but her friend won't let her. "Are you having work done on the restaurant?"

But when Mickey finally manages to hold her friend's eyes, they pool with apology.

"Tiff?" Mickey pierces her with a hard stare, feeling a creeping dread. "What's going on?"

"I didn't want to say anything. You came back here to celebrate . . ." Tiffany blows out a defeated sigh. "Buzz sold the restaurant."

"What?" Their joined hands fall apart. Mickey blinks at her. "But he was going to sell it to you guys."

"He was. Then this developer swooped in and offered him all this money . . ." Tiffany shrugs weakly. "Oh, Mick. We couldn't compete with his bid. He bought up the lot next to ours, too. He's building some new-age spa resort."

Mickey's eyes flick helplessly over Tiffany's face, not sure what she's searching for. A swell of outrage blooms in her chest. "But Chowder's been there forever. How could Buzz agree to that?"

"I don't blame him, Mick. He wants to retire someplace warm. He needs as much money as he can get, and Danny and I always knew we couldn't swing what the property is worth."

But Mickey's heart still hammers with hurt. "That's bullshit. You guys have been running that place for years. It's about loyalty. It's about legacy."

"Mick, I love you, but we both know it's about the bottom line. You of all people do."

Even as she nods, Mickey tries to rearrange her worried frown into an agreeable smile, but she can't. The sting isn't Tiffany's fault; her oldest friend can't know how deep her words cut, or how close. Mickey thought she left the uncertain world back in Baltimore, and that coming back to Beech House would be to return to the safety of the familiar, the predictable.

She never imagined the earth here could be shifting under her dear friend's feet, too.

"Tiff. I . . . I don't know what to say."

"There isn't anything to say. It is what it is. Things are changing." Tiffany tilts her head expectantly, her eyes flashing, and for a second, they could be teenagers again, working the counter shoulder to shoulder, their plans and dreams stuffed snugly in the pockets of their jean shorts with their hair elastics and Chapsticks, everything possible. And longing fists around Mickey's heart. "And it's not just Chowder's. The last few years, things have really blown up around here. Have you had a chance to walk the beach?"

"Not yet," Mickey says.

"Well, get ready. All these new places are going up. So many of the old summer cottages just—whoosh—gone." Tiffany shakes her head. "I'm telling you, Mick. It's bad. Pretty soon Beech House is going to be the only one left standing."

5

1948

Like every summer house on Oyster Point, the Welches' cottage had a name: the Sandpiper. As Cora navigated the brick path to the mint-green front door, a strawberry pie balanced on her damp palms, she kept her gaze fixed on the carved wooden sign that swung from the center of the home's porch. She had wanted to wear her sturdier shoes, the ration-free slip-ons that she had lived in standing on her feet all day at the restaurant, but she knew Harry would rather see her in something prettier and more festive, so on went her white summer pumps. Now, her tapered heels threatening to stay wedged in the wide gaps between the herringbone pattern of the walkway with every step, she wished she had stuck with her first choice.

An uneven brick sent her teetering. The pie tipped, and she sucked in a panicked breath.

"Careful, darling."

Harry's hands jerked out to steady the dessert. Disaster averted, her husband's eyes flickered fretfully over her face as she took a moment to settle her racing breath.

"Are you feeling all right?" he asked.

"I'm fine." Cora tightened her grip on the metal tin,

grateful she'd chosen a sleeveless apron dress in the growing heat. "I'm just nervous, that's all."

"Nervous? What for?"

She stared up at him, his pale lashes blinking furtively with anticipation. Did she really have to explain?

"These are your friends, Harry. People you've known forever. How can I not worry they won't be sizing me up?"

"These are our neighbors. They're hardly Inquisition soldiers."

But tremors of concern still fluttered as he touched her arm to urge her forward again. Closer now, she could make out waves of delighted squeals coming from behind the house, and her nerves pulsed freshly. Harry had guessed the guest list to be no more than three or four couples, but the volume suggested more. Had Lois Welch invited the whole of Oyster Point?

"They just want to meet you, sweetheart," Harry said, squeezing her elbow as they climbed the porch steps. "They just want you to feel at home."

Cora wanted that, too, more than anything, to belong on this beautiful finger of earth he'd brought her to, to weave herself into the quilt of its history as quickly as possible. Over a week on the Vineyard and she already she felt at home in Beech House's kitchen. It was, after all, the place she had spent the most time in, and certainly the room where she found the most purpose. She would admit to being excited at seeing it updated. Already she had ideas of how to make it more efficient, brighter, warmer. For starters, she wanted more storage. Cabinets and drawers. Maybe a pantry. And an uninterrupted stretch of counter space to work at, like she'd enjoyed at Marigold's. She'd even started a collection of clippings for reference, photographs of modern kitchens she'd cut out of magazines, advertisements of finishes and appliances. She planned to show them to this elusive cabinetmaker when he finally came to start work, whenever that might be. To say she was growing impatient was an understatement.

Harry rapped on the front door, then swept a hand through his hair, palming one side smooth. "You have nothing to worry about, darling. Really."

"I just know how people can be, Harry. You're from here and I'm not."

"Never mind all that." He dropped a quick kiss on her temple, so swift that Cora didn't even have time to catch his gaze. "There's no you or I now, sweetheart. Only us," he whispered, seconds before the front door swung open and Lois Welch appeared, gliding forward to greet them as if on ice skates.

* * *

"Everyone's out on the deck," Lois said cheerfully as they followed her brisk lead through the kitchen. "Cora, that pie smells divine. You can just leave it on the counter. I can't wait to put it out for dessert."

Cora set down the tin and gave her damp palms a quick rub down the sides of her gingham skirt, enjoying a flutter of pride before Lois steered them out to the crowded porch.

Her husband's estimate of the guest list had been off by quite a bit. Cora guessed there were at least three dozen people occupying the deck and spilling onto the lawn, many of whom turned when she and Harry appeared, bright-eyed and expectant, as if the two of them had stepped through a stage curtain, which, in a way, she suspected they had. When Harry's hand closed around hers and squeezed, Cora felt a pang of relief cool her flushed cheeks.

On the rolling lawn, several children, the oldest no more than six or seven, Cora thought, ran in and out of a playhouse, shingled just like its full-sized inspiration, while a teenage girl in a pink romper trailed behind them, collecting the toys they left abandoned in their wake.

"This must be the famous Cora." A barrel-chested man in a maroon sport shirt appeared, his green eyes bright. "Ned Welch." He took her hand and shook it gently, his palm as warm as his smile.

"Irene, Phil!" Lois waved toward the hors d'oeuvres table. "Come meet Cora!"

A blond woman in a polka-dot cocktail dress approached with her hand outstretched, a cigarette held behind her, and introduced herself. "Irene Middleton. Your hair is to die for. Tell me you get it colored or I'll just expire from envy on the spot."

Cora laughed and ran her hand self-consciously under the shelf of curls. "Blame my father. His is even redder."

"I blame him entirely," Irene teased as she swung her cigarette to her right. "This is my husband, Phil."

A wiry man in a mustard short-sleeved sport shirt struggled to stuff a cracker into his mouth. He clapped his hands clean before he extended one, but still a smear of crab dip ran the length of his thumb. Cora didn't hesitate to accept his shake, not wanting to embarrass him, and wiped off her hand discreetly in her patch pocket.

Phil Middleton smiled. "She really is too pretty for you, Harry."

"Hey!" Lois swatted Irene's husband playfully on the shoulder. "You didn't say that about me when you found out Harry and I were together."

Harry and Lois had dated? Cora blinked at Harry.

"He didn't tell you? Stinker." Their hostess reached between them and poked a coral nail into Harry's sleeve. "We were sweethearts."

"We were ten," Harry said, his voice taking on a playfully stern tone. "And it barely lasted a week. Don't go giving my wife the wrong idea, Lois."

"Then I probably shouldn't tell her about our wedding ceremony in the Bennetts' boathouse, should I?" Lois swiveled to deliver the next part to the whole of her audience. "His sock monkey officiated. The bridesmaids wore galoshes. It was a real gas."

Laughter bubbled all around them. Irene leaned forward.

"You have to tell me where you found that darling dress, Cora."

Cora looked down, as if she'd forgotten what she'd put on, which should have been impossible considering the amount of time she'd spent deciding. "I wish I could tell you. I've had it so long I don't even remember."

Ned Welch clapped his hands and rubbed them briskly. "Who needs a drink?"

"Martini for me," said Harry.

"And what about you, Cora?"

When their host stepped back to reveal the spread of liquors on the table, Cora's gaze lit immediately on the bottle of whiskey and a memory sparked: unwinding with the waitstaff after closing at Marigold's. She missed the liquor's smoky taste—Harry never kept whiskey in the house—but she missed sharing the drink with her coworkers even more.

The chance to revisit those moments was too tempting.

"Whiskey, please," she said.

Harry's eyes snapped to hers. "Since when do you drink whiskey?"

"Coming right up," Ned said, tipping the bottle over a glass and handing the pour to Cora.

Phil elbowed Harry. "Gorgeous *and* a whiskey drinker to boot?"

Harry leaned in as Cora sipped. "And you were worried you wouldn't fit in?" he whispered. "Half of these men will be in love with you by the end of the night."

"Hardly." Still Cora offered Harry an appreciative smile over her glass.

"How's the construction going up there?" Ned asked.

"As good as can be expected—you know how it is," Harry said with a tinny chuckle, a strange sort of laugh Cora had never heard from him before they came to the Vineyard. "They tell you a week and it turns into three."

A sympathetic groan rumbled through the group.

Ned rested his glass against his chest and swirled it, making the ice clatter. "Lo said you hired some fellows from down-island?"

"Brothers," said Harry. "Dempsey. I hoped to go with Johnson, but he's booked through the fall. Seems everyone is making up for lost time this summer."

"Can you blame them?" asked Lois. "I heard the Talbots will have to wait until August."

"Isn't Audrey due end of July?" asked Irene, tapping off ash onto the lawn.

Lois nodded somberly. "Just what a new mother needs, poor thing. A houseful of dust."

"Smart move on your part then," said Phil, swinging his glass between Cora and Harry. "Getting all that mess out of the way before you have little ones crawling around."

"Now don't push the poor girl," Irene said. "They're only just married."

"Better get started soon, though." Phil chuckled and leaned against Harry. "How many bedrooms in that house of yours? Five? *Six?*"

"Don't listen to my husband, Cora," Irene said, turning to blow smoke over her shoulder. "He won't be happy until we have ourselves a baseball team."

"Not true," Phil said. "I'd settle for basketball. That's only five!"

* * *

By eight thirty, the sun had sunk low on the horizon, washing the ocean and the bluff in shades of lilac and cornflower. The Sandpiper's deck, once loud and crowded, had thinned and quieted, the rambling groups of many whittled down to just a few. In the bathroom, Cora gave her lipstick a freshening coat, her pinned hair a quick fluffing. It had been such a pleasant night, everyone making her feel welcome, included. The knot of her earlier nerves seemed almost embarrassing—why had she been so worried? She scanned the small space, committing the décor to memory, the delicate nautical blue-and-white print of the wallpaper, the matching soap dish and towels, everything bearing some beach design. No wonder Harry had suggested she ask Lois for guidance on how to update Beech House's rooms.

Back outside, Harry found her before Cora could find him.

"There you are," he said, sweeping her into his arms. "Having a good time, darling?"

"Wonderful," Cora said as he leaned in for a kiss. His lips tasted of salt, his breath smoky with alcohol.

"And you were worried they wouldn't like you as much

as they like me." He snorted. "Heck, I'm worried they might like you more."

Cora started to laugh, but the sound faded quickly as she gave in to a yawn. "Sorry, darling," she said. "I didn't realize I was so tired."

"Just a few more minutes? Ned wants to give me a tour of the new courts."

"You do that," she said, smoothing the curled points of his collar. "I'll go on ahead and meet you at home."

Home. The word sounded both strange and satisfying.

Harry scanned her face, looking briefly alarmed. "Are you sure you can find your way back on your own?"

"It's just a few yards on the beach, Harry. I don't expect to cross paths with any grizzly bears."

"That's my brave girl. Promise you'll wait up?"

Cora reared up on her tiptoes to land a kiss on his chin. "Promise."

* * *

But after a few minutes on the beach, Cora realized she may have been hasty in her jest—never mind her confidence. With Harry as her guide hours earlier, the sun still high, she hadn't had to worry about knowing which dune hid which house. Now in the fuzzy light of twilight, the humps of roofs all looked the same from the shore. When she saw a path sliced through the dune grass, she gratefully followed it up the bluff, deciding she'd have a better chance of finding Beech House from the road. Barefoot now, her heels dangling from her hand, she walked the soft shoulder, relief soaring when she spotted the sign for Beech House at the top of the driveway.

Coming down the drive, she saw a truck parked, its

driver's-side door left open, the interior light on. A brown-haired man sat inside, leaned, really, one leg stretched out, a booted foot resting on the truck's running board, his head bent studying something in his hand.

She felt a flicker of alarm and slowed, unsure if she should advance or wait for the man to leave—assuming he would?—but he glanced up before she could decide, looking relieved as he climbed out of the truck, tossing whatever was in his hands behind him onto the seat.

"Mrs. Campbell?" he said, approaching. He was tall and lean. She guessed him to be a few years older than she was, maybe even closer to Harry's age of twenty-eight, but in the milky light, it was hard to be sure. Looking past him, the driver's door closed now, Cora could read the familiar label on the side: DEMPSEY BROTHERS CONSTRUCTION.

"Can I help you?"

"I'm Max Dempsey," he said. "Hope you don't mind—I just came by to grab a few tools for a job I'm finishing up."

"Oh," she said brightly, recognition sparking. "You must be the cabinet brother."

But when he chuckled, she clapped her free hand to her cheek, realizing what he found so funny. "That makes it sound like you're part of a vaudeville act, doesn't it?" she asked sheepishly.

"Well, if you've ever seen the three of us trying to do the foxtrot, you'd know that's not far off." His eyes, Cora thought, were the sort that kept smiling even after his mouth stopped. "But, yeah," he said, "I'll be the one fixing up your kitchen."

Her kitchen? The instinct to correct him pressed at her, to clarify that it was Harry's mother's kitchen far more than it would ever be hers, but Cora rather liked the sound of it too much.

"I tried knocking first," he said.

"My husband and I were at a neighbor's."

He pointed to her hand. "Must have been quite a party."

Cora glanced down reflexively, forgetting that she held her shoes. Her bare toes were dusted with dirt from the road. She would need a scrub brush for the bottoms of her feet before getting into bed.

"I'm sorry if I scared you just now," he said.

"Honestly, I was more scared about not finding my way home before it got fully dark. It's easy to get lost around here."

"That's the great thing about an island. You can't really get lost. Eventually you come back to the same spot."

She smiled appreciatively. "Makes sense."

His blue jeans hung low on his hips. She wondered what Harry would look like in them.

"I'll be back in the morning to get started," he said. "Eight too early?"

"Eight's fine," Cora said, but as she watched Max Dempsey start back to his truck, worry sparked. What about all the dishes? Should she empty the shelves out for him?

"Is there anything you need me to do?" she asked as he climbed inside. "To get ready for you tomorrow, I mean?"

The truck's engine rattled to life. He shrugged and flashed her an easy smile. "I like coffee."

"Coffee." She nodded. "Got it."

When the truck was nearly out of sight, Cora turned to see Harry climbing the lawn, a basket swinging from one hand. She met him halfway, glad to feel the grass already damp with dew, hoping it would be enough to wash her feet clean.

Her husband's eyes were glassy, his cheeks flushed; exertion from his match or maybe just the pink of too many drinks. Cora suspected a bit of both. She peered into the basket, the uncut top crust of her pie looking yellow in the porch light.

He stared past her. "Was someone here?"

"The man who's going to work on the kitchen," she said. "His name is Max. He came by to pick up some tools. He's going to start tomorrow."

"That's swell."

Harry tried to find his footing on the uneven rise of the lawn, weaving noticeably. Cora slid her arm around his waist to steady him, thinking of how he'd done her the same favor a few hours earlier to save her sliding pie, the same pie he returned with now. Disappointment fluttered in her a bit, but Cora tamped it down as they climbed the grass for the porch. There had been so much food there already—no wonder it had slipped Lois's mind to set out her contribution.

And anyway, summer had only started. There would be many opportunities ahead to impress her husband's dear friends with her cooking. Whole weeks of them.

6

1999

When the determined fingers of sunlight finally reach the side of her face, Hedy throws off her sheet and declares her surrender. She's been awake for a while now but had lingered in bed, trying to get swept up in the pulpy paperback she pulled off the shelf last night, then, when that didn't take, skimmed over some listings. Now that she's up, she pads to the bathroom sink. Her mother and Michelle are at work in the kitchen. Hedy has already heard the sounds of their efforts rising up the stairs. The years apart haven't dimmed the spark of their connection one bit. Hedy suspected it would be so. But as happy as she is for her daughter, she feels a shameful pang of envy, too. When Cora and Michelle are cooking together, Hedy always feels a bit like a third wheel; her mother and daughter are such a flawless engine, a perfect team. It's a partnership that has always seemed to come naturally to the two of them, from the time Michelle was young. For Hedy and Cora, the partnership has been far more difficult to form.

It never helped that Hedy was a daddy's girl from the start, but Hedy has known plenty of daughters who enjoy connective tissue between both of their parents—if not equally, then at least in equally rich ways. But for her and

Cora, their seam has always been a weak one. Even now, nearly fifty, Hedy still wonders where she and her mother connect. In the months after her father died, they had spent a good deal of time together. Hedy had hoped she and Cora might find a path to each other in their shared grief, but then the news of her mother's engagement had brought any forward motion to a complete halt.

Hedy had told Michelle that she hadn't met Max Dempsey when Hedy was younger, but that wasn't entirely true. She hadn't lied to her daughter as much as spared her a complicated truth. The summer Hedy turned fourteen, one of the porch treads rotted through and a man showed up to fix it. Hedy had been in her bedroom, tucked into the window seat, when a truck rumbled down the drive. From her perch, she'd watched her father meet the driver when he climbed out. Something in her father's pace, the stiffness in his legs and arms as he marched toward the man, had caused alarm to skitter down her back. Their conversation had been brief, with her father doing most of the talking, though Hedy had been too far to hear anything. When the man drove off, Hedy assumed that he had forgotten a tool, so that night at dinner, she innocently asked when the man was coming back to replace the step. Her father, in the middle of cutting his pork loin, froze with his knife still stuck in the meat, and said in a low voice: "Ask Lois Welch." Hedy watched his nostrils expand in the seconds before he resumed his sawing, and with far more vigor. When she turned to her mother for explanation, Cora wordlessly set down her napkin, pushed back from the table, and cleared her plate to the kitchen.

Hedy didn't need to ask Lois Welch. At fourteen, she'd spent enough summers on the island to understand that, in addition to heading up fundraisers and organizational committees for Vineyard events, another of Lois Welch's main jobs was president of Oyster Point's rumor mill. Whoever the man in the truck was, he'd done something to earn him an unsavory reputation.

But despite Lois Welch's fondness for gossip, Hedy didn't dislike the woman. After all, Lois had been her father's friend almost their whole lives and always made a point of telling Hedy she was every bit her father's daughter. There had even been several times growing up when Hedy had watched her father and Lois Welch in conversation, tipped toward each other in laughter over a shared memory, when Hedy had secretly wished her father had married Lois Welch, had fantasized about what it would have been like to have two parents who were true islanders—an admission which filled her with equal parts longing and shame. Hedy loved her mother, but sometimes she just wished her mother tried harder to fit in, to be like the other mothers on the Point, who arrived with new clothes every summer, who met for drinks at the club and made sure to get their nails done on Fridays in time for their husbands' return.

But it would be the following summer before Hedy would understand that whatever the man in the truck—whose name Hedy had since learned was Max Dempsey, and who had been the one to rebuild the kitchen in 1948—had done, he had done so with her mother. At a retirement dinner at the country club for one of her father's partners, Hedy, invisible in the bathroom stall, had overheard two women at the mirror talking about one of the waitresses, whose marriage to Max Dempsey was breaking up, and would Cora finally get her chance now? Unable to shake the comment, Hedy confronted her mother the next day, only to have Cora say that Hedy must have misunderstood—an explanation that

Hedy embraced gladly, *gratefully*—and let the matter dissolve over time.

Then, six months after her father died, Hedy arrived to find Max Dempsey's truck in Beech House's driveway once again . . .

Another burst of clatter sails down the hall, pulling her back to the present. Hedy's glad her daughter and her mother have this time together, especially knowing that this will be their last summer at Beech House, a fact that Hedy and Cora have yet to share with Michelle.

As she rakes a comb through her hair, melancholy flares again, but Hedy tamps it down with a few final strokes. No more stalling. She needs coffee.

But downstairs, she's surprised—and a little disconcerted—to find her mother alone in the kitchen, puttering at the island. Hedy was hoping for the buffer of her daughter. Her upstairs musings have left her feeling agitated, and the last thing Hedy wants to do is be edgy with her mother so early in the day.

She pours herself coffee and tips her face into her mug, the brew strong and faintly floral.

"I thought I heard Michelle up."

"She is," says Cora. "Tiffany stopped by."

Hedy moves to the window and looks out, seeing her daughter and her old friend standing close in the shade of the beech. She can't quite make out their expressions. She wonders if Tiffany has confessed her news about losing Chowder's, despite her intention to keep it a secret until after the wedding, and guilt shifts in her stomach. It seems Hedy isn't the only one looking to spare her daughter bad news just now.

Moving to the fridge, Hedy pokes around inside, hungry

but not sure for what. Mornings usually find her inhaling a piece of toast or a muffin on her way to a showing. She's never sure how to eat when she's on the road. Too many choices, too much time.

Her mother points to the bread box on the counter. "If you're hungry, there are still some of those store-bought scones you brought."

Store-bought. The phrase is as good as swearing in Cora Campbell's holy kitchen of homemade.

"They're not poisonous, you know," Hedy says.

"Oh, good. Then be sure to eat them up so we can get rid of them."

Hedy plucks one from the box and fixes Cora with a disapproving frown. "You, Mom, are a food snob."

"Fifty years on this earth with me and you're just now realizing that?"

"Forty-nine." Hedy rips open the scone's plastic sleeve and breaks off a crumbly corner. "And I'm going to savor every last day of it, too, if you don't mind." Although she's not sure why she's bothering. Already at work, she's felt the unspoken assignment of her advancing age. How the photographer who took her most recent headshot suggested she try wearing a scarf to hide her softening neck, how he offered her a deluxe touch-up package. He never said the word "old" outright, but Hedy's not an idiot. She doesn't see any of the younger real estate agents wearing scarves or turtlenecks.

"Don't dread it," her mother says, taking a Tupperware container from the fridge. "A woman's fifties can be a wonderful time."

A sharp retort climbs up her throat, but Hedy drowns it in a long swig of coffee. Her mother has never understood the constant pressure Hedy faces to stay young-looking in her field—or out of it. How Cora never had to worry about fitting in, or keeping up. And on only a quarter cup of coffee, Hedy's not about to try to educate her.

She makes her way to the window and scans the back lawn as she sips. An older woman in a block-print tunic walks carefully down the bluff toward the water, a little boy bounding ahead of her, leaping every few feet as if he's trying to take flight.

"I see the Welches are here already," Hedy says.

"They're watching Timmy's little boy, Andrew, this week," her mother says without looking up. "They want to bring him to the wedding and I said that was fine."

Hedy spins back to Cora, nearly spilling her coffee. "You invited the Welches to the wedding?"

"Well, of course. We invited everyone we know on the Point." Cora frowns at her. "Why do you look so shocked?"

"Because most of these people were Dad and your friends, not . . ." Hedy lets the rest of her point sink in her throat but it's too late. Her mother's lips purse with hurt.

Remorse floods Hedy's chest. So much for a smooth take-off this morning.

"Mom, I didn't mean . . ."

"Hand me the microplane, will you?" Cora asks stiffly.

Hedy pulls open the drawer and the clutter of gadgets slides into view. She squints as she searches, as if the sheer volume of kitchen tools is painful to behold. Which it is, frankly. What will they do with it all?

She finds the long grater and hands it to her mother. "I really wish you'd let me make some calls about estate sales. You have to start thinking about where it will all go."

"You and Michelle will take things."

"I live in a two-bedroom town house, Mom."

"Yes, but there are things you want, aren't there?"

Her mother's hazel eyes sparkle with certainty or hope, Hedy can't decide which, and something shifts inside her, wobbles like a knocked glass, teetering before being righted again. While her heart breaks for her daughter having to say goodbye to Beech House, Hedy feels a shameful degree of relief, too: Being at Beech House without her father has been hard—the thought of being here with her mother and a new man seems impossible. Weak as it may be of her, Hedy doesn't want to have to face that grief again.

Her mother picks a lemon from the basket and rubs it over the microplane's fine little blades, sending a flurry of zest snowing down into a small glass dish and the fresh fragrance of the citrus oil into the air.

"Every time I think about telling Michelle I'm selling Beech House, my heart nearly stops beating," Cora says.

Hedy breaks off another bite of scone. "This is a lot of house to care for, Mom. At any age. People downsize when they get older. Michelle's not a child. She'll understand you have to sell."

"Don't be so sure. You saw her last night. She burst into tears the minute she walked into the kitchen," Cora says with a sigh. "Of course she would. She's like me. She feels things deeply."

Hedy dumps the rest of her scone into the trash and claps her hands clean of crumbs. "Just because I didn't break into tears at the end of *Terms of Endearment* doesn't mean I don't feel things, Mom."

"Don't be like that—you know what I mean. You're your father's daughter. You're logical like he was. Clinical when you need to be. It's not a character flaw."

Then why did Hedy always feel like her mother meant it as one?

"I just expected Michelle to be more excited," Cora says. "Didn't you?"

Hedy frowns. Can her mother really not understand why her granddaughter—never mind Hedy—might have reservations about this wedding?

"You and Max is all very sudden for her, Mom. You can't expect Michelle to come in here doing cartwheels."

Her mother sets down the microplane and levels her with a quizzical look. "I'm talking about her restaurant, Hedy."

"Oh. That." For the second time that morning, blooms of rueful heat soak her throat.

Cora wipes the last few curls of zest free with her fingertips. "I mean, here she is, a huge success, not to mention that she's sharing that success with someone she loves—a dream come true—but you wouldn't know it to talk to her."

"She did seem a little distracted when I called her about coming," Hedy admits.

Her mother looks up. "You don't think things with her and Wes are rocky, do you?"

Hedy shrugs, reaching for her coffee. "Don't ask me, Mom. If there was trouble in paradise, you'd know before I would."

"Oh, Hedy . . ." Her mother's eyes are soft, pitying. "That's not true."

"Of course, it is. Michelle always tells you things first. We both know she does."

"Not everything," Cora defends.

"The big stuff, Mom. The important things."

"That's only because it's easier to tell me. Michelle

doesn't have to worry about upsetting me the way she does with you. You're her mother. The stakes are higher."

Hedy buries a skeptical frown behind her coffee.

"But now you know how I felt when you always went to your father with news before you came to me." Her mother's smile is teasing, yet Hedy still feels herself bristle.

"So this is some kind of retribution?"

"Oh, good grief. I only meant . . . Never mind." Cora blows out a tired sigh and resumes her grating, sending the room plunging into a tense silence again.

Hedy pulls in a defeated breath of her own. "I should really call the office," she says.

"Don't they know you're on vacation?"

She's quite certain that spending what might be her last visit to her family's summer home watching her mother marry another man doesn't qualify as a vacation, but this comment, Hedy keeps to herself.

"My work is round the clock, Mom," she says instead. "If I don't find a buyer a house, someone else will."

Her mother's gaze remains even. "You don't have to talk to me like I'm dim, Hedy," she says tightly. "I used to be a working woman, too, you know."

Hedy has heard the stories of her mother working as a cook in her great-uncle Theo's restaurant during wartime. She doesn't doubt Cora experienced some of the stress that comes with a fast-paced job, but a few years helping out in the family diner isn't the same as building a career as a single woman in the high-stakes world of real estate. Yet another point Hedy won't make aloud.

The quiet returns, and with it, the tightness in Hedy's chest. She doesn't want to leave the room on a sour note.

"Why not start making a list, Mom," she suggests. "Things you want to keep. Go room by room."

Hedy steels herself for yet another of her mother's well-worn comparisons—*You and your father and your lists*—but it doesn't come. Instead, Cora's face softens with a wistful smile. Her hands fall to the stretch of butcher block and run fondly over the surface.

"I want to take my island."

"Mom . . ."

Her mother's eyes rise, flashing with determination. "You think I'm joking."

But Hedy knows her mother is completely serious. In the event of a fire, most people would rescue family photo albums, but Hedy knows her mother would try to rip the island from the floor to save it, or maybe just throw her body across it to protect it from the flames. Hedy had never understood Cora's devotion to the quirky collection of drawers and cabinets in the middle of the kitchen floor, but now she can't help wondering if her mother's love for it has always had more to do with the man who built it for her than the structure itself.

Cora continues to stare at her expectantly. "Why can't I take it?"

"Because it's installed, it's an attached good," Hedy explains as calmly to her mother as she does to all her sellers. "Meaning you can't remove it without causing damage to the property. So no, you can't take it with you."

"Well, shoot." Little waves of wrinkles undulate across her mother's forehead. "If I'd known, I'd have asked Max to put it on wheels that very first day."

7

1948

A streak of daylight stretched across the bedroom ceiling. Cora stared up at the shimmering ribbon as Harry shuddered with his release and collapsed on top of her, her husband taking in several hard breaths before he rolled off. His leg still slung over hers, she wondered if he might fall back asleep.

After she and Harry had made love for the first time, Cora couldn't understand how he fell so deeply asleep, or so quickly. Lying there, her mind had been racing, she'd never felt more awake, more aware of herself. But for Harry, the act had seemed to have the opposite effect.

It wasn't as if Cora hadn't known what to expect. She had absorbed the expertise of her dearest friend, Lizzie, who had been married a whole two months and already made love to her husband, Walter, more than a dozen times—making her an authority by comparison—when Cora had pulled Lizzie aside two nights before her own wedding. As she'd listened to the even rumble of Harry's snores, Cora had blinked up into the shapeless indigo, waiting for the lines and corners of their ceiling to come into focus, for her racing heart to slow, and wondered how long before her own body would quiet as her husband's had.

Since arriving four days ago, she and Harry had made

love twice in Beech House. This morning was the third time. The sky through the window still bruised with dawn, he'd drawn her against him, drowsily nuzzled the back of her neck while his hand had come around to stir her, caressing her until she turned to face him, finding his mouth there and open, catching his hungry groan in her throat. Maybe it was something about the nearness of the sea and its churning surf, the inescapable rhythm of the tide, but here on the island she felt an excitement about making love she hadn't felt before, an anticipation, possibility, even. Why did sex only have to be about getting pregnant? Couldn't there be room for simple exploration? Just a few days before, floating in the ocean while Harry sunned on the beach, she'd had the urge to peel off her suit and feel the salt water on her bare skin. She'd gotten her suit down as far as her waist, gasping at the sensation, before she looked up to find Harry marching in to join her and covered herself.

The mattress creaked. Cora turned her head to find that Harry had risen up on his elbow and was smiling down at her, a secretive sort of smile. As if he waited for her to ask his joke. Another beam of morning light had broken through the sheers. His pale blond hair and eyebrows looked as if they had been dipped in gold.

"What?" she asked finally.

"I have a good feeling this time. I think this one took."

Took. Like a mechanic working on a car, sure that with this twist of the key, the engine would turn over at last.

"Any reason in particular?" she asked.

"Your appointment tomorrow." Her doctor's visit. Harry had insisted she be seen by their summer physician, a man named Dr. Fisher who had known Harry practically since he was born. "It makes sense, don't you think? Like carrying an umbrella to make sure it won't rain. You're seeing the doctor about . . . well . . . so wouldn't it just figure that making the appointment would do the trick?"

It was a clumsy analogy, but Cora smiled anyway, even though she wasn't sure she liked to think of getting pregnant as a trick. Although it certainly seemed tricky for them.

Harry shuffled closer and took her hand from where she let it rest on her stomach. "I shouldn't feel nearly this good after so much gin last night, but I do. It must be all the salt," he declared, thumping a fist against his chest as if he were taking in a bracing breath of arctic air. "I always forget that it really is the best hangover cure. That, and a roll in the hay with my best girl." He dropped his grinning mouth on hers and she let his kiss smother her chuckle. He'd always fancied himself a rogue, even though the racier phrases never seemed to sound right coming from him. Like an older person trying to use the language of the younger set. Like an ill-fitting suit.

"I could make us an omelet," she suggested. "With that leftover asparagus?"

"That would hit the spot," he said.

Cora padded to the bathroom to wash and then changed into her yellow-striped house dress. At the mirror, she ran a brush through her hair, making a side part and keeping it flat with a pair of pins. She liked what the sun had already started to do to it. Only a few days here and golden streaks sliced through the dark red. She'd be careful, though. The salt water, everyone warned her, would be harsh. But Cora loved being in it, loved the bracing cold, the sizzling foam, the powerful pull of the tide, all of which had surprised her, having spent so little time at the shore growing up. Surprised Harry, too. Alarmed him, really. Their first day down at the beach he'd hovered over her as she floated beyond the surf line, lecturing her about currents and riptides, as if she were a child still learning to swim.

When she came out of the bathroom, Harry was standing at the window, the sheer drawn back in his hand.

"Looks like we might have to wait on that omelet," he said. "Must be that kitchen fellow parked in the driveway."

"He's here already?"

"Just sitting in his truck with the door open. I suspect he's waiting for us to get up."

Cora's hands slowed on the tie of her house dress, a panicked thought tearing through her as she surveyed the room, counting all the open windows. Just how long had Max Dempsey been out there? Long enough to hear the even knocking of the headboard, or, God forbid, the victorious groan of her husband's—?

Her face burned. "You don't suppose he . . . ?"

Harry turned to her. "What?"

She stared at him, exasperated. Couldn't he guess? "You don't think he heard us, do you?"

"Of course not. Although . . ." Harry's eyes narrowed. "If that's a challenge, then I'm game for another round," he said, grabbing for her.

"Don't joke." She snaked out of his reach. "Because if he had, that would be so embarrassing."

"I wouldn't worry. He doesn't look the sort to be easily embarrassed."

"As if you can tell something like that about a person just by seeing them through a window," Cora said, sliding into her summer sandals. "And anyway, I was talking about me."

"Of course you were, sweetheart," Harry said, giving her

rear a teasing pat as he passed. "Let him in, will you? I need a shower and a shave."

* * *

A person could believe what they wanted to believe, so as she opened the screen door, Cora believed that Max Dempsey had not, in fact, heard the sounds of their coupling from the front seat of his truck. Otherwise she wouldn't have been able to hold her smile—let alone his gaze—as he crossed the driveway in easy strides to where she waited for him.

"You did say eight wasn't too early?" His hair was a dustier brown than she'd guessed it last night, but the low light hadn't played any tricks on his eyes. They were every bit a shimmering gray-blue.

"Not at all," she said. "My husband will be down in a minute."

Max paused on the doorstep to drag the soles of his work boots over the straw mat, though Cora didn't know why he bothered. A few days here and she was already finding sand everywhere, in sinks and drawers, sprinkled in their sheets like talcum powder. The other day, she'd even discovered some in her casserole when she'd crunched down on a gritty bite of noodle.

Living this close to the water, she didn't see how it was possible to keep sand out of a house, and she wasn't even sure she wanted to. Growing up in the city, mud and dirt were the enemy her mother spent her days relentlessly battling. But beach sand seemed somehow pure, inherently clean. Cora didn't mind finding it everywhere, didn't mind the tickle of it on her bare feet. She rather liked it.

She stepped back to let him in. "No tools?"

"Not yet. I'm only looking around today, just familiarizing myself with the space and taking notes," he said, scanning the room. He whistled through his teeth. "Boy, not much storage, is there?"

"That was my first thought, too." Cora trailed him as he toured, cinching the belt of her dress a little tighter. "I don't think they did a great deal of cooking," she said, almost apologetically, as he swept back the curtain below the sink to reveal a collection of lobster pots.

"Most summer people don't," he said, moving on to inspect the stove. "Or they just let other people do it for them." She couldn't decide if there was an edge of something in the man's voice, something damning, maybe.

"It's my husband's family house," she said.

"Well, it's yours now." Max pulled a small leather-bound notebook from his shirt pocket, the book dwarfed in his strong fingers, and split it open. "So now you'll personalize it, make it the way you want it," he said. "What do you have in mind? Lots of cabinets or less? More counter space?" He moved his pencil as he talked, drawing shapes in the air. There was something magical in the motion, as if he were casting some kind of spell over the room. Cora thought of the clippings she'd been collecting, the pictures she'd torn out of magazines. But now the vastness of his question, the breadth of possibility, overwhelmed her. What did she really know about designing a kitchen?

"I'm not sure," she said. "What do you think would look right?"

He shrugged. "It's not my kitchen," he said, matter-of-factly but not at all harshly. "It doesn't matter what I think. I'm not going to be the one cooking in it."

She turned to take the kitchen in freshly, to let her imagi-
nation wander with her gaze, emboldened by his request and
the affirmation that it was indeed her kitchen now.

So what *did* she want?

Their kitchen back in Boston was functional but cold.
Metal cabinets and a dark countertop. Since it was only a
rental, she'd never dared imagine something else, but this . . .
this could be just as she wanted it.

Possibility thrummed like hummingbird wings.

"Don't feel like you have to decide this minute," Max
said. "We're just getting started. Every room is a process, but
especially kitchens." He cut her a quick look. "They're very
personal, you know."

An interesting observation, Cora thought. Particularly
from a man.

"You must cook," she said.

"Me?" He chuckled low. "I can fry an egg. That's about
it."

"Your wife, then?"

"No wife." He smiled. "As my married brothers remind
me daily."

She laughed, training her gaze away from his. He was a
good-looking man. Those sparkling eyes. No doubt he had
options.

"I'm just going to make a few quick sketches for my own
reference." Max plucked the pencil from behind his ear and
pointed it at the banquette. "Mind if I sit down?"

"Please."

He took a seat on the end, his long legs reaching the other
side. She scanned his profile, trying to decide how old he
was. She'd guessed him a few years older than her the night
before, but now she wasn't sure they weren't the same age.

He was deeply tanned, and his heavy brow made a sharp shelf above his eyes. Realizing she was staring, she swept her gaze to the stove.

"I promised you some coffee, didn't I?" she said cheerfully. As she measured out the grounds, the quick, hard scratching of Max's pencil filled the quiet, and it occurred to her for the first time that he would be in this house, in this room, quite a lot in the weeks ahead. That his company would become a constant, and she wasn't entirely uneased by the thought of having someone in her kitchen with her. She had loved the noise and activity of the restaurant's kitchen, the busyness of it. Loved it so much that after she'd stopped working there, she'd asked Harry to do his work at their breakfast table at home while she cooked their dinner. He'd tried for a while but found the small surface too difficult, the chair too hard. And all the clatter of the pots and the tap-tap of the chopping. When he'd abandoned her for the sanctuary of his office again, Cora had asked for a radio, hating the tomb-like quiet of cooking alone, but the crackle and sizzle of the announcers hadn't felt right, hadn't felt warm, so she kept it off.

"Are you sure I can't offer you something to eat?" she asked.

Max chucked his chin at the sideboard. "I wouldn't turn down a piece of that pie over there."

Confused, Cora glanced where he pointed and saw the strawberry pie she'd made for the party. After all the activity of last night, she'd forgotten Harry had brought it back.

"I'm not sure you want that," she said. "It's awfully stale by now."

"Why not let me be the judge?"

"All right."

No sense in letting it go to waste, Cora thought as she cut him a generous slice and set the plate and a fork beside him, hearing a moan of approval through his chewing even before she'd stepped back to the sink.

"Boy, if you think this is stale," he said, "then I'm not sure we share the same meaning of the word."

She smiled, feeling a pleasant warmth at her throat from his compliment. "You're just being polite."

"Polite would have been not asking for a piece in the first place."

When she laughed, they shared another smile, letting their amusement hang on an extra beat while he continued to eat. Almost finished, he moved the plate to the side and resumed his sketching.

"There are all kinds of things you can do to personalize a kitchen," he said. "Last month, I put together a new kitchen for a lady in Sandwich. She likes to bake, so I built in slots for all her cookie sheets, right next to her stove. Another job, I made compartments in some of the drawers to help keep spice jars organized."

"Clever," Cora said, drawing down three mugs from the shelf. She wondered if he could do that for her, too. It drove her mad trying to keep all the jars in place on the top of the stove; they were always tipping and rolling off.

"But that's for later. Right now, we're concerned with the overall plan. The big picture."

Through the screens came the sound of tires grinding over gravel. Cora leaned back to check the window and watched a caravan of trucks rumbling down the driveway. The other workmen were arriving.

She considered the room again. "Do you have to get rid

of all of it?" she asked. "Because I rather like that butcher block over there."

"Then we keep it," Max said. "I'm not a big fan of new for the sake of new. Sometimes it's best to fuse the two." His pencil danced across the page again. Glancing over, Cora watched him write at the top in capital letters: *WISH LIST*. Then, below it: *butcher block STAYS*.

"Sorry to keep you waiting!" Harry blew in, damp hair combed back and shiny like pulled taffy, his hand already outstretched. Cora stepped back to clear his path, grazed by a fragrant breeze of mint soap. "Harry Campbell. Good to meet you."

Max climbed to his feet. "Max Dempsey."

"You have your work cut out with this one, I'm afraid." Harry hitched his fists on his waist and scanned the room gravely, as if they were explorers surveying a rugged mountain range.

"I've seen older," Max assured him.

Harry squinted. "Done a lot of kitchens on the Point, have you?"

"Not here, no. But Edgartown. Oak Bluffs. A few on the cape." Max shrugged good-naturedly. "The big cottages all look alike."

Again, that hint of indifference. Maybe he, like her, wasn't an islander, either.

"Any idea how long all this will take?" Harry asked, making a vague sweep with his hand.

"Depends on the job," Max said. "But I work in parts. Try to do chunks at a time so you always have someplace to cook." The last part he said directly to Cora. She smiled, grateful.

"Not to worry," said Harry. "I'm headed back to Boston in a few days, so there's no rush."

Cora whirled around and blinked at her husband, startled at the news. "When was that decided?"

"Just last night, sweetheart. I thought I told you."

Prickles of worry fired around the base of her scalp, but she managed to rearrange her strained features into an agreeable smile, remembering they weren't alone.

In the tense quiet, Max Dempsey studied his sketchbook, shifted on his booted feet.

"I'm sure you can manage on your own here for a few days." Harry cupped her cheek. "And you know Lois and Ned would love to have you over for dinner while I'm gone," he said, swinging an arm around her and tugging her close, so swiftly that Cora had to brace herself against his chest, unbalanced by the speed of his embrace. He rubbed her upper arm vigorously, as if she had been rescued from freezing water and needed warming up. "Whatever my darling girl wants. A brilliant cook should have an equally brilliant kitchen." One more rub and Harry released her. "I just need to check on a few things in the office," he said, already crossing back for the door. "Bring my coffee around when it's ready, will you? And a slice of pie, too. Great meeting you, Max."

In Harry's wake, the air remained charged with his praise. Cora felt her cheeks still flushed with modest heat. "I'm sure every husband thinks his wife is a wonderful cook."

"Maybe," said Max, "but I can offer a second opinion, and your husband is right." He scraped up the last bite of pie and clapped his hands clean. Cora watched him tuck his notebook back into his shirt pocket.

"Done already?" she asked. "But you haven't even had your coffee."

"Next time," he said. "This was a good start. Keep thinking about what you'd like this room to look like and I'll come back tomorrow with drafting paper so we can start putting things down, give them real shape."

Her head spun, a dizzying mix of excitement and nerves.

"Actually," she said, moving to the sideboard. "I do have a few ideas . . ." She pulled out the pile of clippings from the linen drawer and handed them to him.

"Well, all right." Max Dempsey took the stack and fanned through them, his gray-blue eyes flashing. "See? You do know what you want." He tugged his notebook from his pocket again. "Most people do, in my experience," he said, smiling as he slid the collection of cutouts into the pages. "They're just waiting for someone to ask them."

8

1999

"Tiffany didn't want to come in?" her grandmother asks when Mickey returns to the kitchen. Cora is at the island, picking calmly through a bowl of crabmeat, but Mickey detects a tightness in the air that not even the sweet fragrance of freshly zested lemons can loosen. What argument has she missed?

"She had to get back to the restaurant," Mickey says, looking intently between her mother and her grandmother, as if Mickey is a parent who has walked in to find a broken dish on the floor and is waiting for the guilty party to confess.

Her mother shoves on a pair of readers and picks up the *Gazette* from the counter. "Did you tell Tiffany about the clambake?" Hedy asks as she scans the front page.

"She'll be here." As much as Mickey wants to know the source of the obvious tension in the kitchen, she has other, more pressing questions. "Did you know that Buzz is selling Chowder's to a developer?"

Her grandmother's fingers slow in the bowl. She bobs her head slowly. "I saw Buzz at the market a few weeks ago and he could barely look me in the eye. He's terribly torn about it."

"He should be, Grams. Chowder's is an institution."

"You mustn't be mad at him, Michelle. He's on his own now. He has to do what's best for him."

But as she reaches into the fridge for the tub of ricotta, Mickey feels a childish spark of betrayal. Not her grandmother, too? She'd been sure Cora would share Mickey's ire. Chowder's had also been a huge part of Mickey's grandparents' world here.

"I know it's Buzz's place to sell to whoever he wants," Mickey says as she tears off the tub's plastic lid, "but that doesn't mean I have to be happy about it."

When Mickey reaches under the island for a mixing bowl, Cora stops her.

"The filling can wait," her grandmother says, gently moving the bowl of crabmeat and the container of ricotta to the side. "Why not cool off with a swim first?"

"I didn't bring my suit," Mickey says, not wanting to admit she doesn't have one to bring. At Beech House, you can arrive without a toothbrush or even clean underwear, but to arrive without a swimsuit is cause for banishment. Almost as unforgivable as being on a diet. But in the last two years, forget getting away to the beach; Mickey's been lucky to find time to soak in a tub for ten minutes—what does she need with a swimsuit these days? Several times Wes has suggested they travel to the Eastern Shore, or maybe see the ponies on Chincoteague, but Mickey could never justify spending the money, let alone the time. Now she wishes she had, thinking of dashing into the surf together, of winding herself around him in the waves and then coming up for air on the beach, rolling into each other on sunbaked towels. What if she doesn't get the chance now?

"Check the closet in the Béchamel Room," Cora says. "There's bound to be one of your old suits in there." A good bet. Summer's end always found one or two forgotten swim-suits left drying by the outdoor shower, invariably added to the bursting basket of communal beachwear that had been collected for who knew how many years and was rarely purged.

The wall phone chimes, rattling. "I'll get it," Cora says, dragging her hands down her apron before she picks it up. Mickey waits, anticipation pounding that it might be Wes calling her back, but a few nods and Cora hangs up.

"That was the florist wanting to confirm delivery," her grandmother says, carrying a pencil to the refrigerator and adding another check mark to the to-do list tacked under a lobster magnet. "Now I'm just waiting to hear back from the caterers, and the party rental service about the chairs."

Mickey stares at the ingredients in front of her. As much as she wants to cook with her grandmother, her heart isn't quite in it after Tiffany's news.

"I just wish someone had told me earlier," Mickey says.

Lines of remorse grow deep in her grandmother's fore-head. "Don't be angry with us, sweetheart. Tiffany didn't want us to say anything. She knew you'd be upset and she didn't want to spoil the celebration. Not just the wedding, but your success, too."

"Too late for that."

Mickey is sure she has mumbled the response, but as soon as she looks up, her mother and grandmother both wear a wide-eyed look of alarm.

Hedy blinks at Mickey over her readers. "What is that supposed to mean?"

For a foolish second, Mickey thinks she can brush off their inquiry, but her grandmother is already shaking her head. "We knew something was off," Cora says firmly. "We knew it the minute you walked in the door." She glances toward Mickey's mother and the two women share a knowing look.

Hedy slides her paper to the side. "What's going on, Michelle?"

"I've just gotten a little behind on some bills, that's all."

"How little?"

"I don't understand," Cora says. "The restaurant is doing so well. You have great reviews. You're in *Gourmet*, for goodness' sake."

This is always the hard part to explain. Looking in, everyone assumes filled tables mean they must be making money hand over fist. It's an understandable assumption. Once upon a time, Mickey would have thought the same thing.

"How far underwater are you?" her mother asks.

Far enough that I've been keeping it from my boyfriend and that I rushed off to this wedding without him, is the answer Mickey should give but doesn't.

Her grandmother steps closer. "Why didn't you tell us right away that you were having trouble managing the restaurant?"

"Because I thought I could handle it, Grams."

"What does Wes say?"

Mickey picks up her coffee and downs a lukewarm sip to stall.

Her mother sweeps off her glasses. "He doesn't know?"

"I was going to tell him," Mickey defends. "But then I got your call about the wedding and it just felt like the wrong time—"

"You have to tell him, Michelle."

"I will," Mickey says, "when I get back."

"Not when you get back," Cora says. "Now."

"But we're in the middle of making the ravioli." Mickey motions to the dirty mixing bowl they made the dough in. "And I have dishes to clean . . ."

"I'll be *plongeur* today, chef—better you clean your conscience instead," her grandmother says sternly, sliding the bowl out of reach and hitching her chin toward the door. "Use the phone in the study. You'll have more privacy."

Mickey looks over at her mother, hoping for aid, but Hedy's narrowed blue eyes remain resolute. Whatever fight had divided the two women while Mickey was talking to Tiffany has clearly evaporated with Mickey's confession. The last time Mickey saw this united a front between her mother and grandmother was when Darren Savage stood Mickey up for the summer formal and a bag of spoiled clams mysteriously appeared on the front seat of the young man's Mustang the next morning.

"Before you go." Her mother reaches into the fridge for the pitcher. Mickey's grandmother is already pulling down a tumbler from the cabinet.

"A dose of liquid courage," her mother says, handing Mickey a generous pour of lobster daiquiri with a tender smile. "Something tells me you're going to need it, kiddo."

9

1948

Dr. Reginald Fisher looked every bit as warm as his picture in the waiting room, Cora thought with relief as she settled into the upholstered chair on the other side of his polished desk. His graying hair was fine and curly, wispy like dandelion fluff ready to be blown to the wind, and his eyes were a soft brown. When he spoke, two dimples stayed creased in his full cheeks, giving him the impression of a continual smile. In front of him, a notebook sat open, a few lines already written at the top of the page. Something about her and Harry, no doubt. Or maybe just about her?

She settled her straw clutch on her lap, not sure why she felt nervous. This was, after all, a friendly visit, a chance for her to be introduced to the Campbells' family doctor on the Vineyard, no different from meeting the Welches or any of the other neighbors on the Point. Still, her fingertips worried the purse's raffia flowers. It did please her to see an abundance of healthy-looking plants on the windowsill behind his chair, several blooming with white flowers. She thought of the potted African violet that her doctor in Boston, Dr. Schwab, kept on the edge of his desk, how it always looked so parched, its leaves so limp. *What does it say about a fertility doctor who can't make a houseplant bloom?* she had whispered to Harry after their first appointment.

"Harry couldn't come with you today?"

"There was some kind of emergency at the bank," Cora explained. "He was still on the phone when I left."

"Too bad. I was looking forward to seeing him." The doctor sat back, causing the chair's brown leather to give up a gentle creak, and laced his fingers over his white coat. "I understand this is your first time on the Vineyard?" His smile was as relaxed as his pose and Cora felt her own pulse settle a bit. "And what a spot you have out there on the Point," he said.

She nodded enthusiastically. "We're very fortunate."

We. The pronoun seemed to stick in her throat, strange and insincere. As if she were being deceitful in using it. After all, she'd only been on the island a few weeks.

But why should it feel strange? Hadn't even Max Dempsey said she needed to start thinking of Beech House as her house, too?

"Harry must be glad to be back," the doctor said. "I'll bet he's already busy practicing his backhand."

"You know he plays?"

"I know he wins. I'm sure he's told you that he holds the record for youngest Half Shell Tournament champion?"

Only a dozen times. Cora smiled. "He's mentioned it, yes."

"We're all looking forward to this year's event, having everyone back on the island. After these last few years, how hard they've been . . ." He gave up a soft sigh. "It feels almost like coming out of a tunnel, doesn't it?"

Cora thought of the Sumner Tunnel in Boston, how she would always have to squint for several moments to adjust to the glare after over a mile in the dark, the light almost painful.

The end of a long, dark tunnel, spilling them all out into the brightness of this summer.

Yes, she liked that comparison very much.

"So . . ." Dr. Fisher slid on a pair of reading glasses and leaned forward to scan his scribblings. "When Harry and I spoke on the phone, I explained that it isn't customary to test for pregnancy unless there is a medical reason—"

"A test?" Cora blinked at him, startled heat crawling up her throat. "Doctor, I don't know what Harry told you, but I can assure you I'm not pregnant."

"Oh?" The doctor's warm brown eyes flicked quizzically at her over the top of his glasses.

Cora pressed a hand over her hair, tilting her face enough to hide an embarrassed flush. "I'm afraid Harry is a bit impatient," she said. "Sometimes I think he confuses the gestation period of a human with that of a hamster."

Dr. Fisher released a low laugh. "That would be quite a trick."

"The thing is, doctor . . ." She gripped the top of her clutch with both hands tightly, as if the purse were a steering wheel. "I think . . . no, I know . . . Harry is concerned that we're not . . . well, that *I'm* not . . ."

"Conceiving?"

Cora nodded quickly, immeasurably relieved for his rescue. "I think he wonders if there's a certain way," she said. "Maybe something we're not doing?"

Dr. Fisher set down his pen. "Cora, when someone's used to plugging in numbers to get the right answer—which you and I both know Harry does for a living—the uncertainty of the reproductive process can be exasperating. Even alarming." He paused to sweep off his glasses, folded them carefully, and set them to one side. "But the fact is that there are many reasons why couples, even the healthiest ones, don't always get pregnant right away."

"But we've been trying for nearly a year, doctor. And Harry says that's too long."

"And if Harry were here, I'd remind him of his area of expertise, which isn't, last I heard, obstetrics." When Dr. Fisher laughed quietly, Cora smiled, gratitude stilling the butterflies that continued to flutter in her stomach. "I don't know what your doctor back in Boston has told you, but a year isn't uncommon. I have patients who've conceived after two, sometimes three years."

Fissures of hope shot through her. "Then you don't think we should be concerned?"

The doctor held her gaze. "Are you concerned?"

Cora picked at the ragged corner of her thumbnail, the urge to confess to him so strong. He had such a kind face. So much kinder than Dr. Schwab, whose white caterpillar brows were always fixed in a perpetual V of disapproval.

"The truth, doctor?" She blew out a weary sigh. "I'm concerned that I'm not concerned."

The confession out, Cora searched Dr. Fisher's face expectantly, her racing heart slowing when a warm smile stretched across his face.

He shook his head patiently. "Don't be," he said simply.

She allowed a grateful breath to escape her tight chest, and another smile stretched across his round face, his dimples deepening.

"You came here for my advice, so here it is." Dr. Fisher closed his notebook and folded his hands over the top. "Don't worry about getting pregnant. Enjoy your summer, enjoy your marriage. Swim in the ocean, go for a sail. Put your efforts into other things." He leaned in. "Do you have hobbies, Cora?"

"I like to cook," she said.

One brow arched skeptically. "I meant things you do for pleasure."

She smiled. "That is what I do for pleasure, doctor."

"Then Harry is a lucky man."

"So he claims." Cora patted her curls, pushing them up to get air at her damp neck. "He's even hired a man to update our kitchen."

"That's just the sort of thing I'm talking about," Dr. Fisher said, nodding. "What you need is a project. A distraction. Then you'll see." His smile grew so wide, his eyes were swallowed to sparkling slits. "Nature will take its course."

* * *

Pulling into Beech House's winding drive a half hour later, Cora didn't startle anymore at the collection of trucks and wagons that filled the crescent of gravel, or marvel at the clutter on the front lawn where the workmen had turned the grass into their construction staging area, their equipment and supplies always seeming to expand overnight like proofed dough. When Cora spotted Max Dempsey's dusty-blue truck in the configuration, she felt an unexpected burst of relief, Dr. Fisher's advice floating back to her as she turned off the car, buoying her steps as she crossed the drive for the door to the kitchen wing. *What you need is a project. A distraction . . . Nature will take its course . . .*

Once through the entry, she slowed upon seeing Max at the sink, a measuring tape stretched between his opened arms.

He flashed her a welcoming smile over his shoulder. "Morning."

"Good morning," she said.

He lowered his arms, and the tape retracted with a high-pitched whir as it snapped back into the case. He wore a work shirt just a shade lighter than his blue jeans. Cora wondered if he knew that the color matched his eyes.

"I just stopped by to take a few more measurements," Max said, shoving the tape into his pocket.

She glanced through the doorway, curious if Harry was done with his phone calls and moving about the house, but the great room was empty.

"I also wanted to drop off some sketches for you to look at." Max directed her gaze to the banquette, where a pile of pages sat. "Those clippings you saved were helpful. Gave me a good sense of what you want."

Cora remembered his pocket notebook, how her heart had jumped when he'd written *WISH LIST* in big letters and then slashed a thick line underneath it.

She crossed to the table and picked up the top drawing carefully, admiring the crisscross of pencil lines.

"They're rough," Max said as he came beside her, standing close enough that his sleeve brushed her arm. "Just ideas."

She caught a breath of him, dark and earthy, like warm metal. It always struck her, the smell of other men. She was so accustomed to Harry's aftershave, the minty scent he'd worn forever. How strong it had been whenever he'd come to the restaurant and sat on his usual stool at the counter, always detectable, even through the pervasive haze of sautéed garlic and tomato sauce, when she'd lean in to set down his plate or refill his coffee.

Max laid out the drawings in a grid and stepped back,

folding his hands over his chest, letting a few moments pass before he asked, "Any one in particular jump out at you?"

Cora scanned the drawings slowly, possibility prickling. They were all different—and all beautifully rendered. Some with more cabinets, some with more drawers. But her gaze always returned to one in particular, which featured a large work surface in the very center of the floor: a long, high table that reminded her of Marigold's cooking space.

"That one," she said. "I don't think I've ever seen a kitchen like that in someone's home."

Max chuckled. "Me, neither."

When Cora glanced up at him, he wore a sheepish smile. "I just remember you saying you didn't like having your back to everyone, so I thought, why not just put something right there in the middle of the action, forward facing? Most people nowadays want an open floor plan, but I'm not sure how many of them like to cook the way you do. Or can, for that matter."

If he meant the point as a compliment, Cora wasn't certain, but she warmed with it all the same.

"And this room is so big. It just seems like an awful waste of space, otherwise," he said, pushing a hand through his hair. Unlike most of the men she knew, he didn't seem to have decided on a part, but rather swept it all back in one great wave, letting it fall where it wanted.

Cora moved her gaze from the page to the room and then back to the page again, trying to envision what he intended. The new cabinets and countertops on either side of the sink and stove were easy to imagine, but a table in the middle of the floor?

"And you could put the . . . what would you call it? A workstation?"

"I've heard it called an island," Max said.

An island on an island, Cora thought with a smile. "You could attach it right to the floor, then? Make it permanent, I mean?"

"That would be the idea, yeah." Max leaned forward to point on the drawing. "And I could put shelves underneath it. A place for your mixing bowls, or pots. And drawers, too, so your measuring cups and spices and all that could be close."

As he swept his finger around the sketch, Cora imagined herself moving through the space, all that room to spread out her ingredients, to prep and cook and serve . . .

"I love it," she breathed.

"Good." Max gathered the drawings back into a pile and rolled them up. "I'll be another few days finishing up the job in Edgartown, then I'll be back here for good. The benefit of a bare-bones space is that you don't have to worry about the delay for demolition. There's not much here to tear down and haul away. We can talk finishes later. Materials, colors, all that," he said, clapping the roll of drawings against his thigh as he moved to the door. "And I want you to know, you won't hurt my feelings if you want metal cabinets and drawers. Just because I'm a cabinetmaker doesn't mean I have to make yours, okay?"

Cora smiled. "Okay."

But as she followed Max Dempsey to the door, a realization sparked: This man, this relative stranger, hadn't just designed a kitchen—he'd designed a kitchen especially for her.

Gratitude overwhelmed her. Her skin flushed with it like a fever.

"Thank you," she said as Max pushed open the screen.

He turned in the doorway, considering her for a moment before he offered her a bemused grin. "I haven't done anything yet."

*   *   *

The office door was closed when Cora walked through the downstairs to find Harry a few minutes later. She leaned against the raised panel, hearing her husband's laughter on the other side before she dared to open the door a crack. Hearing the squeak of the hinges, Harry spun around in his chair, the phone still at his cheek, and waved her in.

"Friday at noon, then," he said into the receiver, his eyes fixed intensely on her as he talked. "I look forward to it, Mr. Reynolds."

Hanging up, he leapt from his leather chair. "Tell me everything, darling girl," he said, breathless with excitement as he came around the desk and took Cora in his arms. His eyes flicked longingly over her face, and she might have been exasperated with him if he didn't wear such a look of unabashed hope. "It's good news, isn't it?"

"Oh, Harry . . ." She set her hands on his chest, feeling the furious racing of his heartbeat under her fingers. "Why did you request a test? You didn't really think I was pregnant, did you?"

His smile fell. "Then you didn't bother?"

"What would have been the point? My period only just ended, remember?"

"Oh." He frowned, looking utterly dejected. "Because when you came in here just now, you looked so happy, I thought . . ."

A flicker of remorse sparked in her stomach—Harry had mistaken her excitement about Max's kitchen design for good news from her appointment. No wonder he was confused.

She flushed with guilt, eager to buoy his dimming optimism. "Dr. Fisher assured me that we have no reason to be concerned," she said brightly, snuggling into his arms. "He says there's nothing worrisome in a couple taking a year or more to conceive."

"That's not what Dr. Schwab said."

"Maybe Dr. Schwab doesn't know everything, Harry," she said, leaning back to meet his narrowed gaze.

"Did Fisher have any suggestions?"

"Just that we try to focus on other things, to let it happen in its own course. Me, especially, he said." She smoothed the wide triangles of her husband's sport collar. "I told him we were redoing the kitchen and he seemed very pleased about that."

Harry snorted. "Probably because he hopes for a dinner invitation."

"Don't be mean. He only meant that we shouldn't be putting so much pressure on ourselves. That we should spend this summer enjoying being here together. And that having a baby will happen in its own time."

"Maybe," said Harry. "But it won't happen in the kitchen. Unless we can convince that Dempsey fellow to build us a bed in there, too." His frown righted itself into a devilish grin.

"Very funny." Cora wanted to tell him about the work station—island—Max had designed but didn't want to change the subject when her husband was looking so cheery again.

"Are you hungry?" she said instead. "I thought I'd make us tuna melts for lunch with that sharp cheddar I bought."

"That sounds delicious—and just the thing," Harry said,

turning his wrist to check his watch. "I have one more call to make, then I promised Ned a match at one. Better get the practice in while I can. God knows how soft I'll get back in Boston for a few days. Promise me you'll call Lois while I'm gone. Have her take you to the club. We're members, you know. One lunch with her there and the whole of West Tisbury will know who you are." Harry shifted to look past her. "Is Dempsey still here?"

Cora shook her head. "He won't be back until the end of the week."

"And you're sure you don't mind him being here while I'm gone?"

"He's very friendly. And you know I like company in my kitchen." *My kitchen. Our house.* Cora bit back a smile, feeling a foolish prickle of pride. She was quite getting the hang of this now, wasn't she?

"How friendly, exactly?" Harry tightened his grip around her waist, looking down at her with a playful scowl. "Should I be jealous?"

"Says the man who married Lois Welch."

"She was Lois Kern then. And it was never consummated."

"At ten?" Cora exclaimed. "I should hope not!"

He tickled her sides until she shrieked, then dropped a kiss on her mouth, pulling back just enough to search her eyes. "I know you think I'm bonkers for being so impatient, sweetheart. It's just that we've put our lives on hold long enough. First my parents, and then the war. And it doesn't help that everyone has already started their families and we're so far behind . . ."

Far behind what, exactly? Cora wondered, feeling a fresh twinge of frustration.

She frowned up at him. "It's not a race, Harry."

"I know that, darling."

But Cora wasn't so sure he did.

She lowered her hands from his collar, but he swept them up again.

"I just can't wait to see you holding our child." Harry bent his head and rested his forehead against hers. "Is that so terrible of me?"

"No." Cora caressed his jaw, the tiny square of strawberry-blond whiskers he'd missed shaving that morning, poking out from his freckled skin at the edge of his chin. "Not terrible," she whispered. "Not even close."

Harry released her and returned to his chair. Cora reached down to the framed photograph of their wedding day that he kept on his desk and admired it. How happy they looked in front of his parents' grand fireplace. Her simple ivory satin gown. Harry's tidy suit. Her bouquet, a heavy waterfall of white roses that had fallen almost to her knees. How glorious it had smelled.

She sighed. "I still don't see why we can't put this one up on the wall with the others."

"We've been over this, sweetheart," Harry said, wheeling his chair back to the desk. "Only people who've been married at the house can be added to the wall. Those are the rules."

"But if it's our house now, why can't we make new rules?"

"Because it would be bad luck. My mother always said so."

Cora set the photograph back down, thinking sulkily that it hadn't been their fault they couldn't marry at Beech House.

"But I promise you, darling, as soon as we can, we'll in-

vite the whole Point here to watch us renew our vows some-
day and then we'll have a proper photo to hang, all right?"
Harry said, snatching up the receiver before she could agree.
"Now be a love and let me make this one last call."

10

1999

Despite her grandmother's request for donations to a food pantry in lieu of wedding gifts, the study is cluttered with packages when Mickey steps inside, so many that the damp smell of the room's sea-soaked wood walls is masked by the powdery fragrance of wrapping paper. Mickey has to move a gold-foil box off the desk chair, huge but surprisingly light. She sets it down carefully atop a nearby stack of more presents, afraid of dropping it, her hands shaking so much with nerves. A part of her—and it's a shameful, weak part—hopes that Wes won't be able to come to the phone, that she'll be granted a few more hours of clemency, but the rest of her knows she's put this off too long.

Taking in a deep breath, she punches the number and waits, hearing her heart thump back at her against the earpiece. She swigs her daiquiri and swallows hard.

"Piquant, this is Nina."

"Nina, it's Mickey." Is her voice shaking, too? God, she hopes not.

"Mickey! Hi! How's it going over there?"

Over there. Nina makes it sound like Mickey has just gone down the block for a few hours. Like she hasn't crossed into another universe, light years away from Piquant, which is how it suddenly feels.

"Everything's great." Mickey winds the cord around her fingers. "What are we looking at for reservations tonight?" she asks as casually as she can, because that's usually one of the first things she asks Nina at preservice, and as much as she wants to talk to Wes, she doesn't want to give her manager a reason to suspect anything's wrong.

"Let's see . . ." Pages rustle, Nina checking the book. "Booked solid. And one, two . . . six on the wait list."

Mickey knows she should feel a swell of relief at that number—especially for a Tuesday night—but her heart still pounds. "Is Wes around?"

"He and Lucas are at the bar, tasting. Julianna came by with those reds you requested."

Alarm skitters across Mickey's scalp. Wes's ex-girlfriend, Julianna? What were the chances there was another rep with the same name?

"Hang on, I'll go get him."

Nina puts Mickey on hold, leaving her with Piquant's piped-in piano jazz and the image of Wes listening to Julianna talk about tannins and body, her asking if he can taste the black currant, if he thinks it's tight enough, using words like "buttery" and "firm." One of Mickey's most cherished memories with Wes is when they were looking to build Piquant's wine list and he took her to a tasting in the Shenandoah Valley. How much fun it was trying to pair dishes with varietals, how turned on she got just watching him swirl his glass, his wide palm cradling the bowl . . .

The line clicks and Mickey sucks in a startled breath.

"Me, again," says Nina. "Wes said he wants to take the

call from the office." Probably best, Mickey thinks. When he blows his top at her, he'll be out of earshot of the staff downstairs. "Hey, did Wes tell you about last night? Chelsea and Pete got engaged! It was so romantic. Wes made a hazelnut tart and stuck the ring right in the middle. God only knows what that man will think of when it comes time for the two of you to make it official—"

"Got it, Nina, thanks." Wes's voice breaks in, warm and cheery, and the other line clicks off.

Mickey pulls in a deep breath. "I didn't mean for you to have to leave the kitchen."

"Yeah, well, I don't think you want me sharing the dream I had about you in front of the staff," he says.

The pounding behind her chest migrates lower. So much for hoping he'd make this confession easy on her. "Very funny."

"More like, very dirty." She can hear him grinning through the phone. "So how's it going there, Beautiful?"

The groan of her desk chair reclined sounds in the background. He's getting more comfortable while she's becoming more undone.

"It's going great. So far, anyway." Mickey manages a short laugh.

"Prewedding jitters everywhere, I'll bet."

Yes, she thinks, *but ironically not from the bride.* "How's everything there?" she says instead. "Nina said you've been full."

"Packed. I told her we need to put up the sign again for servers. The staff could barely cover the floor."

She feels a pinch and looks down to see that she's wound the cord around her index finger tight enough to turn the tip bright red.

No more stalling. "Wes, I have to tell you something . . ."

"Okay, shoot."

Mickey takes another swig of her daiquiri, swallowing too fast this time. Needles of chill pierce her forehead. She squeezes her eyes shut.

"Mick, is everything okay? Did something happen there?"

She leans forward, her head between her knees the way they tell you to sit when you're airsick, but she still feels sure she's going to throw up. "It's nothing here, no."

She waits in the quiet for him to prompt her again, but the line remains silent.

"Baby, I think I may have screwed up. No . . ." Mickey pushes out a resigned breath against the heel of her hand. "I screwed up."

The line hushes. After a moment, Wes comes back on, his voice lowered with alarm. "Screwed up how?" Another beat. "Did you sleep with someone?"

"No!" She bolts upright. "Absolutely not. It's nothing like that."

"Then what?"

She swears she can hear his jaw click tight.

"We're kind of . . . sort of . . . behind on a few bills."

Wes pulls in a breath and blows it out against the mouth-piece. "On how many accounts?"

The sting of tears starts to burn. Mickey squeezes her eyes shut to stem them.

She swallows to moisten her dry throat but her voice still comes out squeaking like a rusty hinge.

"All of them."

The silence this time is so stark, Mickey fears Wes has hung up.

When he finally speaks, any hint of his earlier grin is gone.

"You swore to me you had everything square, Mick."

"And I did," she says, hearing the desperation in her rising voice. "But then we got rolling and I lost track of a few bills and then a few more . . ."

There's a rustle on the line and Mickey suspects it's the sound of him standing up and pacing in front of the desk.

"I guess that explains why Robb's didn't deliver this morning," he says, and Mickey winces. Their beer supplier. "Is there anyone we're paid up with?"

"I prepaid for the year with P and J's to lock in a good rate, so at least we don't have to wash our own tablecloths." She lets out a weak chuckle and regrets it immediately.

"Tell me you're not actually making a joke about this."

"Sorry," she mutters.

"Jesus, Mick . . ." He exhales loudly. "I can't understand why you would keep this from me. We're supposed to be partners."

His voice is rough with emotion, more from the injury of her betrayal than anger, she decides, and suddenly it hurts to breathe.

"I didn't keep it from you—"

"You didn't tell me. That is literally the definition of keeping something from someone."

She bites at her thumbnail. "I thought Julianna wasn't a Kline rep anymore."

"What?"

"Nina said Julianna is there with some reds."

There's a stunned beat of silence, then Wes blows out an exasperated breath. His voice drops an octave. "You've been keeping the fact that we're underwater from me for

months and you're worrying about a wine rep I dated a million years ago?"

"Because I wouldn't blame you if you wanted to—"

"For fuck's sake, Mick. I'm hanging up now."

Panic knots in her chest. Her face flares with it. "Wes . . ."

"Tell your grandmother I said congratulations."

"Wes—"

The click of disconnection sounds, landing in her stomach like a stone. Mickey keeps the phone against her ear for
another moment, as if there's a chance he might pick up again,
before she settles it softly on the receiver and drops her head
into her hands.

11

1948

"And you promise you'll call Ned and Lois if anything comes up while I'm gone?"

From the other side of their bed, Cora handed Harry the rolled necktie with a weary sigh. "For the hundredth time, yes," she said, watching him tuck it neatly into his suitcase between two folded striped oxfords. She'd never been a fan of the tie's loud geometric print, but he'd acquired it at a swap the year before and refused to part with it. "You know, I spent whole weeks on my own before you came along, Harry Campbell."

"Yes, but not in Beech House—and not with a circus of construction workers banging about," he said as he disappeared into the bathroom. Cora wanted to assure him that she'd managed to hold her own just fine in her uncle's restaurant, the only woman in a kitchen of line cooks and dishwashers, most of whom came to work hungover and as polite as feral cats. A few men with hammers were no match for her.

"I'll have plenty to keep me busy," she said instead when he emerged with his shaving kit a few moments later. "I'm going to plant my kitchen garden, remember?"

Harry cut her a wary look. "I'd wait until the workmen clear out. They're liable to trample all over it."

He'd made the point already but Cora couldn't wait. Her herb seedlings were quickly outgrowing their tiny pots. She had to get them into the ground.

"I also promised Max I would move out the dishes so he can install the first set of cabinets he's built when he comes back," she said, changing the subject rather than argue with him.

"Good," Harry said. "If there's any issue with purchasing or supplies, I've left instructions to move ahead with whatever is needed. I don't want anything held up if they can't reach me right away. And you know where I keep the checkbook in case of emergencies, right?"

She nodded patiently. He'd reminded her twice already.

He dropped the suitcase's lid and snapped the brass fittings closed. "Do you suppose the kitchen will look much different when I get back?" he asked as he pulled on his summer-weight jacket and tugged on the cuffs.

Cora shrugged. "I'm not sure a person can transform a kitchen in just a week."

Even though she might have hoped otherwise. The sooner the renovation was finished, the sooner she and Harry could host a party for his friends. Already Cora had menus planned. She'd even unpacked the boxes of her late mother-in-law's collection of American Limoges, laying out the twenty-four-piece settings on the dining table. All through their courtship, Cora had heard plenty of stories about what a gifted hostess Harry's mother, Beatrice, was. Known as Busy Bea for her ability to organize a huge party at a moment's notice, Bea Campbell's dinner parties had been, according to

Harry, the highlight of the summer season on the Point. But having spent over two weeks now in her late mother-in-law's sparsely appointed kitchen, Cora had realized that while Bea Campbell owned the place settings for a party of fifty or more, her spare collection of kitchenware barely fed a half dozen; Bea may have been an expert hostess but she was clearly not an expert cook. Her lavish parties were always catered—no wonder Harry had been so thrilled to learn that Cora cooked food as well as she served it.

Working at Marigold's had taught Cora how to be a great hostess, to know what people needed and when. To make sure that they had clean utensils, or when their coffee was too low or too cool, to add a splash to warm it up before they had to ask. So while she may not have possessed Bea Campbell's gregarious personality, Cora had full confidence she could hold dinner parties impressive enough to honor her late mother-in-law's legacy, and she was anxious for the chance to prove it.

"Now where is that blasted car?"

Cora looked up to find Harry at the window, scanning the driveway.

"I still don't know why you're bothering with a taxi and leaving me the car," she said. "I can call for a taxi if I need to go somewhere."

"An emergency might come up—and I'd feel better knowing it's here," he said, then lowered his voice to a whisper. "Just whatever you do, don't park it anywhere near their trucks."

* * *

For the rest of the day, clouds rolled over the sun, keeping the wind brisk and the upstairs blessedly cool. Cora was still in the kitchen when the hall clock chimed and was amazed to count four bells. Had she really been almost three hours packing up the kitchen? Scanning the space, she decided her hard work certainly showed. When Max returned tomorrow, he'd find the room ready for him, just as she promised.

She only wished she could as easily relocate all the leftovers she had amassed in the refrigerator. Before leaving, Harry had promised to do his part to eat what remained from the previous night's dinner—a particularly luxurious meal of roasted brussels sprouts, striped bass, and a plum compote with fresh whipped cream—but he'd run out of time.

Cora wondered if any of the workmen might take some leftovers home to their families, assuming any were still around. She was skeptical; the clatter and thumping of activity had quieted in the last hour.

She crossed to the screen door to check and was startled to spot Max's truck parked under the beech. He wasn't scheduled to work today. She searched the lawn, then moved to the sink to check the view from that window, seeing him in conversation with a man in overalls, and a flutter of pleasure shuddered briefly in her stomach. Had he been there all afternoon? She wondered why he hadn't stepped inside and felt a twinge of confusion—or was it . . . no, surely it wasn't . . . hurt. How could she feel hurt? But the desire to connect with him, even to say hello, overwhelmed her. Or maybe she was simply lonely, though that explanation didn't sit right, either. Harry hadn't even been gone a full day yet—was she honestly lonely after a handful of hours without him?

She had no doubt Max would appreciate the leftovers. He had certainly enjoyed the bowl of corn and shrimp chowder she'd given him a few days before.

Cora worked quickly to fill a plate and draped the serving with a clean dish towel. When she stepped outside, she
was relieved to find Max still at his truck, loading a length
of lumber into the bed. He glanced up as she approached.

"This is a surprise," she said.

"A good one, I hope," Max said as he came around the
back of the truck to meet her. He wore a tan-colored sport
shirt. She wasn't used to seeing him in short sleeves.

"I thought you were working down-island today."

"Listen to you." He grinned as he brushed off his hands.
"Talking like a proper islander, already."

"Trying, anyway," Cora said, feeling her face warm
pleasantly at his good-natured teasing.

"I'm just here as a chauffeur today. I'm giving Ricky a
ride home."

She held out the plate. "Then I hope you're both hungry."

Taking it, Max lifted the corner of the towel, his eyes
widening with awe.

"Now, the roasted brussels sprouts aren't as crisp the next
day, but they should still taste fine," she said, "and you can
reheat the compote. Just make sure to add a splash of milk
to keep it from drying out. And the cream sauce over the fish
has fresh tarragon in it, which can be a little strong for some
people's taste, so you won't hurt my feelings if you don't care
for it—" She glanced up to find Max staring at her, blinking
somewhat dazedly, and she felt a flicker of embarrassment,
suddenly aware that she had rushed out impulsively, that she
had made such a gesture in front of all the other men, rambling on about her food as if she were James Beard.

She folded her hands behind her back. "I didn't mean
to give you such a speech. It's just a little something I made.
It's hardly precious."

"Are you kidding?" Max shook his head. "This is a feast. I feel like I just sat down at the Dunes." The Vineyard's most expensive restaurant—Harry had promised to take her when he returned. Cora felt her skin flush with the high praise. "All that's missing is someone tucking a napkin into my collar."

She laughed, and their eyes met, holding an extra beat. A rush of air bloomed in her chest. Her hands still behind her, she laced her fingers together and squeezed.

"It's not that special," she said, breaking their gaze. "But please take it. You'd be doing me a favor. My husband will be gone a week and it won't keep until then."

"But what will you eat?"

"Don't worry about me. I'm looking forward to my oatmeal."

"Hold on a minute." Max squared her with an arched brow. "You give me a five-course meal and you're left with oatmeal?"

"Oh, it's not just any oatmeal. I used to make it for the waitstaff after closing—it got to be a tradition at the restaurant. We'd gather up any leftovers from the day—crumbled bacon, pieces of pie, croutons, hash browns—and just dump it all in with butter and cream. Everyone called it Cora's kitchen sink oatmeal. We'd all sit at the counter after closing and unwind with big bowls. I can never make it when Harry's home."

"Doesn't have the taste for it, huh?"

"I'm afraid not," Cora said, not wanting to tell Max Dempsey that Harry's dislike of her oatmeal had little to do with taste and everything to do with association—or that the reason her husband resented the reminder of her work in the restaurant was the very reason she cherished making it.

"Well, thank you," Max said, reaching into the open passenger window to set the plate on the seat.

The man he'd called Ricky arrived with a thermos tucked under his arm. "Thanks for waiting, Max." Ricky tipped his head at Cora. "Evening, ma'am."

"Good evening," she said, stepping back as Max walked around to the driver's door. "I've cleaned out the shelves and the sideboard. Is there anything else I can do?"

"That's plenty." He opened the door and climbed in. "See you tomorrow at seven."

"Perfect." Excitement coursed through her. *Come even earlier*, Cora wanted to tell him. *I doubt I'll be able to sleep.*

But she just gave a short wave instead, then forced her trembling hands into the deep pockets of her apron and turned for the house.

12

1999

In the kitchen, Cora slows her pacing around the island and sighs loudly in the direction of the doorway where Michelle exited minutes earlier to call her boyfriend.

"Mom, please come sit down," Hedy calls to her from her post at the banquette, where Cora's daughter has been poring over the real estate section. "Watching the door isn't helping."

"I'm just so anxious," Cora says as she crosses with her coffee and eases herself onto the bench. "She's been in there a long time. Do you think that's a good sign?"

Drumming her fingers against her mug, she looks expectantly at Hedy, but her daughter's attention remains fixed on the paper. If Hedy shares Cora's concern, she doesn't show it. But Hedy has always been better at keeping her emotions in check, Cora reminds herself. Like her father. Cora suspects that kind of cloak is a good quality to have in sales negotiations.

It is not, however, of any benefit in the negotiations between mothers and daughters.

Cora drums louder. "Do you?"

"Do I what?" Hedy asks absently, continuing to scan the newspaper.

"Think it's a good sign or a bad one that Michelle's been in there so long?"

"I have no idea, Mom."

Cora folds her arms and sits back. "You're being awfully cavalier about all this."

Now her daughter looks up over her readers. "What is that supposed to mean?"

"I thought you liked this young man."

"I don't know him."

"But you know Michelle likes him. Loves him, I suspect."

"That's her business," Hedy says, returning to her listings. "I've never met him."

"Or maybe you don't want to meet him."

Cora's daughter levels her with an exasperated stare. "That's ridiculous. Why wouldn't I want to meet him?"

"Perhaps the same reason you never wanted your father to meet any of the men you dated after you divorced Grant."

It's a nerve Cora knows better than to so much as graze, and now she's gone and hit it squarely. *So be it,* she thinks stubbornly. If there's one thing she's learned through her romance with Max, it's that life is too short not to say what needs to be said.

Hedy slaps the newspaper closed, takes off her readers, and sits back.

"I'm right, aren't I?" Cora holds her daughter's even gaze, refusing to budge.

"If given the chance, I would gladly meet Wes, Mom."

"That's not what I was referring to, and you know it."

Hedy sweeps up her mug and climbs out of the banquette. "I'm not having this conversation right now."

"When, then?" Cora says, twisting in her seat. "You've barely visited in the last three years."

At the counter, her daughter empties the last of the coffee into her mug and shoves the carafe back onto the plate. "That's not true, Mom. I've been back several times."

"Once," Cora clarifies. "And you didn't even stay the weekend."

"You know how busy my work is. Real estate is twenty-four-seven."

"People take time off, Hedy."

"Sure. People who don't care if they lose sales," her daughter mutters before she tips her face into her coffee.

Determined not to let Hedy create any more space between them, Cora rises to follow her daughter to the counter, but before she can get there, Michelle appears in the kitchen doorway.

Her granddaughter looks numbly between them, her eyes red-rimmed, the tip of her nose pink, and Cora's heart sinks.

"I think I'll take that swim after all," Michelle says, her voice so thin it's nearly a whisper.

Cora glances back at Hedy, seeing alarm flicker over her daughter's even expression.

Hedy steps forward. "Oh, sweetheart . . ." Her hands outstretched, she crosses to meet Michelle and leads Cora's granddaughter to the island. "How did Wes take it?"

"Not well. He's really angry."

"Of course he's angry. You've been lying to him."

Hedy's words are harsh but her delivery, Cora is relieved to hear, is gentle. Still, Michelle's features remain tight with strain.

"Give him time, darling," Cora says, joining them at the island. "If he loves you, he'll forgive you."

"I'm not sure it's that easy, Mom," Hedy says.

Cora shoots her daughter an arched brow. So much for motherly encouragement.

"Are you sure you don't want to talk about it?" Cora asks tenderly. "I can make a fresh pot of coffee. Or maybe just stick with that pitcher of daiquiris?"

Michelle tries to laugh, but it's a half-hearted sound. "I think I'll switch over to water right now," she says, tipping her chin in the direction of the beach. "And anyway, I'm not about to spoil your magic weekend with my mess."

"Maybe a good rinse in the ocean will help," Cora says. And she would know. In all her years living by the sea, she's never known a single pill or serum with the healing powers of salt water. Certainly none as good when it comes to treating wounds of the heart.

"Love you both." Michelle gives them each a quick hug, then disappears through the doorway.

In her wake, the room sinks into silence.

Cora claps a hand to her cheek and sighs. Surely her daughter is thinking the same thing she is?

"You realize we can't possibly tell her about selling the house now, Hedy. After everything she's dealing with, losing her restaurant and maybe her boyfriend, too . . . Telling her she's going to lose Beech House will be too much."

"I know," Hedy says, pinching the bridge of her nose. "But we can't keep it from her anymore, Mom. You saw how upset she got that we didn't tell her about Chowder's. Not to mention what hypocrites that would make us—telling her she shouldn't hide something from her boyfriend, meanwhile we're doing exactly that to her? You know I'm right."

Maybe, Cora thinks as she and Hedy raise their mugs in unison.

Or maybe not . . .

Cora swallows her coffee slowly, possibility prickling.

Just because she's too late to protect her granddaughter from the fall doesn't mean she can't try to cushion her landing, does it?

13

Despite Cora's speed in boxing everything up, Max spent the first two days of work on the kitchen outside, on the porch, where the workmen had set up sawhorses and their larger tools and where he was building the frame that would become the workstation—or island, as she had to remind herself. Despite Harry's advice to wait until the men finished their repairs, Cora began planting the herb garden she had been planning since she first learned they would be spending their summer at Beech House. She'd come prepared, arriving with seedlings: thyme, basil, oregano, and parsley to start. Her great-grandmother Marigold, whose talent for cooking had inspired the name of her uncle's restaurant, had kept her own kitchen garden in an old washtub on her fire escape in Brighton. Growing up, Cora had learned which herbs to pick and how to harvest them, how much or how little to use, whether to add them during cooking or only at the very end.

But on the third day, back from the nursery with a few more seedlings, Cora stepped into the house to find two cabinets in the middle of the kitchen floor with a length of wood on top of them and gasped. "It's beautiful!"

Max smiled. "It's getting there." His thick hair, always tousled, seemed wavier today. The humidity, no doubt. Goodness knew Cora had been fighting to keep hers flat and neat all morning. "It's nowhere near finished, obviously," he said as she set down her tray of tiny pots on the banquette. "But at least we can get a sense of scale and proportion in the space."

She walked around the island, marveling at the dimensions. It was even grander than she'd imagined.

"Do me a favor, will you?" Max said. "Pretend to be preparing something at it. I want to get a measurement on the height so I know how much to add to the base before I nail anything down."

Cora stepped up to the edge, carefully, the way someone might be fitted for a wedding gown, she thought with a small smile as she put out her hands over the unattached countertop and mimed herself stirring, reaching below for something, reaching across.

"Good height?" he asked.

"Perfect."

Max glanced down at her feet and squinted at her white-and-brown spectator pumps. "Those heels are pretty high. Do you always wear heels when you cook?"

"Actually, no. Usually I wear slippers or go barefoot."

"Then take them off," he said, plucking the pencil from behind his ear, "and let's measure from there."

"All right." Reaching down to her slingback pumps, Cora felt a flush of self-consciousness, enough that her fingers struggled to loosen the strap, as if she were shedding her dress and not just her shoes, then chastised herself for it. Still she swore she saw Max shift his gaze to a spot on the ceiling while she pulled her feet free. Had he felt an unexpected spark of intimacy in the moment, too?

Barefoot, she stepped close to the island again, finding the work surface a tad too high now.

"Glad we checked," Max said, dropping down to notch one corner with a quick pencil tick. He stood up again, hands on his waist. "Now I'm thinking I can build a shallow drawer between the cabinets . . ." From his back pocket, he pulled out his little notebook, flipping to the sketch he'd made of the island and adding fresh marks to the drawing. "And below that, slats to hold cookie sheets and cooling racks."

She nodded quickly. "And maybe even cookbooks?"

"Absolutely." Max swung his pencil toward the open space between the two cabinets. "And I'll notch the drawer so you won't have any pulls poking you in the stomach while you work."

"I would appreciate that," she said, laughing. Was there anything he didn't think of?

Max scratched out a few more lines on the drawing, then a few more on the frame itself.

"That carrot cake you sent me home with last night was delicious, by the way," he said, glancing up from his notebook.

"Do you like fish cakes?"

"Love 'em."

Good. She'd needed to use up some leftover cod and made more than she could eat. "I'll pack you some of the remoulade I made to go with them, too."

One of his eyebrows shot up. "Remou . . . ?"

"Remoulade. It's made with mayonnaise. Sort of sour-sweet."

"Sounds fancy."

"It's really not. It's quite simple to make."

"For you, sure." He grinned as he shoved his notebook back into his pocket. "You know, you keep this up, and I'll be as wide as this island."

"I doubt that," Cora said, her gaze falling reflexively down his body before she forced her eyes to the other side of the kitchen. Through the doorway, she spotted a burst of color on the table in the dining room. What in the world . . . ? The bouquet was a collection of carnations, bursting out of a milk-glass vase. Cora walked quickly to reach it.

"Those came for you while you were out," Max said as she carried the flowers back into the kitchen. "I figured they'd be safer in the other room while I was working." He smiled. "Your husband must miss you."

"Maybe just my cooking," she said with a small laugh, but even as she admired the fringed edges of the pink blooms, she felt a girlish heat spread across her cheeks. She couldn't remember the last time Harry had sent her flowers. She plucked the envelope from the stems and pulled out the notecard.

> To the best chef that island will ever see. Sorry I couldn't
> hand deliver these but you know I can't stand being on
> a boat. Marigold's still misses you. Don't be a stranger.
> Love, Uncle Theo

Cora stared a long moment at the words on the card, trying to will away the tears that pricked behind her eyes, but her vision blurred quickly. Dear, sweet Theo. Cora could just see him placing the order for the flowers, leaned over the counter in his sauce-and-grease-stained apron, drafting the card on a napkin or maybe an old order ticket and laboring over every word.

Her heart swelled behind her ribs.

"I take it your husband writes as good as you cook."

She looked up, startled, first at Max's question, then at

the realization that she'd allowed her longing to show on her face. She stuffed the card hastily back into the envelope.

"They're actually from an uncle of mine back home," she said, blinking to stem another burst of tears. "I worked at his restaurant while he was deployed."

"And he let you leave?"

Cora let out a small laugh, grateful for the levity, even if the compliment caused another shudder of yearning to coil in her stomach. If only she'd had the choice to stay. But she wasn't the only woman to find herself having to hang up her work hat when the war was over and men returned to fill the jobs she and so many other women had done in their absence. Done and—in Cora's case—genuinely loved.

"It wasn't really Theo's choice," she said. "I was only filling in while he was away. I knew as soon as he came back to Inman Square, he wouldn't need me in his kitchen any-more."

"Did you say Inman Square?" Max jammed the handle of his hammer into his belt and turned to her. "My dad's brother lives in the Port."

Cora blinked at him. "Not really?"

Max nodded firmly. "Went there every summer when I was a kid. Uncle Rich used to take us to the candy company—"

"Squirrel Brand!"

"That's the one," he said. "And there was this place in Inman Square we used to get blueberry pancakes as big as truck tires—"

"Poppy's Diner!" she exclaimed. "That's right next to my uncle's restaurant!"

"You're kidding?" Max leaned back and shook his head. "Well, heck, if I'd known that then I'd have parked myself at your counter and ordered up your food all damn day."

Cora laughed. "You would have had to wait a long time. I would have still been a little girl."

"Good point. Wow . . ." His eyes traveled her face slowly, his mouth spreading into a wistful grin. "How about that."

"How about that," she repeated, hearing the same awe in her own voice. They continued to stare at each other a long moment, enjoying the remarkableness of this shared connection. In the silence, the room felt different, like the air before a storm—unsettlingly still but charged with electricity.

"Knock, knock!"

Cora spun to find Lois Welch letting herself in through the screen door, her neighbor's gaze sliding between her and Max, then down at Cora's bare feet.

Cora felt her face flame.

"I hope I'm not interrupting?" Lois asked brightly.

"Of course not." Cora stepped back from Max, so quickly that she knocked her hip on the edge of the island but bit back the sting of pain into her lip. "Lois, this is Max Dempsey. Max, this is Lois Welch."

Max nodded. "Pleasure to meet you, ma'am."

"The famous cabinetmaker," Lois said. "Cora talks about you constantly."

More heat soaked Cora's already warm face. "Not really," she said with a nervous laugh.

"Aren't those lovely!" Lois cried, her attention shifting to Theo's bouquet. She looked back at Cora. "Maybe Harry can be forgiven for leaving you alone so soon after all."

Even as she drew her lips into an agreeable smile, Cora knew she should correct Lois about the identity of the sender, but the explanation stuck in her throat. Harry had made a point of suggesting Cora keep details of her world back in Inman Square to herself, focusing instead on building their new life together on the island, and she had already folded herself so nicely into their close group. The last thing she wanted to do was muddy the waters . . .

In the strained silence, Cora glanced at Max, meeting his gaze only for a moment before she looked away, feeling the heat of culpability rise to her cheeks. She already felt thoroughly embarrassed by Lois's claim that she spoke of him often. Now Max would surely be wondering why she hadn't told Lois the truth about the flowers. Hadn't they just spent the last few minutes sharing fond memories about the same place—a place she remembered she was supposed to forget?

"We should let Max get back to work, Lois," Cora said, stepping around the banquette to steer them to the door, suddenly eager to be where a breeze might cool her flushed face. "Shall we talk outside?"

When they were past the screen door and down to the lawn, Lois wrinkled her lips into a teasing smile. "Well, he's quite the dreamboat, isn't he? No wonder you haven't been by the house this week."

"Oh no, it's nothing like that," Cora said, and maybe a little too quickly, she thought when she saw Lois rear back with a laugh.

"I'm only kidding, silly." Lois darted forward. "About you, I mean. I'm completely serious about that tall drink inside. Lucky you. These roughnecks are rarely anything to get excited about."

Cora's stomach knotted. She'd heard the term many times growing up but it was hardly used as a compliment. Surely Lois didn't mean to be so rude.

"Well, no more hiding," Lois said. "Irene and I are

having lunch at the club tomorrow and we won't take no for an answer. Pick you up at eleven?"

At last—a promised trip to the famous club.

Cora let her tight lips soften into an appreciative smile. "Eleven is fine."

"Dress code is neat casual," Lois said as she turned to go with a wink. "And shoes, too, of course."

14

1999

The suit's silver straps are so frayed that Mickey worries they will snap like old rubber bands as she tugs them over her shoulders, the once glittery knit of her old one-piece stretched out and pilled. She's just grateful she still fits—well, barely—into it. She remembers how sexy she felt in it when she bought it the summer she turned seventeen. Her first grown-up bathing suit, scooped low in front and cut high on her hips; the first one that didn't have racing stripes or straps as wide as packing tape, and in a color other than the usual finger-paint shades of red or blue. She turns in the dresser's old mirror, wondering what Wes would think of her in it, and a jab of regret pierces her chest. Her mother and grandmother's optimism is appreciated—her mother's decidedly more measured than Cora's, no surprise there—but Mickey can't muster any of her own. Wes's anger was expected, maybe even bearable; it's the fear that he has lost trust—never mind faith—in her that is responsible for the knot in her stomach, a tangle that keeps getting tighter the more time that passes. The distraction of a swim will be short-lived but welcome.

She pulls back on her ribbed tank and shorts, pushes her bare feet into flip-flops, and heads down the hall, slowing at the linen closet for a towel. At the bottom of the stairs, the ancient, beloved collection of straw beach hats still dangles, their wide brims cracked from salt air, holes worn in their crowns from where they've been unceremoniously jammed back onto their hooks over the years. Mickey takes one out of tribute more than necessity. As bad as she knows the sun is for her skin, she wants to return to Baltimore with a little color, something to remind her. As a girl, a Beech House summer tan was the best kind of keepsake. Now she wonders how much longer she will be able to call the constellations of dots across her face freckles and not sunspots.

At not yet noon, the sun won't have baked the sand to its midday broil, when the simple act of reaching the path barefoot is like a hot-coal walk, done usually as a shrieking sprint. Mickey abandons her flip-flops and takes her time descending the sandy bluff, letting her heels sink hard with each step. The wind greets her, a glorious pummeling of salt and heat, combing her loose hair behind her and ruffling the tufts of grasses and tendrils of beach pea that erupt from the sand. The tide is high, the water a dark cobalt. The private beach is mostly empty, its only occupants a young couple cuddling under an umbrella and a small boy building a sandcastle at the water's edge. An older woman sits in a beach chair near enough to keep watch—his grandmother, Mickey suspects. Or maybe even great-grandmother. The woman's back is to Mickey; she can't tell for sure.

Tiffany was right to warn her of the change in the view. Mickey counts at least three new homes rising up from the bluff, and another, a tower of framing bones nearing completion as a fourth, its fat, fresh timbers oddly flesh-colored in the sun, dwarfing one of the original cottages beside it. The little boy's collection of pails has rolled a good distance from where he works, crouched over a fence of sand towers almost as high as he is. When the foamy surf tumbles over one of the neglected buckets and swallows it, Mickey drops her hat and towel and hurries down to the water, dashing in to her shins before she can rescue it, stifling a shriek at the numbing chill.

She walks the bucket back to the boy, and he squints up at her fiercely when she holds it out to him, little lips pinched defiantly, as if she's come to claim his castle.

"What do you say to the nice lady, Andrew?"

The woman's raspy voice carries down the beach. Mickey turns to watch her rise cautiously but somehow regally from her folding chair and walk toward them, her gait long and sure. She wears a flowing block-print tunic and wide-legged linen pants. Most of her face is hidden under a wide-brimmed sun hat and sunglasses with lenses as big as coasters, but still recognition flares.

Mickey squints. "Mrs. Welch?"

The woman slows.

"Michelle Campbell," Mickey says, seeing that she hasn't yet made the connection. "Cora's granddaughter."

"Of course." Lois Welch's drawn cheeks rise in a smile. "Good grief, I hardly recognize you. Welcome back, dear."

"Thank you," Mickey says. "It's good to be back."

Lois draws off her sunglasses. Her lids, looser with age, are still brushed heavily with blue shadow, her lashes still thickened with mascara.

"Ned and I have heard wonderful things about your restaurant," she says. "New York, is it?"

"Baltimore," Mickey corrects her gently. She knows that for many people, especially people in the Northeast, opening an East Coast restaurant in any city other than New York doesn't deserve the same degree of applause, and Lois Welch's smile, more consolatory than congratulatory, confirms it.

"I think the last time I saw you, dear, was at the funeral."

"I haven't been back since, I'm afraid," Mickey admits.

"Well, you'll have to come by the club. I know everyone would love to see you."

Mickey offers a polite smile. "That would be nice," she says, even though she has no intention of taking Lois Welch up on the invitation. Even when Mickey's grandfather was alive, the country club, with its stiff-cushioned chairs and unseasoned food, was never her taste, in any sense of the word, despite all the times Mickey's mother insisted on going when they visited the island. Once, just ten, Mickey had brought a few threads of dill in her pocket at Cora's urging, only to have Hedy shoot Mickey a withering look when she sprinkled the herb over her fish before the waiter had left their table. The whole ride back to Beech House, Mickey had tried vainly to argue her case. "How is it any different than adding pepper or salt?" she'd asked. "Because those are already on the table," her mother had answered sharply. "And because you're ten years old and you're not the chef." *Not yet*, Mickey had thought.

The little boy begins filling a different bucket, grunting with exertion as he scoops heavy shovels of wet sand.

When Mickey looks up, she finds Lois Welch studying the horizon in the direction of Beech House. "I trust it's a whirlwind of activity up there," Lois says. "I saw the tent on my way down to the beach."

"Things seem to be coming together."

"I offered to help with the arrangements—we know an incredible florist, but your grandmother assured me she had it under control." Lois's eyebrows draw together into a worried point. "How is your mother handling it all?"

Mickey waits a beat, not entirely sure how to take the question or Lois Welch's sudden, evident concern. She can't help thinking the woman is sniffing for signs of drama in the house.

Once a gossip, always a gossip.

"She's doing fine, Mrs. Welch, thank you for asking."

But Lois's furrowed brow doesn't relax. She continues to study Mickey as she taps the end of her folded sunglasses against her chin. "I'm sure this is all very overwhelming."

"It was a surprise, for sure."

"Of course," Lois says, bobbing her head slowly. "I can imagine it was for you both."

The older woman's smile is sympathetic, but Mickey feels a strange unease, as if there is something more to Lois's point: that maybe the engagement announcement wasn't surprising for anyone else on the Point.

"Well." Lois snaps open her sunglasses and slides them back on. "Just shows what patience can bring."

Mickey frowns, not following. *Patience?*

"But then, I always told your grandmother, that's what makes her such a good cook. Me, I always take my cakes out too soon. I just can't stand to wait," Lois says with a little laugh. "Your grandfather was the same way. Not that I have to tell you, dear." The older woman's attention remains on her grandson, but Mickey is sure Lois Welch is seeing something else. Her voice is suddenly as far away as her gaze. "He was so eager to throw your poor grandmother into our little pool. Right into the deep end. And, God bless her, she was a good swimmer . . ."

With a startling roar, the little boy brings his fists down on his castle, sending sand spraying. Mickey jumps back.

"Oh, Andrew, do be careful!" Lois smiles and releases a heavy sigh. "It all worked out somehow, though, didn't it? But I knew they were suited. Anyone could see it, really. Truth be told, I always envied them a little."

Mickey nods, just grateful to find her bearings in the conversation again. "My grandparents did make a wonderful pair," she says.

Lois Welch stares at her strangely, a tremor of something close to confusion briefly pinching her features, Mickey thinks, before the woman's gaze shifts, fixing on a spot behind Mickey. Lois's face lights up with a slow smile as she says, "And speak of the devil."

Turning, Mickey tents her hand over her eyes and sees that a tall, white-haired man has appeared on the rise, dressed in khaki slacks and a loose Henley shirt.

He looks at Mickey for a moment, then gives her an easy wave. As if he knows her. As if they are old friends.

15

1948

The Oyster Point Country Club was sheathed in the same weathered gray shingles as Beech House, and even boasted a similarly sprawling deck, but somehow it felt less warm to Cora as she followed Lois and Irene up the wide stone steps to its entry, giving her hairpins a last-minute tap to secure them, the wide straps of her garnet jumper dress a few straightening tugs. She'd spent far too long that morning debating what to wear—not that she had many options. In the weeks before coming to the Vineyard, Harry had pleaded with her to visit Filene's, to replace her older apron dresses with brighter, sleeker styles, but Cora had put him off, too comfortable in her existing wardrobe. But now, as she stepped into the dining room and saw the array of pastel wrap dresses and boldly printed peplum skirts, she wished she had taken her husband's advice.

She'd ask Lois and Irene if they could recommend a good boutique and go shopping as soon as Harry returned.

The club's dining room was a sweeping space, lit up with crisp white tablecloths and polished silver. Huge windows ran one length of the room, overlooking the sloping lawn that feathered gently into the bay.

On the way to their table, Lois slowed their course to introduce Cora to several guests, all of whom looked up briefly from their shrimp salads or cocktails to offer her a smile before they asked how Harry was and, more important, why he hadn't come to the club yet. Cora tried desperately to remember each name, employing a memorization trick she had learned from working at the restaurant to remember regular customers' names and lunch orders, but by the time she, Lois, and Irene had finally reached their table at the window, Cora's brain felt fuzzy, stuffed like an overpacked suitcase.

The place settings gleamed, the starched napkins in the center shaped remarkably like flower blossoms. Cora tipped hers gently, trying to understand its construction without pulling it apart. At Marigold's, they had used paper napkins, self-serve in metal dispensers. If she was going to fit in hosting formal dinner parties here on the island, she would do well to learn a few impressive decorative napkin techniques.

Irene perused the day's specials. "I can't believe Harry hasn't brought you here yet."

"They've only just arrived," Lois defended before Cora could respond. "And they've been so busy with the house."

"Which is all the more reason to come here and get out of the fray," Irene said. "Let someone else make dinner."

Lois swept up her menu. "Don't forget—Cora actually likes to cook, remember?"

"Not me," said Irene. "I'd be here every meal if Phil would agree to it."

"Order the bisque if they have it," Lois said, patting Cora's hand for emphasis. "It's marvelous. If I weren't pregnant, I'd order it myself, but shellfish right now is just . . ." Lois made a fluttering motion with her fingers in the direction of her stomach and rolled her eyes.

"The bisque really is sensational." Irene plucked her

cigarette purse out of her handbag and unsnapped the clasp. "Better than sex, I swear."

"Irene!" Lois chided.

"Well, sex with Phil, anyway," Irene said, grinning as she slipped a cigarette between her teeth. "So maybe it's not so great after all."

Cora scanned her menu, startled at the selection. She'd expected high prices but these seemed foolish. Crabmeat au gratin for two dollars? Endive and beet salad for a dollar?

"It really is too bad," said Lois, twisting in her seat to scan the room. "I was hoping there'd be a better crowd today. We were looking forward to giving you the rundown on the usual suspects, Cora. Get you up to speed on everyone before the next party."

"At least Poppy is here," Irene said, tipping her chin to an alarmingly thin woman sitting alone a few tables away who seemed to swim in a lilac suit, her graying blond hair combed up into loose rolls, two angry streaks of rouge on her drawn cheeks. "But then, Poppy is always here."

Lois turned to Cora and lowered her voice. "Poppy Donovan. Her husband Clive works in Hartford and leaves her here all summer. She practically lives at the club. She'll nurse a martini and a bowl of soup for a whole afternoon just to chat up the busboys and waitresses. They laugh at all her jokes and she leaves them an enormous tip. It's really quite painful to watch."

Cora stole a quick look at the woman, who was, at that moment, smiling up at a young man in a white jacket who held an impressive stack of dirty plates. He looked somewhat charmed, Cora thought. "Maybe they enjoy her company," she said.

Irene snickered, as if Cora had made a joke, but when

she didn't laugh, Irene stared quizzically at her. "You're not serious?"

Cora bristled, not sure why she couldn't be.

"The least one of them could do is tell her to blend in her rouge, for God's sake," Irene whispered. "Does she apply it with a butter knife?"

Cora set down her menu, still feeling a flutter of sympathy for the old woman despite their teasing.

"I just can understand how someone might get lonely if their husband left them alone for long periods of time, that's all," Cora said.

"Unless their husband leaves them with the company of a dishy cabinetmaker, she means," Lois said, exchanging a knowing look with Irene over her menu.

Cora glanced between them, lost for a second, then she felt her face flush with understanding.

"Oooh, that's right." Irene tapped her cigarette on the side of the crystal ashtray. "Lois filled me in on your carpenter. What's his name again?"

"Max Dempsey," Cora said quietly.

Irene blew out a ringlet of smoke as she smiled. "Mimi Ferguson knows who he is. He did some work at their cottage in the spring. She said he's quite a dreamboat. A smile that could melt steel." Irene stared expectantly at Cora. "She said he looks like Burt Lancaster."

"You know, he does!" Lois tapped Cora's hand. "Don't you think so?"

Cora reached for her glass. "I hadn't really thought about it," she said, downing a quick sip of ice water, grateful for the burst of cold.

"Harry must be mad to leave you alone with him," Irene said.

"Harry isn't the jealous sort," Cora said. "He has no reason to be."

But Lois's lips remained a teasing curl. "Maybe you should convince Phil you need new cabinets, Irene."

Irene snorted. "Wouldn't that be a trick?"

When the waitress arrived to take their order, Cora felt a swell of relief.

"Lois tells me the kitchen already looks very different," Irene said when they were alone again. "Something about a table in the middle? What in the world?"

"It's called an island," Cora said, grateful to have the conversation shift away from Max. "Wait until you see it. You won't believe how amazing it is."

Another young woman, brunette, appeared with a coffeepot and carefully added to Lois's cup first, then Cora's. When she reached Irene's cup, the girl tipped the pot slightly, sending a splash onto the tablecloth.

"I'm so sorry, ma'am" she gasped. "I can change it out if you'd like—"

Irene brushed her away. "Just leave it," she said curtly. She rolled her eyes, barely waiting until the girl had left the table before she leaned in to add, "That's exactly why Phil never tips here."

Cora stared between them. "Never?"

"People rarely do," said Lois, snapping her napkin loose and draping it over her lap. "Half the time these young girls are off in a corner gossiping, or out on the porch flirting with the caddies while our dishes are getting cold."

"And goodness knows the dues here are high enough they could pay them more," Irene said, tipping cream into her coffee, "so if they feel slighted, they can take it up with the management."

Cora flushed with outrage. She wanted to say something, to assure them that to refrain from tipping was not only rude but criminal, that servers and bussers, even at fancy country clubs, depended on tips to make a living wage, but the subject turned to silver patterns, and Cora let the speech die in her throat.

* * *

Wanting to walk off a bit of her meal, and growing dizzy from Irene's cigarette smoke, Cora asked to be dropped off at the top of the drive. At this late hour, she knew she would find the driveway and the house both empty, the workmen off today, including Max, so when she came around the bend to find a strange black car parked in the shade of the beech, she slowed.

A blond woman in an embroidered peasant top and a pale blue skirt stood at the door, knocking.

"Can I help you?"

Hearing Cora's voice, the woman spun. She was quite pretty. Cora guessed her to be twenty, maybe twenty-one. She looked Cora full in the face for a strange moment, her eyes blinking as if with recognition though Cora was certain she'd never seen her before.

The woman stepped down to the grass. "I'm looking for Max Dempsey. He's supposed to be working here?"

"He is, yes," Cora said, "but he's off today. He'll be back tomorrow."

The woman shifted on the block heels of her brown oxfords, as if trying to decide something.

Cora extended her hand. "I'm Cora Campbell."

"Betty," the woman answered, accepting her shake. "Betty Meyer." She worried the strap of her handbag, shifting it higher over her shoulder. "I saw you earlier today, actually."

"Oh?"

"I wait tables at the country club. You came in at the end of my shift."

"Oh!"

Cora recalled the sweet young brunette who had waited on them, and wondered if they were friends, and if they compared notes on guests, especially the difficult ones like Lois and Irene. When she'd worked at Marigold's, Cora and the other waitresses had always commiserated about demanding customers. Those who groused over burnt coffee, or eggs cooked too long or not long enough. But today Cora had been the guest and not the server, and the reminder left her uneasy.

"And you know Max?" Cora asked.

"Yes, I'm his . . . I'm a friend."

A friend. Cora may not have been an expert on innuendo—as today's lunch conversation had proven—but she knew enough to read the expression of someone who felt affection for another. Betty Meyer's face had turned a distinct shade of pink—the shade of desire, of hope. This woman was more than just a friend to Max Dempsey. Cora wondered if Max knew it, too. His mention of his brothers pressing him to marry flashed back at her.

"Would you like to come in?" Cora asked, sweeping a hand toward the door. "I could make us some coffee. And I have some banana bread. Just made it this morning."

Betty's head bobbed with a knowing smile. "You're the cook Max is always raving about." Cora felt a prickle of pleasure, though she tamped it down. Always? She doubted that. "Thank you, no, I can't stay."

"Maybe you'd like to leave Max a note?" Cora suggested. "I'll make sure to give it to him tomorrow."

"That's all right," Betty said, stepping back toward her car. "I'll just try his house."

His house. The thought of where Max Dempsey went when he wasn't here filled Cora with a sudden and strange longing—was it odd that she didn't know where he lived?

But why should she? Why should she know much about him at all? As much as she enjoyed his company, as grateful as she was for his skills and his dedication to building her a beautiful kitchen, Max Dempsey wasn't a friend. Or, at least, he shouldn't be. Lois and Irene's teasing at lunch still stuck in her thoughts, guilt fluttering. Cora was a married woman. Max worked for her husband. He was there to do a job.

And she'd do well to remember that.

The recollection of their lunch conversation sparked another memory, another tremor of regret.

"Betty, could I ask you a favor?" Cora said, reaching in to her purse. "The young woman who waited on us, brown hair, blue headband—"

"Linda," Betty said.

Cora smiled as she freed a five-dollar bill and held it out. "Would you see to it that she gets this?"

"Of course," said Betty. "But you really don't have to do that, Mrs. Campbell. Guests rarely tip at the club. It's not expected."

"Maybe not," said Cora. "But as someone who knows how hard waiting tables can be, I think it should be."

Nodding with an appreciative smile, Betty took the money.

"And please," she said. "Call me Cora."

16

1999

At ten forty-five, when Beech House finally settles into the hush of sleep after a long afternoon that stretched into an even longer night, Hedy pokes her head out into the upstairs hall and waits several beats for sounds of movement. Hearing nothing but the stillness of the close night air, she flips a towel over her shoulder and pads barefoot down the stairs. Thirty-five years after the first night she snuck out of Beech House, she still knows what floorboards to avoid as she slips through the great room, and how far she can open the porch door before it gives a betraying squeak. The air outside, tinged with damp, is still warm and soft as she crosses the wide porch and steps down to the lawn, the cold dew startling on the bottom of her bare feet as she crosses into the watery dark of the bluff.

The deep roar of the surf is muffled by the rise of grasses and juniper. A few more strides and she clears the edge, hearing the roll of the waves fully, as if someone has opened a door, and she feels the welcome pressure of the salted wind. Several minutes in the dark now, her eyes have finally adjusted. There's just enough moonlight that she can see the phosphorescent foam at the edge of the surf, as frothy and tantalizing as the head of a draft beer.

That *Jaws* movie be damned—she still loves a midnight swim.

And Hedy can't recall a time when she's ever needed the cleanse of salt water more than she does tonight. Coming here, she anticipated the complicated feelings she would have over her mother getting remarried, but she now has the added weight of worry that her daughter has run her new restaurant nearly into bankruptcy, not to mention possibly ruined her relationship over her poor management skills.

She loosens her wrap and lets it drop. Gooseflesh flares instantly across her skin, as much from expectation as chill. The sand is cool as she heads for the water and enters slowly, the way a person might enter their childhood home, cautious but reverential. The cold stings her ankles but she presses on, eyes squeezed closed as she charges forward, a trick she taught herself as a child, imagining the navy water as a tropical green to trick her brain into feeling warmth. She pulls in a deep breath and goes under. Sinking into the still, silent world of beneath, long enough to coat her fully before she bursts to the surface again, varnished with seawater.

When she's cleared the pier, she reaches down and peels off her suit, careful to hold it against the rush of the current, the cold bracing on her newly bared skin. She leans back and lets the water carry her while she blinks against the short sting of salt. The rush of water is bath-like, heavy and soft at the same time. All that salt, it keeps a woman light, allows her to rise more easily than in fresh water. And she can't remember when she has ever felt quite so heavy.

Her heart still can't believe that her father is gone, and now her mother is marrying another man. And inviting the whole Point to witness it? Hedy's not sure why the guest list rattles her so—her mother is right that it's her prerogative to invite whoever she wants—but having all of her father's friends there seems so . . .

Hurtful.

There it is: the word Hedy didn't say aloud earlier.

And what of her mother's comment about Hedy not wanting her father to meet any of her suitors after her divorce? Is that really what Cora has believed all these years?

Hedy submerges for a moment and bursts up, slicking back her hair with her free hand.

Okay, yes, maybe she was cautious about bringing men around after Grant. And why shouldn't she have been? Her father took the breakup of her marriage so very hard—which wasn't surprising, considering Grant's father was a partner at the bank and Hedy had known Grant almost her whole life. This was exactly why she should never have married him, but their match had been so long in the making, and her father had been so happy at their engagement, so blissful. Hedy, of course, had known from the minute she and Grant first made love that the union was a mistake. Everyone had told her that it took time to grow comfortable in one's sexual skin, but Hedy knew that wasn't why she didn't enjoy sex with Grant. She didn't love Grant Heller. She loved that her father loved him. And she foolishly believed that would be enough.

She sweeps her hands through the water, the gentle lap soft in the night's hush, her thoughts shifting with the current. Can't her mother appreciate how difficult this wedding is for her? The memory of those strange, fraught moments involving Max Dempsey that Hedy has lately recalled return to her. Something secretive about Max all those years ago. Hedy didn't press her mother for an explanation then. Should she now?

Tilting, Hedy catches a mouthful of seawater and coughs, her balance gone. Her feet scrape the sandy bottom. So much for trying to float tonight.

She pulls her suit back on and climbs out of the surf, the air bracing as she spins herself into the heavy warmth of the towel, waiting for her body temperature to readjust as she rubs herself dry, then swings back into her cover-up and climbs the beach, then the bluff, following the two squares of yellow-gold on the home's second floor, lights she left on in her room. Since she didn't want to turn the porch light on and announce her departure, the rest of the house and the lawn is a shapeless pool of blue-black, staying so even when Hedy nears the porch. She can barely make out the edge of the deck.

Almost there, she hears movement behind her and spins reflexively, straight into the blur of a tall shape. She gasps, so startled she brings up her arms, hears the crack and thud of her elbow making contact and then a man's voice hissing: "Shit."

Hedy scrambles back, her heart racing, desperate to secure a berth between herself and whoever has appeared. A streak of light from the office window—a forgotten desk lamp—illuminates the grass that separates them, and the man staggers into it.

"I'm Tom," he says. "Max's son."

Hedy slows, catching her breath. Relief swells. She claps a hand to her chest. "I thought you were a prowler."

"Sorry. I would have called, but I didn't want to disturb anyone."

So much for that plan, she thinks as she takes him in in quick bursts—a graying buzz cut, a collared white button-down, khakis. "I'm Hedy," she says. "Cora's daughter."

"I figured."

He offers her a hand and she shakes it warily. "I'm sorry about . . . It was reflex. You just came out of the dark—"

"It was my fault," he says, pinching the bridge of his nose. "I'm fine." But as soon as he steps fully into the fringe of light, Hedy can see the trickle of blood running from one nostril.

"Oh God, you're bleeding!" She swings off her towel and holds it up to his face. He takes it from her and claps it against his nose.

He chuckles, the low rumble muffled behind the towel. "I've known women who wanted to deck me, but usually they've at least met me first."

* * *

They enter through the kitchen wing, Hedy first and Tom trailing. She points him to the banquette and rushes to the sink to wet a dishcloth. Holding the cloth under the tap, she looks over her shoulder to find him leaning back.

"Don't lie down," she says. "You want to keep your head above your heart. Try to lean forward a little bit, too."

He pulls himself upright again, her beach towel still covering most of his face, and squares her with his one visible eye. "Are you a nurse?"

"Real estate agent. You can't believe how many people get nosebleeds from the stress of buying a house." She hands him the damp cloth. "Use this to pinch your nostrils. Gently."

Squinting, he does as instructed.

"Can I get you a drink?" she asks, moving back to the counter. It's the least she can do.

"Sure. Whatever you've got. So long as it's strong."

The bottle of rum they've been using to make lobster

daiquiris sits on the counter. Hedy scoops out a handful of cubes from the ice bin and drops them into a tumbler.

"What were you doing skulking around out there, anyway?" she asks as she pours a long splash.

"Looking for the spare key," Tom says, his voice sounding stuffy from the pressure of the towel. "My dad said they kept one under one of those big pots on the patio."

"It's the green one," she says, handing him the glass.

"Good to know."

When he removes the towel to take a hard sip, Hedy sees him clearly for the first time. She's fairly certain Cora mentioned he was an architect and it wouldn't surprise her. He's handsome in that smooth, put-together way of other architects Hedy's met, tanned, the kind of even color someone gets from sailing or golfing, and his eyes are a startling gray-blue. He's Max's son, all right.

He looks pointedly at her hand. "Where's yours?"

"I don't like to drink before bed. It disrupts my sleep." A symptom of menopause, or so her doctor has kindly informed her, but she's not about to share this information with him.

Tom frowns at her. "First you almost knock me out then you make me drink alone?" He grins. "I may have to talk to the manager of this place."

Hedy rolls her lips, biting back a smile. What the hell, she thinks. After the day she's had, she won't sleep tonight regardless. "Fine," she says, rising.

She walks to the counter and pulls down another glass.

"I really am sorry for startling you like that," Tom says. "I had to wait until the last ferry to get a spot. I was thinking I was going to have to spend the night in my car."

"You know, there's this amazing new invention called a reservation," she says as she unscrews the bottle's cap.

"So I've heard."

He must be hot in those khakis, she thinks as she pours herself a generous shot and walks back to the banquette. The house is especially warm tonight. She'll remind him to grab a fan from the hall closet before he settles in. She can't remember if she left one in his room after she made up the bed.

He reaches his glass over and taps hers. "Cheers."

"Cheers."

They each take a sip in toast. Hedy enjoys the bolt of warmth that soaks her throat when she swallows, the rum sweet, laced with vanilla.

"We made up the Remoulade Room for you." When Tom squints at her, she says, "My mother named all the guest rooms after cooking sauces." He didn't know that? "I thought you'd been here before."

"I have. Just never for a night."

"Oh."

"So what kind of sauce is a rema . . . what did you call it?" he asks.

"Remoulade." She grins. "You'll have to ask Cora. Or my daughter, Michelle."

"She owns the restaurant, right?"

A sigh escapes her. "For now."

"Is she planning to sell?"

"Not planning, no." Hedy meets his quizzical gaze over her glass.

"Running a restaurant is tough enough," Tom says. "I can't imagine owning one. I dated a woman after my divorce who

managed a restaurant in Tribeca. Still does, as far as I know."
He takes a sip, eyeing her as he swallows. "Are you married?"

"No."

"Divorced?"

"Yes, though Grant and I were in divorce court longer
than we were actually married." He continues to study her,
as if he's waiting for something more. "It was for the best,
trust me." The ice shifts in his glass, his rum almost drained.
"More?" she asks him.

"Why not?"

She walks to the counter, grateful for the excuse to move
and for the break in the subject of marriage after her musings in the water, and returns to her seat with the bottle.

"I can't believe we've never met before this," Tom says
as she adds more rum to both of their glasses.

"I'm sorry for not reaching out when all this started. I
should have."

"Don't apologize. I could have done the same. I've been
out flat at work with this new build on the cape. It started
out as a writer's studio—one room—and now it's a three-
bedroom guest house. The client's run through four deco-
rators already."

"I know the type."

"I'll bet." He studies her over his glass. "How long have
you worked in real estate?"

"Twenty-six years."

"I bet you have some stories."

"Oh, you have no idea." Hedy picks up her drink and
swirls it, letting the sweet smell of the rum float up before
she takes a short sip.

"And your daughter's name is . . . ?"

"Michelle. She's upstairs. She came in last night." Hedy steals another look at him. "Do you have children?"

"A son," Tom says. "He's in Switzerland."

"What does he do there?"

"Jack's a ski instructor in Saint Moritz."

"Wow."

"He likes it."

"Well. What's not to like?"

"Exactly."

They both sip their drinks, letting the room fall quiet. When Hedy looks up, she meets Tom's gaze, his pale eyes questioning, and she understands. It's as if they are on a first date, having struggled through the awkward but required stretch of cursory small talk, and can now move on to real subjects.

"So . . ." he says.

She traces the rim of her glass and sighs. "So."

"This is all . . ."

"Surprising?"

"That works," Tom says.

He shifts on the bench, clearly needing to stretch his legs. They're long, like his father's.

"How do they seem?" he asks.

"Good, I guess. Happy." Hedy shrugs. "My frame of reference is fairly narrow. I haven't really spent much time around them before this week. You?"

"A few times. Once for my dad's birthday last year. Another time when I was on the island for a client."

"I used to come here more when my daughter was younger," Hedy says, "but these past few years I've just been so . . . busy." She tips her face into her glass, feeling a spark of guilt for the thin excuse. Her absence has had nothing to do with her schedule and everything to do with not knowing how to be here without her father. But maybe Tom Dempsey already suspects her lie. Maybe, like her, he's struggling to see his father with someone new. If they knew each other better, Hedy might dare to ask him, but they are strangers. And it's late.

Tom swishes what's left in his glass, then drains it. "Well. I think I better get myself upstairs before I fall asleep right here," he says, rising.

Hedy smiles reflexively, a memory flickering. Coming downstairs one morning to find thirteen-year-old Michelle asleep on the banquette bench, her fingers and hair sticky with dried dough after staying up all night to perfect choux pastry for the two trays of chocolate-covered éclairs she vowed to bring to the Point's annual Half Shell tennis tournament.

"Thanks again for the drink," Tom says, grabbing his bag.

Hedy rises, too. "Sorry again about your nose."

"Sorry about your towel."

"It comes out," she says. "Good night."

"Good night." He's almost to the door before he slows and turns back. "Which room is mine again? Mustard or mayonnaise, was it?"

She smiles. "Follow me."

17

1948

Rain fell in sheets. Cora woke the next morning to the relentless pounding of it on the roof and pulled in a panicked breath, fearful of which cracks in the ceiling the plunging water would squeeze through. The roofers had made great progress in the last few weeks, but Beech House possessed so many gables, so many eaves with seams to keep snug. She pulled on a short-sleeved brunch coat, tied it around her waist, and walked briskly through the upstairs, listening for the telltale patter of drips from leaks, and was relieved to find only a small, shimmering puddle in one of the bedrooms off the kitchen wing, the same one she'd noticed when they first arrived. At least the rain would help her just-planted herb garden, she thought, as she slid a bucket into place.

There was no question the bad weather would keep the roofers away, but not Max, she hoped, as she pushed her feet into her summer sandals. Even though Max was a remarkably tidy carpenter, sweeping up as he went— much like a chef, Cora had thought on more than one occasion, remembering how Theo had taught her to clean her workstation as she cooked—loose nails and splinters were still a risk, so she never dared to go barefoot. She made her usual path around the stacks of finished drawers and cut lumber and door panels that had been filling up the kitchen in the past week as Max completed pieces in his workshop and delivered them to Beech House to be installed. If she had to put a percentage on it, Cora would say the kitchen was half completed. The cupboards around the sink and stove had been put in but awaited their drawers. Half the cabinets had been hung but some still needed doors, and the stretches of countertop had been cut but not yet installed. The same was true for the island's generous rectangle of butcher block, which bridged the two cupboards beneath it, though Cora had fixed herself a tomato and cheese sandwich at it the night before, unable to resist testing it out.

She glanced at the clock, wondering if she had time to make her marinade before Max arrived. She'd bought bluefish for Harry's return that night, his favorite, but first she would need to soak it in buttermilk to draw out the fishy taste. As she searched for a bowl, anticipation grew warm in her stomach, imagining how Harry would bound up the steps, how he'd swing her into his arms. In her husband's absence, she'd felt longing in a way she hadn't known before, found her thoughts drifting to intimate moments, the sensation of his fingers tracing her hip bone, the curve of her breast. Her body, it seemed, felt softer to her recently. Her senses somehow heightened. Even now, the clean smell of the cabinet's fresh wood seemed particularly fragrant, and it pleased her.

The fish in its pool of buttermilk, Cora set it aside to start the coffeepot. Scooping in grounds, she saw a flash of blue through the sheers above the sink. A few minutes later, Max blew through the side door, breathless from his sprint through the rain.

"I guess that answers my question of whether it's lightened up out there," Cora said to him. "Maybe you should build an ark instead of cabinets today."

Max laughed as he dragged his boot soles over the straw mat. "I just might." He pushed both hands through his wet hair, slicking it back, and Cora thought fleetingly of Lois claiming he resembled Burt Lancaster. The tousled hair. The strong nose. Those gray-blue eyes.

Cora could see it.

When a bloom of heat spread across her collarbone, she returned her gaze to the coffee before Max could catch her appraisal, grateful to find it ready.

"Something smells good," he said, rubbing his palms down the front of his denim shirt to dry them.

"It's probably the fresh dill. I'm experimenting with a new marinade for this bluefish steak. Coffee?"

"Please."

She glanced at him as she poured two cups. "Do you like bluefish?"

"It's not my favorite," he said, wrinkling his nose. "Too oily."

"You've just never had it cooked properly, then. Or eaten it fresh enough." She handed him a mug. "Bluefish can get awfully gamey if it isn't cooked right away."

"Is that an invitation?"

She laughed. "I'm afraid my husband Harry isn't much for sharing his bluefish. He's coming back tonight."

"Well, good." Max took a quick sip, then a second. "I was worried there wouldn't be anyone to eat all those delicious leftovers while I'm gone."

Her cup nearly to her lips, Cora slowed. "Where are you going?"

"Just back to the shop," he said, setting his mug on the island. "I still have the rest of the drawers and doors to make. It shouldn't take me more than a week."

Even as she smiled, Cora felt a strange flicker of loneliness. She'd grown so used to his company in the past few days. But Harry would be back. Maybe it was best.

Max crossed to the stack of panels that rested against the far wall and sorted through them. "What time is he due home, your husband?"

"Three or four. He's supposed to call this morning to confirm."

"I'll be sure to be out of your hair by then."

"You're hardly in my hair," she said, maybe a little too forcefully, she feared, as she gave the marinade a vigorous whisk.

Max pulled his measuring tape from his pocket and stretched it across a cabinet's opening. "Those flowers are holding up."

Cora looked back at the bouquet where she'd set it on the banquette, the mention bringing back a memory that made her flinch.

"You're probably wondering why I let Lois Welch think they were from my husband," she said.

"I'm not." The tape snapped back. He scribbled something in his notebook. But the need to explain seemed suddenly urgent. The possibility that Max might think her a liar, almost crushing.

Cora set her whisk to rest against her bowl and turned to him as he continued to measure another stretch of cabinets. "People here don't really know anything about my old life, and Harry seems to think I shouldn't make a big deal about any of it, so it just seemed easier to let Lois think . . ." She swallowed the rest of her explanation. The confession, once imperative, now seemed foolish. Worse, shameful.

But Max's eyes shone with understanding. He lowered the tape measure. "It's not my business, but you shouldn't feel like you have to hide where you're from," he said, as if he knew what she feared, even without her saying it. "People here like to think they're worth more because they come from money. They're not."

Feeling another bloom of heat, Cora picked her whisk back up and began swirling the marinade again, quicker now. She pulled a lemon from the basket, the sounds of her scraping it over the grater's tiny blades blending with the zip and whir of his tape, then the scratches of his pencil over his notebook pages.

"So do you do that a lot?" he asked as they worked.

Cora felt a flicker of dread. "Lie?"

He let out a small chuckle. "Make up recipes."

"Oh, that." She felt a sheepish blush burn across the bridge of her nose. "Harry teases me every time I open a cookbook. He says I'm biologically incapable of following a recipe without adding my own twist to it."

"I kind of guessed you're someone who likes to make up her own rules."

Was she? Cora flushed at the suggestion. She'd never thought of herself as a contrary person. And she certainly didn't want to be seen as such here. If she wanted to fit into the world of Oyster Point, she would, for lack of a better comparison, have to follow the recipe of life here.

Max walked back to his collection of finished drawers. "That can be hard in a place like this."

"What can?" she asked.

"Being your own person. Having your own thoughts."

He swung his pencil toward the window. "I can't tell you how many times I go into one of these big houses to change something up for someone and the first thing they ask is, 'So how did you do it for Mr. So-and-So?' It's like they want to make sure they're just the same, you know? Like there's some guidebook they're all following."

Cora knocked the whisk clean on the side of the bowl. "I think most people just want to fit in. To belong."

"It's understandable," Max said with a consenting nod, and yet Cora had the feeling Max Dempsey wasn't someone who worried about fitting in, or who might have felt obliged to hide things about his past to do it. As she cleaned a clove of garlic, she felt another flutter of remorse—then another, deeper in her stomach, of envy.

Maybe it was easier for men not to worry as much about belonging, she thought as she minced, so distracted with the possibility that she let the knife get too close. The blade nicked her thumb and she let out a small hiss, more from frustration with herself than from pain.

Max lowered his tape and looked over. "You okay?"

"I'm fine," Cora said, giving the small cut a quick inspection before rinsing it under the tap. "Just another scar to add to the collection." She wiped her finger dry on her skirt and gave a self-deprecating laugh. "I'm afraid my career as a hand model will have to wait."

"You want to compare scars?" Max said, climbing down from the ladder. He pocketed his tape and walked toward her, holding out his hands. "Get a load of these."

How different his hands were from Harry's, Cora thought as she appraised them. Broader, the knuckles and veins so much more pronounced. No freckles sprinkled across the backs. Even the nails. Where Harry's were long and tidy,

Max's were squared and uneven, the cuticles stained with dirt.

He tilted his right hand and pointed to a scar that traveled the length of the meat of his thumb. "My first time using a chisel," he said. "And this—" He held up his left thumb, the nail misshapen. "Trying to rush through a job on a drill press."

Cora grimaced. "It went in?"

Max gave a resigned nod. "Now let's see you beat that."

She presented her hands as he had, wiggling her fingers invitingly. "While kitchen tools don't tend to impale, I do have a burn mark from my first time using a hand torch on a crème brûlée that I'm rather proud of," she said, directing his attention to a heart-shaped stain on her palm.

"Impressive." Max took her fingers into his for a closer look. The heat of his hands was startling. It raced up Cora's arms like gooseflesh. She wondered if he could feel the thrum of her pulse where his index finger circled her wrist.

He turned her right hand gently in his left, the hard pad of his thumb grazing the peak of her pinky knuckle where the skin was scarlet.

"What about here?" he asked.

"I wasn't paying attention and I caught it on a hot pan handle."

Max winced. "Looks like it hurt."

"A little," she said, suddenly aware that his thumb had started circling the spot, as if the burn was fresh and he was rubbing invisible salve over the wound. Or maybe she was only imagining the motion. Then why was her heart pounding? And why did the air in the kitchen seem suddenly warm and so very still?

Looking up, she found his gaze waiting.

When the trill of the telephone sailed out from the other end of the house, Cora sucked in a startled breath, not sure if the reaction was from the surprise of the sound, or the shock of his touch. She tugged herself free from Max's hands and felt color rising to her face. Grateful for the rescue of the telephone's ring, she excused herself and rushed through the great room, reaching across the desk to grab the receiver off its hook, her heart still pounding as she answered: "Hello?"

"Hello, darling."

She smiled at Harry's voice and sank into his chair, willing her racing pulse to slow. "I was hoping it was you."

"You were expecting someone else?" he teased.

"Of course not," she said, touching her cheek and uneasy to find it still warm. "How are you?"

"Tired. Ready to come home. How was yesterday's lunch with the girls?"

Had that been only yesterday? It seemed months ago somehow.

"It was a lovely time," Cora said, even as the memory that flashed back first was how quietly outraged she'd been when Lois and Irene had boasted about not tipping the waitstaff. She wanted to tell Harry but refrained. A few days earlier she had pointed out that Lois had made a snide comment about the condition of their patio furniture, and instead of agreeing that it had been rude, Harry had grumbled that he'd been meaning to replace the old collection since they arrived. It was quite clear Lois could do no wrong.

"Did Lois introduce you to everyone for me?" Harry asked.

"There weren't many people there, but she did her best."

"Oh, I'm sure she did. How's everything at the house? Are the men still working on the roof?"

"They didn't come today. It's pouring here," Cora said, spinning the chair to face the window, where necklaces of rain snaked down the glass.

"Too bad. It's a beautiful day here. Not that I would know, holed up in my office."

"Poor darling."

"Don't feel too sorry for me. Roger took us out for lobster thermidor last night."

"How was it?"

"Edible, but nowhere near as delicious as yours."

"Good." She wound the heavy black cord around her fingers. "The men did start on the porch repair, though."

"Super. I promised Ned we'd have them over when I got back."

Cora felt prickles of anticipation travel up her arms. At last, her chance to impress his friends—their friends—with her cooking and her skills as a hostess.

"How's the kitchen?" he asked.

Cora turned the chair back to the door, looking down the hall to the kitchen doorway. "It's coming along nicely. I can't wait to show you."

"Will I need a map to find my way around?"

She laughed into the receiver. "Not yet. But you may bump into things in the dark for a while."

"Hmm. Sounds dangerous." Harry sighed. "Ready for me to come back?"

"What do you think? I've put some bluefish in a marinade."

"Sounds scrumptious. What about dessert?"

She wound the phone's thick black cord tighter around her index finger and let her lips slide into a wicked smile. "I was thinking you could just have me."

Harry sputtered out a startled chuckle. "Listen to you! What's all this about?"

"What? Can't a wife miss her husband?"

"It's advisable, yes." Cora could hear the smile in his voice. "I'll be on the two o'clock ferry, sweetheart. Hopefully that cabinetmaker fellow will be gone by then."

Cora glanced up, sure Max was too far away to hear, but she lowered her voice just in case. "Do you know he has family in the Port? Isn't that remarkable?"

"It's hardly the other side of the world, darling. I'm not sure how remarkable it is."

"Yes, but he even knew Marigold's."

"Hmm. No doubt he's trying to butter you up so I'll give him more work."

Cora bristled, forcing a softness to her reply even as the desire to defend Max thumped in her chest, but her voice just came out sounding watery and thin instead.

"That's not it at all, Harry."

"Don't be so sure." Her husband sighed, his breath vibrating against the receiver. "You're too trusting, sweetheart. Good thing I'm coming home."

She let the cord loosen around her finger, whatever tremors of excitement she'd felt pulsing through her at his impending return suddenly, disappointingly cooled.

"Yes, it is," Cora said, as if he'd needed confirmation. As if she might have, too.

18

1999

It takes a great many things to make a successful clambake. By the time guests circle around the teeming bowls
of steamed seafood and vegetables, paper plates trembling
in their hands from anticipation, no less than eight hours
of effort have delivered them their bounty. There's corn to
de-silk. Potatoes to scrub. Cheesecloth to cut. Rockweed to
collect from the beach. The pit alone can take hours to dig
out of the sand and line with rocks, the fire another several
to set up and then burn hot enough to cook. Start to finish,
a clambake can take a full day, which means the thing that a
clambake requires most of all is patience.

Mickey had that once, she thinks as she rolls over, sending out a chorus of groans and creaks from the twin's old
springs. She grew up around clambakes, both as guest and
cook. She knows how much time it takes to do it right.
Yet where was all that patience when she was growing her
restaurant? It was no different than cooking, heating up a
pan slowly to avoid burning your food when you added it.
Tiffany was the one who'd made that comparison. Her oldest friend, who could have run a restaurant in her sleep.

Mickey turns onto her back and sighs. She looks up at

the slanted ceiling, at the same configuration of water stains meeting at the seam of the pine boards where the eave connects, the dot-to-dot puzzle she solved a hundred times every summer, when she lost sleep over a broken heart or some other disappointment that seemed so crushing, so life-ending at the time. The memory of her phone call with Wes throbs like a hangover headache. Before bed, she called him at home but got the machine and proceeded to ramble on, hoping he would put her out of her misery and pick up, but he never did. She slept fitfully, too warm despite the fan beside her bed, and woke every few hours, sure she heard phantom rings from downstairs: Wes finally calling back to say he could forgive her, that they could move on from this together. But the darkness was always silent when Mickey opened her eyes.

Down on the lawn, muffled voices sail through the screen beside her bed. The slamming of car doors, then the rumble of an engine. Sitting up, Mickey pulls back the sheers to look down on the driveway in time to see a black sports car disappear around the trees.

Normally she'd be looking forward to a Beech House clambake, up before everyone else, and the first in the kitchen to start prepping, but this morning the prospect of the big party makes her want to pull the covers over herself and hide. What will she say when people want to talk to her about Piquant? The firepit is not even lit, and already knots of worry are tightening in her stomach. Here she is, back on the Vineyard, her dream of owning her own restaurant having finally come true, and instead of feeling pride and excitement to talk about it, all she feels is regret.

A shower with the bracing fragrance of mint shampoo perks her up a bit, but Mickey's pace downstairs is far less brisk than it was her first morning here. This time when she passes the Wedding Wall, she keeps her gaze forward, fearful of seeing only judgment in so many faces.

Not surprising, preparations have already started without her. Even her late-sleeping mother has beaten Mickey to the kitchen this morning. Hedy sits at the banquette working on the seating chart in front of her—a large piece of paper covered with circles—and a sea of place cards spread out around her. Her mother's hair, usually as neat and glossy as a varnished cherry tabletop, has been pulled back into a messy twist and secured with a neon clip that Mickey is sure is hers from a hundred summers ago.

"Cute hair, Mom."

"Don't start," Hedy says. "I'm about ready to lose my last shred of sanity over this seating chart."

Mickey heads for the coffeepot. "Anything I can do to help?"

"Only if you can convince your grandmother to elope in the next twenty-four hours."

"I was thinking more like drawing names out of a hat," Mickey says, adding a splash of cream.

Her mother sighs. "I haven't ruled that out."

A plate of crumb-topped blueberry muffins sits on the island. Mickey breaks off a corner of one and carries it with her coffee to the table.

"Where is everyone?" she asks as she swings into the opposite bench.

"Your grandmother is upstairs trying on her dress, and Max and Tom went to town to get the littlenecks and corn."

That explained the black BMW. "When did Tom get here?"

"Late last night." Her mother sits back and blows out

an exasperated breath, swinging off her readers and rubbing her eyes. "The problem is that I don't know half of these people—and I can guarantee you, most of them would never share a table on this island."

Mickey knows her mother doesn't mean the comment to be rude or harsh—but it's the truth. Hedy is having to blend two very different island worlds, which, even for the duration of a single meal, is challenging.

"What you really need," Mickey says, leaning over for a closer look, "is to clone Lois Welch so you can put one of her at every table. She'd do all the talking for everyone. Problem solved."

She smiles over at her mother, but Hedy can't seem to summon one in return.

"I'm still struggling to see even one of Lois Welch in this mix," Hedy admits quietly.

Of course her mother would be, Mickey thinks, feeling a pang of sympathy as she takes another sip of coffee. The difficulty in merging these two worlds isn't reserved only for the dinner guests.

"Speaking of Lois Welch," Mickey says. "I ran into her on the beach yesterday. She said something so strange."

"We are talking about Lois Welch," her mother mutters absently, still scanning the sea of place cards.

"We were talking about Grams and Granddad—or at least, I thought we were—and she said that they seemed suited from the first. That she knew it the first time she saw them together. And I just assumed she meant Granddad."

Her mother looks up over her readers. "Who else would she be talking about?"

"Max, I guess?"

There's a brief flash of something in her mother's eyes—

amusement or agreement—but Mickey can't decide before Hedy tips her head back down to the chart.

"I'm sure you misunderstood," her mother says, fanning out another section of cards.

Her grandmother sweeps into the room. "Good morning."

"How does the dress fit, Grams?" Mickey asks.

"The skirt is still longer than I'd like," Cora says. "But I don't have the heart to tell Wanda—she's already hemmed it twice—so I'm just going to hem it myself with a little tape."

"Mom, you can't tape the hem of your wedding dress," Hedy says. "That's just not done."

"It's just a few inches." Cora shrugs. "What the heck, maybe I'll just go for it and cut it to a miniskirt." Mickey's grandmother directs this question to her. "What do you think?"

"Don't answer that," Hedy warns Mickey.

"Still no word from the caterer?" her grandmother asks as she crosses for the pantry.

"Not a peep."

"Michelle, have you met Tom yet?"

"Not yet," Mickey says.

Cora emerges from the pantry with a roll of cheesecloth and sets it on the island. "Hopefully it will be less dramatic than your mother's introduction."

Mickey looks across the table for explanation, but her mother's gaze won't rise to meet hers.

Cora stretches out a section of cheesecloth and fishes a pair of scissors out of the drawer. "Apparently, your mother and her future stepbrother got their first fight out of the way."

"It wasn't a fight," Hedy says wearily. "He startled me in the dark and I accidentally elbowed him in the nose. I felt terrible."

"What were you even doing out there?" Cora asks.

"I told you, Mom. I went for a swim."

"In the dark?"

"Haven't you heard? Women over forty-five have to swim at night. It's a public service. When people see our decrepit bodies in bathing suits in daylight, they turn to stone."

"Good grief . . ." Cora groans and looks at Mickey, her teasing smile thinning. Her pleated eyes pool with worry. "Any word from Wes, darling?"

Mickey shakes her head. "Only in my dreams, I'm afraid."

Cora cuts a square of cheesecloth and measures out another. "He'll come around. You'll see."

"I'm not sure, Grams. You better put me to work— otherwise I'm liable to stare at the phone until _I_ turn to stone."

"There's not much to do until the men get back with the food," her grandmother says, adding another square of cheesecloth to the pile. "Why don't you go down and start collecting rockweed for the pit? Buckets are on the porch."

Normally, Mickey would do anything to linger in this kitchen, but this morning she's more than happy for the excuse to leave it.

Especially when she steps around the porch to see Tiffany's van rolling down the driveway. Relief settles over her, the knot of tension between her shoulder blades unraveling, and she lets a wistful smile turn up her lips: The two of them had always made the best seaweed-collecting team on the Point.

"What is this crap?" Tiffany cries with mock outrage as Mickey crosses to meet her, a bucket held out for her to take. "I thought I was here as a guest."

"Nice try." Mickey grabs Tiffany's free hand and tugs

her forward. "You know family never get to be guests at Beech House."

* * *

Mickey waits until they've been in the water long enough that their calves no longer ache with cold before she confesses everything.

"Oh, Mick . . ." Tiffany's eyes swim with apology. "And there I was yesterday, whining to you about losing Chowder's, and you didn't say a word."

"Stop." Mickey would reach across the rock and give her old friend's arm a fond touch if her fingers weren't so slimy with seaweed slick. "You had Chowder's snatched out from under you—I've sent my restaurant over the cliff all on my own. It's my fault. You were right; I have no business running a restaurant."

"When did I say that?"

Mickey smiles. "Only every day we worked together."

They pick up their buckets and wade deeper, moving to the next cluster of seaweed-covered rocks.

"Well, it still sucks," says Tiffany. "Is that why Wes didn't come with you?"

"No, but it's definitely why he won't be coming any time soon." Mickey pulls at a fat clump, but the seaweed clings stubbornly. "I only just told him yesterday."

Tiffany looks up, her eyes wide with alarm. "Oh, shit."

"It's my own fault for waiting." Her hands too wet to get a good grip, Mickey drags her fingers roughly on her shorts to dry them and tries again. "I was just so sure I could fix it and never have to tell him, but . . ." Another tug and the weeds give, blowing up a cold breath of brine. Mickey flings the slippery strands into her bucket.

Tiffany chuckles. "Remember that one clambake when everyone was frantic because they couldn't get enough rockweed and all those people were standing around waiting?"

As if Mickey could forget. There had been a boy—there was always a boy—a neighbor's cousin she was looking to impress. Certain they knew the perfect place to harvest some seaweed, they'd taken out her grandfather's dinghy and found themselves stranded on the sandbar. Instead of being great saviors, they'd needed saving themselves.

"What was his name?" Tiffany asked, squinting with effort. "He looked like Keanu Reeves. God, he was hot. Chip, was it?"

"Kip," Mickey says. And he was incredibly hot—until she and Tiffany got off the boat with their filled buckets and he broke her heart with two words: "Thanks, kids."

"Who calls fifteen-year-olds kids?" Mickey says, the memory still causing outrage.

"A twenty-one-year-old guy, that's who." Tiffany gives her a teasing poke. "You were inconsolable."

"I can't believe I really thought he was going to ask me out."

"I can't believe I let you talk me into taking out the dinghy."

They had been so sure that was the very worst blow life could deal them. Because up until then, it had been. Fifteen years and so much true loss later, family members passed away, both of Tiffany's parents gone, they might long for those simpler heartaches.

Mickey straightens, needing to stretch. Tiffany joins her.

"See what I mean about the houses?" Tiffany says as they scan the view. "They throw them up like circus tents, I swear to God."

The wind picks up, lashing Mickey's face with loose tendrils. Her hands still gooey, she brushes them back with her knuckles.

"How's your mom taking all this?" Tiffany asks as they resume their work, wading in deeper.

"You know my mom. She keeps things close. It's hard to know for sure. But I've been seeing some cracks. I know this isn't easy for her."

"Or for you, either," Tiffany says. "Especially in a place like this, where everyone is in everyone's business all the time."

Mickey slows her search, a thought sparking. "Are people actually talking about this wedding?"

When Tiffany hesitates, Mickey feels a flicker of unease. "What are they saying, Tiff?"

"They're saying . . . God, it's so stupid . . ." Tiffany rolls her eyes. "They're saying Max is the one who got away."

Mickey steps back, abruptly enough that the seaweed sloshes in her bucket, sending up a spray of salt water.

"I told you it was stupid," Tiffany says, giving Mickey's arm a comforting squeeze. "These people can't help themselves. It's pathological. God knows Danny hugs someone when I'm not around and ten minutes later, everyone's talking about how he's having an affair and we're on the rocks. You know it's all bullshit."

Until it isn't, Mickey thinks, even as she offers Tiffany an agreeable nod. But as she resumes collecting, uncertainty continues to prickle. Lois Welch's curious comment flashes back. Was her mother aware of these rumblings, too? Is that why she's been so especially edgy here?

After a few more slippery handfuls, she and Tiffany scan their yields and agree they've collected enough. They carry their buckets up the beach, the glistening tangles of seaweed sloshing, and leave their harvest at the top.

Tiffany looks around. "Do you think we should start on the pit?"

It's not a bad idea. And anything Mickey can do to avoid watching the phone is a bonus.

"Sure," she says, then coaxes her tight lips into a smile. "But if we're on dig duty, then we're going to need beers."

* * *

Mickey climbs the porch and takes the doors through the great room, slowing when she hears her mother's throaty laugh sail through the kitchen doorway. It's not the volume that startles her, but the pitch. It's what Mickey always called Hedy's "agent laugh," the one her mother reserves for people she's trying to put at ease, strangers she doesn't yet know but wants to feel welcome, calm, and something in Mickey's stomach shifts, dips like a pitched boat. Stepping into the kitchen, she stops just over the threshold.

"Look who was in the neighborhood!"

But Mickey's eyes have already locked on his where he stands at the island, between her mother and grandmother, a beer in his hand, looking as relaxed as if he's been here a hundred times before, and every inch of her skin blazes with shock.

"Hey, Mick," Wes says, one side of his heavy brow rising. "I hear I'm just in time for a clambake."

19

1948

They woke late Saturday morning, both so Harry could catch up on his sleep and because they could with the workmen not arriving at their usual seven a.m. to force them from their bed. While he showered and coffee brewed, Cora made them scrambled eggs with chives and cream cheese. The rain had passed and the day promised unfettered sunlight and heat. Cora opened the room's windows to take advantage of the morning's cooler breezes, and several times as she cooked, she thought she heard Max's truck crackle down the driveway and had to remind herself of his absence over the week ahead. Her thoughts slipped to the last time they'd shared this space together, their playful inspection of each other's battle scars just before the phone rang, how she'd felt almost caught by the sound and tugged free of his hands, the reminder causing a tremor of guilt to snake in her stomach. They had, of course, done nothing wrong. They were just having fun. So why did she feel as if she had something to hide from Harry?

"I ran into Lois at the gatehouse on my way home," Harry said as Cora cleared their breakfast plates an hour later. "She pressed for us all to get together, and road-weary as I was, I didn't put up much of a fight, I'm afraid, so I told her tonight for cocktails."

Cora blinked at him—her heart pounding with panic. That was only a few hours away. He was just telling her this now?

"Why didn't you say something last night?"

"I thought you would be excited to have everyone over."

"I was," she said, breathless now with nerves. "I am! But, Harry, these things take time. I'll need to make a menu, and then an order for the market—"

"Sweetheart . . ." Harry arrived behind her at the sink and placed his hands on her shoulders. "Relax. These kinds of things come together at the last minute all the time here. My mother used to pull a party together in a few hours for five times as many guests."

Cora stared up at him, growing warm with outrage. Did he not appreciate the significance of their first party—her first as his wife? How crucial it would be to make sure everything went smoothly?

His gaze held hers, demanding her surrender, but she shook her head.

"You need to give me more time, Harry," she said, her voice edged with the same firmness she used to employ at the restaurant with difficult customers or sloppy line cooks.

After another heated moment, Harry released an exasperated sigh and let his hands drop to his sides, defeated. "Fine," he said wearily. "I'll ring Ned and push them off until tomorrow night. But don't be surprised if they've already got other plans."

Her heart finally slowing its furious beat, Cora smiled as

she sank their dishes into the sudsy water, relief pooling in her stomach, and a tickle of pride at standing her ground.

* * *

"To the next generation of Beech House!"

Harry made the toast on the porch the following evening, his arm around Cora's shoulders to keep her, she suspected, from dashing off for another tray of hors d'oeuvres. After much deliberation, she'd settled on a simple but succulent menu: deviled eggs, salmon mousse canapés, stuffed mushrooms, and crab salad sandwiches. The party itself had, as far as she could tell, been a great success. Now, the sun setting, everyone full, they languished on the back porch, settled into the new patio chairs that Harry had bought, replacing the brittle wicker collection that had lived on Beech House's porch since he was little. The fresh seat cushions were decorated with giant bamboo palm leaves, and so stiff they squealed with strain when everyone sat.

"They're lovely," Lois said, sweeping her hand along the curved arms. "Bamboo?"

"Rattan," Harry corrected. "I thought if we can update the inside, why not outside, too?"

He winked at Cora and she smiled, excitement stirring freshly. While she had been looking forward to their first party so she could impress her husband's friends with her cooking skills, she was equally anxious to give the women a tour of the kitchen. For weeks, she had been sharing news of its development. But now, the space nearly complete, Cora had no doubt they would puddle with envy to see it— and all of its custom touches—for themselves: Imagine Lois and Irene wanting to emulate her instead of the other way around!

Phil wagged a finger at Harry. "Don't forget, Champ. You promised me a match when you got back."

Harry balked. "Tonight?"

"Why not tonight? Didn't I tell you we got lights installed?" Phil dripped salmon mouse on his knee and Cora handed him a cocktail napkin.

Lois set down her coffee. "We should really get back and relieve the sitter."

"Agreed," said Irene, rising. "Emily isn't much of a major general, but she means well. Summer girls don't make the best sitters, unfortunately. Too much mooning over tanned summer boys."

Lois rolled her eyes in Cora's direction. "You'll find out soon enough."

But when the group began to rise in unison, Cora felt a burst of panic. She rushed to her feet, so quickly she nearly spilled her coffee.

"You can't leave yet," she said to Irene and Lois. "I haven't given you the tour!"

* * *

"Like I said, it's not quite finished," Cora said as she led them into the kitchen, fissures of pride and excitement already sizzling around her scalp, "but it's close—and I can show you where everything will go that hasn't yet been installed."

Lois and Irene slowed at the stove, taking in the space.

"It's all Max's design, everything custom," Cora said, moving purposefully to the first cabinet. "Look—they revolve!" She opened the door and gave the three-tiered shelving a spin to demonstrate. "So I can always reach what I need."

"Clever," Irene said with a measured shrug.

"Isn't it? Oh, and on the countertop over there," Cora said, pointing, "Max is going to cut out an opening in the counter for trash, so I can just dump my peelings and scraps right into it."

"Dump them where?" asked Lois.

"Just below," Cora explained, swinging open a lower cabinet door. "There'll be a bucket down here."

"I don't know that I'd like that," Irene said, making a face at Lois. "Having a big garbage hole. Won't it smell?"

"I—I don't think so," Cora said, tamping down a tiny pang of insult at the point—not to mention the women's general lack of enthusiasm. "Now over here on the island—"

"Island—how quaint," Lois said.

"That's what Max calls it."

"But right in the middle of the floor like this?" Irene said.

"It certainly does take up a lot of space," Lois remarked, circling it.

"But look at all it will have," Cora said, tugging out the deep drawer in one of the cabinets, sure this detail would impress them. "Max is going to line the drawer with tin so I can store my flour in there. Just pour it right in so all I have to do is scoop it out. No fussing with bags. And there will be a second one for sugar, but he hasn't had a chance to make that one yet. And this one"—she stepped back to access the shallow drawer under the lip—"will have sections for smaller tools, graters and whisks and measuring spoons. And all this space," Cora said, spreading her arms out over the stretch of butcher block, "to prep or roll out dough or whatever I want to do."

There were other things—the rack for paper towels behind one of the cabinet doors, the extra work surface that would slide out like a desk—but Cora held back, seeing the women's features go slack, as if with boredom. How could they not feel some kind of awe?

"And he's made all this himself?" Lois asked, running her fingertips along the beveled edge of a cabinet door.

"In his workshop," Cora said. "Max cuts them there and assembles them here. He's really very talented."

"All these funny little gadgets," said Irene. "No wonder it's taking the man so long."

"It's different, that's for sure," Lois said, fingering her pearls as she looked around. "Dreamy or not, I think someone has read *The Swiss Family Robinson* a few too many times."

Irene snickered into her glass.

Cora pressed her hands down the front of her skirt, prickling with hurt. Had she really imagined they might have any appreciation for all that Max had made—let alone been envious of her new custom kitchen? After all, both women admitted to hating cooking. But they didn't need to be so mean about it.

"Don't get me wrong," Lois said. "It's all very clever. And I'm sure for someone who worked in a restaurant, it must all make complete sense."

"That's right," said Irene. "Harry was telling us how he used to come in for your . . . what was it? Peach pie?"

Lois brushed sharply at a streak of sawdust on her blouse as if it were a spider.

Cora swallowed. "Lemon meringue."

"Right," said Irene, letting the middle of the word drag out. "Such a darling story. Really, it's like a fairy tale. Like Cinderella, or something."

"But then we always knew our Harry was a real prince, didn't we?" Lois said.

"That's exactly what I said when I teased him about it tonight," Irene said, turning to Cora. "I said he rescued you, just like Prince Charming, and he positively beamed."

Cora felt as if she'd stepped in front of a roaring fire, her whole body suddenly overheated. Her jaw ached, as if someone had glued it shut.

"He hardly rescued me," she said tightly. "I was very happy there."

"Oh dear, I didn't mean to offend you." Irene leaned back and clapped her hands over her heart, crossing them as if she had kneeled for a blessing.

A thread of sweat trickled down Cora's temple. She wiped at her forehead, suddenly needing air.

Irene leaned toward Lois and whispered low, "I think maybe we hurt her feelings about the kitchen, too."

Cora didn't like how they spoke as if she weren't standing right there, but she wasn't about to let them know the weight of their insult. Not just to her, but to Max and all his hard work.

"Hardly," Cora assured them with a short smile. "I'm not so thin-skinned."

But as she returned with the women to the porch to find the men gone, Cora feared she was.

The sun had dropped fully behind the trees. The low light of dusk washed the lawn in a cool silver-blue.

"So much for waiting for that match," said Irene, fishing a cigarette out of her purse. "I'm not surprised. Phil's been champing at the bit to show off the resurfaced court. All those years not being here. It was an absolute disgrace, as you can imagine."

"The Half Shell championship is in a few weeks, Cora," Lois said. "It's a very big deal on the Point. Bragging rights and all that." Cora already knew. Harry had mentioned it more than a few times. "I'm sure it will be quite the event this summer, what with all the years we've missed."

Irene lit her cigarette and exhaled over her shoulder. "Phil fancies himself Bobby Riggs, but he can barely get it over the net."

Harry's comment about rescuing her from the restaurant flooded back to Cora, the need to press her husband on it urgent.

"Which way to your court?" she asked Irene.

"Follow us," said Lois, as they began across the lawn.

"But I wouldn't get too close with those," Irene said, pointing her cigarette down at Cora's white pumps. "That red clay is murder."

* * *

At the fork in the path, Cora parted from the group and followed the sounds of hollow thwacks and guttural cries of defeat to find her husband and Phil Middleton lunging madly across the field of terra-cotta, their bodies darting in and out of the flickering streams of light from the two spotlights that rose up on either side of the net.

She stopped several paces from the cone of the lights and watched the match, both fascinated and alarmed at the intensity of her husband's swings; the groans of joy or agony, depending on who hadn't stretched far enough to save the ball from escape. Curses of frustration filled the humid air, words Harry never used in her company. Cora felt invisible in the dark, independent somehow, and couldn't decide if she liked the feeling or not. On her way to the court, her outrage had been so intense, her need to confront Harry urgent, but now she felt her resolve fading . . .

"Who's that?" Phil tented a hand over his eyes as he squinted toward her, his chest heaving under his soaked sport shirt.

"It's Cora," she called as she stepped into view.

"Hello, darling!" Harry let his racket dangle at his side. "Come to see me pummel our neighbor, have you?"

Phil howled. "In your dreams, Campbell!"

Cora walked to the edge of the clay and Harry met her there, winded. His breath was hot, soaked with gin. Sweat shone at his temples, glued one end of his collar to his shoulder.

A stripe of clay streaked his damp neck. Cora wiped it off.

"Could we talk?" she asked.

"Of course, darling."

She glanced past him to see Phil Middleton watching them, swinging his racket evenly like a metronome. He seemed different to her, somehow. Drowsy, but not with sleep.

"Privately," she whispered. "Please?"

"Sweetheart, I'm in the middle of a match. Can't it wait?"

"Lois and Irene said that you rescued me from the restaurant." Cora swallowed, her pulse hastening at the memory. "Like Cinderella."

"I'm sure they were kidding."

"Well, it wasn't funny. Irene said she teased you about being Prince Charming saving me and that you acted as if it was a compliment."

"I was only making a joke."

"At my expense, Harry." When he reached out to clasp her hand, Cora stepped back, out of reach. "Are you embarrassed by me?"

"What?" Harry blinked at her. "Of course not. Why would you ask that?"

His voice was rising. Cora cut another glance at Phil, flushing with worry to find his continued study. Now the arc of his swing grew longer, like a machete cutting through thick brush.

"Please don't make a big thing of it, Harry. I'm just tired. I was hoping you would come home and we could—"

"Later," Harry said firmly. "I told you I'm in the middle of a match." Her husband staggered back, his racket dragging across the clay, sending up a cloud of red dust. "What do I always say, darling? You're too sensitive."

Tears prickled at the edges of her eyes, but Cora blinked them away, waiting until Harry had reached back with his racket, groaning as he smacked the ball through the cone of light, before she turned and slipped up the path for Beech House.

20

1999

When Mickey fantasized about bringing Wes to Beech House, it usually went something like this: They'd arrive on a flawless June afternoon, maybe near high tide so that the wind off the water would be faintly salty and not quite so tangy when they stepped up to the house. She'd be tempted to take him past her and her grandmother's precious kitchen garden, but she'd restrain herself, leaving that tour for later. They'd enter through the side door, step into a cloud of garlic-and-butter-soaked air, and find Cora waiting for them in the kitchen, where she'd been whipping up a pot of her famous chipotle clam chowder. Then they'd tuck themselves into the banquette with steaming bowls and glasses of cold, crisp beer, and spin tales. Both inherently charming people, her grandmother and Wes would take turns charming each other, and be thick as thieves by the time their bowls were empty . . .

But that's not how it's happened.

And as she stands on the porch, where she and Wes have just excused themselves from the choking silence of the kitchen, Mickey's never felt so torn. As startled as she is that he's just shown up unannounced, her stomach is a whirlpool of need for him. She wants to touch him, wants to throw herself into his arms, but Wes keeps a gap between their bodies, his hands anchored deep in the pockets of his cargo shorts. She tells herself he wouldn't have come all this way to break up with her—that is what phones are for—but her heart still pounds with uncertainty.

Below them on the beach, Tom and Max have lit the fire in the sandpit. The wind off the water is fragrant with fresh smoke, a smell Mickey would normally grow dizzy on, but right now, she can barely breathe. It's all she can do not to jump out of her skin.

She wants to confess that she can't believe he's here, that he came, but she's afraid just the mention will cause Wes to change his mind and get back into his truck, the familiar gray Nissan pickup she can see parked by the carriage house. She still can't believe he got a reservation on the ferry at the last minute.

The breeze blows his dark hair over his forehead. Mickey wonders for a panicked instant if she will never get the chance to bury her fingers in it again.

"I know you didn't want to leave Pete in charge—"

"I didn't." Wes's voice is hard, as rough with frustration as it was on the phone. "I closed the restaurant until Monday."

"What?" Panic squeezes Mickey's chest like a too-tight zipper. "But Nina said we're booked up. All those reservations—"

"Nina called everyone and promised to comp their first bottle of wine when we reopen next week."

"Oh." Her pulse slows, but only for a moment: How can they afford to comp who-knows-how-many bottles of wine?

Mickey swallows, determined to stay focused.

When she looks back at Wes, his dark eyes are there waiting to hold hers.

"Why the hell didn't you trust me enough to tell me we were in trouble, Mick?"

"I did trust you," she says. "I didn't trust myself. I was too proud, too stubborn . . ." But even as she answers, Mickey feels like someone in a game of charades, throwing out words, hoping for the right one, but none quite seem to hit the mark. She turns up her palms. "I just thought I would figure it out. But then I fell behind and I didn't know how to catch up. How to fix it . . ." She presses her fingers to her lips. "What now?" she asks weakly.

He shrugs. "Now we wait. Hope we can recover."

Does he mean the restaurant—or them? Mickey's heart pounds with uncertainty.

Wes steps past her and leans a hand against the column, scanning the view. "So, this is the famous Beech House," he says, pivoting to take in the exterior. "I can see why you love it here."

Mickey eyes him skeptically—he's barely been here, what? An hour? But she can't doubt his claim. Beech House is irresistible, its spell instantly intoxicating. She only hopes its soothing magic will work on him as well as it does on everyone else.

Behind them, the screen swings open and Cora leans out, her apron dusted with flour, her round cheeks flushed from exertion. "Sorry to interrupt, lovebirds. But I need a volunteer to pick through thirty pounds of clams."

Wes raises his hand. "Right here."

"Wonderful." Cora points to Mickey. "And you, darling, have some potatoes to scrub."

Mickey gives a dutiful nod, her eyes locking with Wes's and holding briefly before he steps back and sweeps his arm toward the door.

"After you, chef."

21

1948

After a tennis match with Ned that Thursday afternoon, slick with perspiration, Harry strolled into the great room, where Cora was sorting through the bookshelves, with an announcement: "Get dressed, sweetheart. I'm taking you to the club for dinner." The Welches and the Middletons would be meeting them there, a detail her husband neglected to include until they were through the double doors and Cora spotted Lois waving across the club's dining room, her stack of gold bangles catching the light. In the few days since the party, the sting of Lois and Irene's dismissive words about Max's work—never mind Cora's at Marigold's—continued to burn, despite Cora's efforts to forget them, wishing she could focus instead on the success of her first time as hostess, her first party as Mrs. Harry Campbell.

As they reached their table, Cora vowed to try harder.

"We took the liberty of ordering drinks," Ned informed them, rising while Harry helped Cora into her seat. Two fingers of an amber-colored liquid sat in a glass at her place. "Whiskey, right?"

Cora looked across the table to find Ned smiling expectantly at her. She was relieved to find the same boyish warmth in his puppy-dog eyes that had flickered at her the first time he'd handed her a drink.

"Good," Ned said. "I thought I remembered correctly."

"If only you could remember to scrape that awful clay off your tennis shoes as well as you remember people's drink orders," Lois said, adjusting one of her sunburst earrings.

"First time back, isn't it?" Ned asked, raising his high-ball glass to Harry. "Cheers."

"Cheers," Harry said, then glanced around as he sipped. "Did they change out the bar?"

"Redid the whole other side of the room," Lois said, snapping open her napkin.

"Now if they could just fix the course." Phil swirled his glass, making the ice rattle.

"Whatever you do, don't order the lobster," Irene said. "I came yesterday and they're only serving shedders."

Cora looked to Harry for explanation. Her husband leaned in close. "They're lobsters that have just shed their shells, so there's less meat."

"I don't understand . . ." Cora frowned. "They don't have any shells?"

"They do. They're just soft."

"Then they aren't protected?"

"Not for a bit, no, but they harden eventually."

"And how long does that take?"

Across the table, Irene wrinkled her lips with amusement. "Good grief, you didn't tell us you married a budding marine biologist, Harry."

But Cora didn't feel like laughing. She looked around the table, seeking a sympathetic face, but the only person to offer her a tender smile was Ned.

She spread out her napkin. "I'm just saying it seems unfair to catch them when they're not yet ready."

"What's unfair," said Irene, reaching for her martini, "is charging as much as they do for them. That's the crime."

Phil shrugged. "Better they get boiled alive rather than torn apart on the ocean floor, I say. More humane, don't you think?"

"Phil, please." Lois screwed up her nose. "Are we really talking about this?"

"I don't see why they can't just live with the same shell," Irene said.

Phil snickered as he perused his menu. "Does that mean I won't be getting any more bills from Filene's?"

"Fat chance," said Irene.

The table shuddered with laughter. Cora glanced up to see a smiling blond approach their table, ready to take their order, and recognition fired. "Betty?"

The woman held her pencil against her order pad and pivoted to shine her smile on Cora.

"Oh, hello, Mrs. Campbell."

"Cora," she insisted gently. "How are you?"

"I'm fine, thank you."

"Did you find Max?"

"I did, yes."

"Good, because I realized after you left that—"

Phil cleared his throat pointedly, the sound cutting through their conversation like a blade. In the strained silence, Cora glanced over to find Lois and Irene exchanging a wary look over their menus.

"If you don't mind," Phil said, "the rest of us would like to hear tonight's specials before they sell out."

"Of course. My apologies." Betty's pale cheeks bloomed with embarrassed color even as she spread her lips into an appeasing smile and fumbled to flip to the front of her order pad, reciting the entrées in a bright voice.

Sitting back, Cora felt her own cheeks flush with heat. Not with contrition but with indignation. She turned to Harry, pleading for his defense with her stare, but he kept his gaze fixed on his menu. Was her husband not going to say something to defend her?

When Betty had finished taking their orders, Cora tried to catch the young woman's gaze, but Betty refused to meet her eyes as she briskly took their menus and turned for the kitchen.

* * *

"That was terribly awkward tonight, wasn't it?" Harry said as soon as they were in the car and pulling out of the club's parking lot an hour later.

"Wasn't it, though?" Cora said, relieved. So long as her husband made his loyalty to her known in private, she could forgive him not defending her in the moment—after all, Harry wasn't much for confrontation. In Cora's experience, few men were. Maybe that was why they preferred settling arguments with tennis rackets. "Phil can be so rude, can't he?"

"Phil?" Harry cut her a sharp look. "I was talking about you and that waitress."

Cora spun in her seat. "Me?"

"We're all ready to order and you were chatting her up like you two were friends."

"We are friends, Harry. She came by the house to see Max a few days ago. We talked."

"Wilson comes by the house to drop off the paper every

morning. I hardly plan to invite him to dinner," Harry said, yanking at the gear shift. "I can't believe I have to spell this out for you, Cora. It's just not done, all right?"

"What's not done? Being courteous?"

"Don't be dim." Harry rolled down his window, filling the car with a sour burst of tidal air. "She's a waitress, and you're a member of the club."

"Harry, for goodness' sake, I was a waitress once, too."

At the intersection, he slammed on the brakes, abruptly enough that Cora lunged for the dash to brace herself. Harry swung his gaze at her, his eyes hard.

"I married a girl who had to be a waitress," he said tightly, "and I'd appreciate if you wouldn't remind the whole world of it every chance you get."

Her face burned, as hotly as if he'd struck her. "You had no problem discussing my work as a waitress when you wanted to make yourself look like some white knight to your friends."

"Not this again . . ." He squeezed the wheel and groaned. "For God's sake, Cora, it was a joke. Won't you let it go, already?"

But as she sat back, her heart pounding, Cora knew for certain it hadn't been a joke at all. This wasn't her being overly sensitive, as Harry was always accusing her—her husband really did believe he had rescued her, that he had saved her from a place she had loved more than any other.

Tears burned behind her eyes, but Cora rolled her lips together to stem them, glancing only briefly over at Harry as he sent the car rolling forward through the four-way stop. She hoped he might cast her a tender look, but his gaze remained on the road, both of his hands clenched on the wheel tightly enough that his knuckles glowed white, and silence swallowed the car.

22

1999

From the time her hands were big enough to grip an ear, the duty of de-silking corn for clambakes had always belonged to Hedy and her father. Having inherited her banker father's attention to detail, Hedy was the perfect partner. She can remember them tucked into the picnic table with tall glasses of lemonade, a high stack of freshly picked corn between them, a bag for the silk threads and the outer husks on one side, a bag for the cleaned ears on the other. Carefully, meticulously, peeling back the thin inner husks, not so far back as to detach them from the stalk but only to free the veiny network of silk threads that wove through the kernels, then gently easing the husks back over the corn. The effort should have gone quickly. And yet, for all their expertise, Hedy and her father somehow always managed to stretch out the work, nursing their iced lemonades so long that little moats of sweat would spread out around the bottoms of their tumblers while they talked.

Maybe it's the quiet or the day or the familiar grassy smell of the freshly picked corn in front of her, but Hedy thinks she feels her father's absence more keenly sitting at the picnic table today than she has anywhere else in the house since he's been gone. She wonders what Harry Campbell would think of all this drama, whose problem he would look to solve first. Michelle's, of course. His dear granddaughter. (Hedy may have broken her father's heart by divorcing his dear friend's son, but giving him a grandchild had certainly helped heal the wound.) He would pour her a Coke (even when Michelle became of drinking age, Harry could never bring himself to offer his granddaughter anything but a soft drink), walk her to the table with a pencil and paper, and tell her to make a list. Because like every mathematician, Harry Campbell was a problem solver.

Even when Hedy had come back to Beech House, Michelle only just born, and Hedy was desperate to end her marriage, her father had told her to first make a list. The same technique Hedy tells her clients when they're deciding whether or not to buy a house. Make a list, she says. The pros, the cons. Then see which side has more. The math of life, her father always called it. Hedy would never forget the look on his face when, after tallying the two columns, she announced her answer. The agonizing way his features sank with disappointment as he stared at her. It had never occurred to her father that the math might bring her to the solution of divorce.

"I thought you might need reinforcements."

Hedy looks up to find Tom has arrived with a bottle of rosé in one hand and a Heineken in the other. He wears an olive-green polo that brings out his even tan. In daylight, the threads of gray at his temples are more prominent. He's more handsome in daylight, too, Hedy thinks. Or maybe it's just seeing him without a towel covering half his face.

She winces at the memory. "How's your nose?"

"Great—unfortunately," he says as he swings into the other side of the picnic bench. "I wouldn't have minded missing the stink of low tide this morning."

She laughs. "It did seem particularly fragrant, didn't it? I tend to forget when I'm away too long."

He holds up the wine. "More?"

"Please."

"I'd offer to help, but I can see right now I'm not qualified for this level of detail work."

"I thought architects were supposed to be fastidious," she says.

"When we have to be. Personally, I've always preferred the heavy-lifting part of clambakes. The digging and the fire . . ." He flashes her a grin as he pours. "*The eating.*"

"Done a lot of clambakes, have you?" she asks.

He corks the bottle, sets it aside, and reaches for his beer. "I worked through college at a restaurant on the cape that used to host bakes for big parties and I got pretty good at them," he says, twisting off the cap on the hem of his shirt and taking a quick pull from the bottle. Hedy tries to conjure an image of him many years earlier, slinging seaweed and shoveling sand to make the pit, and it's quite easy to do. His short-sleeved shirt offers a view of strong forearms.

"I hear my dad and I missed some fireworks earlier," he says.

"Oh, don't worry. There'll be more." Hedy glances up to find him studying her expectantly. "I don't know if your father has told you, but the house is going on the market in the fall."

Tom nods gravely. "I had my suspicions."

"Well, my daughter doesn't know yet," Hedy says. "We wanted to wait until after the wedding to tell her." She picks out the threads of silk and drops them into the trash bag. "You can probably guess that I'm not looking forward to that conversation."

"Can I ask you a question—and I don't mean it offensively," Tom says.

"With a setup like that, how can I refuse?"

He grins. "Is there always this much activity when you three get together?"

He's chosen a diplomatic word, but Hedy knows what he really means: drama.

"Normally we can stretch it out over a whole summer," she says. "But with just a few days, you have to cram it all in. We haven't been here together for three years. We've got a lot stored up." She drops a few outer husks into the paper bag on the bench beside her. Does he have a good relationship with his father? The question feels natural, logical, and yet it sits in her throat.

Tom leans back, his bottle held to his chest. "I'm not throwing stones," he says. "Believe me. My father and I have our moments, too. Although these days it's mostly because he takes far too much pleasure in watching my son make my blood pressure skyrocket. Karma, he calls it. I call it gloating." He tips his beer bottle at her. "What about you and Cora? Any gloating there?"

"Michelle rarely gives either of us reason to pull out our hair," Hedy decides is the most straightforward answer— although not entirely the most truthful in light of her daughter's recent, distressing news about her restaurant. "But Michelle and my mother have always been close. The best of friends, really."

"What about you and Cora?"

Hedy lets the half-husked cob rest in her hands, debating

her answer. Despite their easy conversation, she's not about to peel the lid off her relationship with her mother with Tom this early.

He leans in. "I don't mean to pry . . ."

Glancing up, Hedy finds his gaze apologetic, and her fingers resume their careful work.

Maybe she could crack the lid just a bit.

"You're not prying," she says. "It's not as easy between me and my mother. It never has been. I was always a daddy's girl. We were a team. He was a wonderful father."

"I'm sure he was," Tom says gently, and Hedy feels a flush of regret at the force of her answer, the sharpness of it. As if her father has needed defending. Or maybe just acknowledgment.

She tugs on the last leaf of husk, feeling a strange longing in the strained silence, and the unwelcome sting of impending tears. The mention of her father still seems to float in the air between them like a scent.

When she dares to look up again, Tom's eyes are warm as they flick over her face.

"I'll bet that must have made it awfully tough for guys to measure up."

Her lips rise reflexively. "You could say that."

"Didn't want to take another spin around the block after your divorce, huh?"

"Never found anyone worth spinning with," she says, reaching for another ear. "So what about you? How high is your bar?"

Tom swigs, shrugs as he swallows. "Depends on the night. Depends on the woman . . ." He looks up at her and squints one eye. "Boy, that didn't sound good, did it?"

"I think I'm starting to see why women might want to deck you on purpose."

He chuckles. "I started out with a pretty high bar."

"Your ex-wife?"

Tom nods. "Laura. Although she might remember it differently."

"How so?" Hedy asks as she slides her nail into the seam of husk and parts it, feeling the tightness in her chest loosen again. She's always more comfortable when she's the one asking the questions.

"Laura used to tell people I was already on a date when I offered to buy her a drink."

"And were you?"

"I'd been set up by a friend. I was supposed to have drinks with his girlfriend's roommate."

"Ahh." She bobs her head slowly. "So you *were* on a date."

"In theory, yes, but the roommate didn't show up."

Men. "A small detail," Hedy says wryly.

"But a crucial one. Without it, the story makes me out to be a heel, right?"

"So you're saying that your ex-wife liked telling the story in a way that made you look like a heel?"

"It would seem so, wouldn't it?" Tom tilts his head, amusement dancing at the corners of his mouth again.

"And let me guess—when you told the story, there was no setup, no roommate."

"Of course not. The setup never showed. Laura did." He swigs his beer and shrugs. "Timing is everything." He taps his bottle to her glass. "To timing."

"To timing," Hedy echoes, stopping to take a sip of wine.

Tom looks past her to the house. "Seems a shame to let it go, doesn't it?" he asks, then slides a smile in her direction. "Or maybe that's not a fair question to ask a real estate agent."

If only it were that easy, Hedy thinks wistfully. Try as she has to wear her agent's hat this trip, to put aside all the memories of Beech House, to see it as she sees any property, an empty chest awaiting new treasure, she can't, of course. Though there's no question the house feels different to her now with her father gone.

"It must have been in your family for a long time," Tom says. "Some of the wedding pictures on that wall look old." He swirls his bottle. "Is it true that your parents never had their picture on that wall?"

"They weren't married at Beech House," she says. "That's the rule of the wall."

Which makes the fact that Cora and Max will be eligible to join the gallery especially difficult to swallow for her, Hedy wants to confess but doesn't.

Tom continues to scan the house. "It would make a great inn. Maybe your daughter could take it."

"Michelle?"

"You said she's selling her restaurant? Maybe she could open one up here at the house."

"She's not selling. At least, she doesn't want to."

"What about you?" Tom asks.

Hedy shakes her head. "It's not the same house for me anymore."

"I understand," he says, waving his hand. "Don't listen to me. All this end-of-the-world, Y2K stuff. A new millennium and I just keep thinking I should do something big. Something crazy." He leans forward. "Want to go skydiving?"

She lets out a startled laugh. "Are you kidding? Not in any millennium!"

"Good—me, neither," he says, tapping her glass with his bottle again before sitting back. Then after a moment, he grins. "What about just diving off the pier?"

But even as Hedy rolls her eyes, she's still laughing.

23

1948

Phil Middleton leaned back in his beach chair and rolled his head toward them all. "Whatever you do," he said, raising his sunglasses for emphasis, "don't let Chuck's wife make the crab cakes this year. I'd sooner choke down a tennis ball."

An agreeable laugh rumbled through the group, and Cora managed to add hers at the last minute. The three couples and the four children had been at the beach for hours, and her mind had been drifting, her gaze with it. Even though they were too far down the shore to see Beech House behind the bluff, she still found her attention pulled in its general direction. After a week away in his shop, Max had arrived that morning with the last of the cabinets and drawers, and Cora felt as antsy as a child on Christmas Eve. She was anxious to see the kitchen finished at last. And she would admit, though only to herself, that she maybe wanted to see Max, too . . .

"It's too late to tell Martina no," said Lois, tipping her head back to see past the deep brim of her red straw hat. "She's already signed up. The best we can do is have someone make a second batch."

A spread of snacks had been set out in the middle of their cluster of towels and blankets. Cora's contribution, a plate of blue-cheese-stuffed mushrooms, had been the first to disappear, something that should have been a source of pride, but today she struggled to take much pleasure in the compliment. Try as she had to forget the episode at the club, she couldn't shake the feeling that something had shifted in the group, her earlier and unconditional welcome no longer guaranteed. She felt, quite frankly, like a scolded child left at the table with a full plate of food, not allowed to leave until she finished every bite.

The Middleton boys lobbed an enormous beach ball around the perimeter of their gathering. Timmy Welch trailed them, demanding a turn.

"I hear Forester's the man to beat this year," Phil said, leaning back to adjust the waistband of his tropical print trunks, the elastic snapping with a loud smack. "Vic said he's been getting lessons."

Harry scoffed. "Donald Forester couldn't beat me with a hundred years of lessons," he said, reaching into the cooler for a soda.

"Hand me one, will you?" Ned asked, leaning over.

"It has been a few years since your last win, Harry," Lois reminded him with a teasing smirk. "Careful you haven't gotten soft."

A rainbow flashed, the ball bounced at the edge of the blanket, sending up a shower of sand, and Irene gasped. "Simon, you and Arnold take that silly ball further down. You're getting sand all over the kabobs!"

"You heard your mother, boys," Phil said, around a foamy mouthful of deviled egg.

"I will admit my wife's cooking has made me a little softer in places," Harry said, patting his stomach over his blue cabana shirt.

"I think Lois was talking about your head," Ned teased.

Phil snorted. "Yeah, but which one?"

Laughter erupted and Cora scanned the view to hide her flush. For a moment, she caught Ned Welch's gaze and appreciated the brief but apologetic smile he offered her, glad to know she wasn't the only one who found Phil Middleton's humor distasteful.

"Don't tease him, Phil," Irene said. "Not all of us can be master chefs like Cora, can we?"

"Speaking of which," said Phil, "how goes the kitchen job?"

"He's in there now," Harry said. "Supposedly finishing up today."

Cora met her husband's confident smile and returned it.

"Boy, I swear it feels like he's been working in there forever." Phil pointed his bottle at Harry. "Be careful he's not bleeding you dry. They do that, you know."

"Max would never," Cora said, her defense too quick and too sharp she realized with a bloom of regret when she saw Harry's face shine at her with surprise.

Ned smiled. "I'm sure it will all be worth it," he said, breaking the strained silence.

Cora offered him a warm smile back, grateful for his rescue.

"I suppose this is what we get for wanting to grow up so damn fast," Phil muttered.

Lois lifted her face to the sun. "We certainly did know how to have fun back then."

Harry snorted and glanced at Cora. "Lois's idea of fun was to trick me into taking her father's brand-new cutter out without his permission and get us stuck on the sandbar."

"And didn't a tree branch poke a hole clean through the jib?" asked Ned.

Lois's lips stretched into a self-satisfied grin. "Boy, did Daddy snap his cap."

Cora wanted to ask what a jib was but didn't dare.

Harry wagged a finger at Lois. "You were always getting us all into such terrible trouble, wicked girl."

"Someone had to," Lois said with an unapologetic shrug. "Such a bunch of altar boys. I would have been bored out of my mind otherwise."

Cora pried a scallop shell from the sand and worried the grit from its delicate ridges, trying to think of an excuse to get back to the house to check on Max.

"What about you, Cora?"

She spun toward Irene, seeing herself reflected in the woman's white-framed sunglasses.

"What about me?" she asked.

"Surely you have stories of summertime mischief? Dashing in and out of parties all night long, driving your father mad with worry?"

Cora rubbed at the shell, mining her memories for something, anything, that might be considered remotely scandalous to impress them but nothing surfaced.

"Don't be shy," Lois said. "We're all friends here."

Were they, really? Even as she kept her polite smile intact, Cora felt flickers of doubt at the claim that she hadn't felt before.

"There wasn't a lot of time for parties, I'm afraid," Cora said. "The only time I was dashing was to get back and forth from the restaurant. It was a ten-block walk."

Phil scanned her slowly. "Probably how you got those fantastic legs . . ."

"Phil, the bucket!" Irene cried, snapping as she pointed to where one of the boys' pails had been snatched by the surf.

"Damn," Phil muttered, screwing his soda bottle into the sand before he bolted from his chair, yelling as he dashed down the beach, "Arnie, dammit. Pay attention!"

Lois sat back against her chair, the ruching of her emerald suit straining around her growing belly. "That's a darling suit, Cora. Where did you get it?"

"Filene's," Cora said, grateful for the change in subjects. "I can't bring myself to do the two-piece ones yet."

"Well, don't wait," Irene said. "After you have babies, you won't want to."

"It's true," said Lois. "Between the stretch marks and the loose skin, you'll wish you could swim in coveralls."

Phil returned, winded, and flopped into his chair with a snort. "We should start tying those things to the boys' ankles like the damn boat at the launch." He reached out. "Hand me another soda, will you?"

Harry looked in the cooler. "I'm afraid we're out, pal."

"We have more up at the house," Lois said, looking pointedly at her husband. Ned began to hoist himself up from the chair.

But Cora was on her feet faster. "I'll go."

* * *

Cora grabbed the cardboard holder of bottles off the Welches' porch and carried them through the thicket of evergreens that separated the two houses, relief blooming when she saw Max's truck still parked under the beech. Nearing the screen, she detected the faint scent of fresh wood, the smell stronger when she stepped inside and pulled in an awed breath.

"Perfect timing," Max said, stepping down from the ladder. "I was just making a few final adjustments." He crossed to join her. "What do you think?"

Cora set down the bottles and clapped her hands to her cheeks. "I'm . . . I'm speechless." With the last section of cabinets hung and the final drawers put in, the kitchen was fully transformed. She took the room in slowly, letting her gaze linger on each surface, but when her scan brought her to the curved valance above the sink, she let out a small gasp.

CORA'S KITCHEN had been carved into the wood.

"The sign doesn't have to stay," Max said. "I'm not much of a carver but I had an extra piece of wood and I just thought, why not? But you won't hurt my feelings if it's not your style. I made it on a separate piece so it's nothing to pop it out and still have a piece underneath to cover the bulb—"

"Don't you dare." Cora turned to meet his eyes. "I love it."

She let him hold her gaze another beat, the room growing warm. The women's tour of the room flashed back at her, the dismissive way they spoke of his design, and guilt and anger pressed at her heart. Why hadn't she defended him better? Why hadn't she defended herself? Max believed her to be so independent, so confident. She wanted to tell him he was wrong about her, that she wasn't as strong as he suspected. She could hold her own in a kitchenful of bullish men, but faced with the Oyster Point scorekeepers, she was as tough as an underbaked cheesecake.

"I wanted to tell you I got a call from my uncle the other day," Max said, his face lighting with a smile. "I told him about you being from Inman Square, how your uncle owns the restaurant next to Poppy's . . ." His smile tilted, turning sheepish. "He said you sound like a great girl and that I should ask you out on a date."

Even as she let a startled laugh escape, Cora felt the heat of pleasure flare across her face, too quickly to disguise it.

Her heart pounded.

"And what did you say?" she asked.

"I told him you were happily married . . ." Max's pale eyes held hers. "And that I was too late."

Cora sank her fingers into the fabric of her wrap, desperate for something to hold on to, the air sizzling with emotion. Leftover sand prickled in her suit, tickling the skin where her thighs met. She glanced at the side of the room where Max's tools had lived for the past month, the space empty now, the only evidence of his weeks of work a small stack of shims, and disappointment fluttered, the unspoken finality of this day settling over everything like dust.

She swallowed. "Then I guess this mean you're . . . ?" The last word stayed stuck in her throat, refusing to come out.

Max nodded. "Almost. Just have a few more adjustments to make," he said, adding with a smile, "then you'll be rid of me for good."

Cora flinched. *For good.* Her stomach lurched, as if she had stood up too fast.

"Don't say it like that," she said, catching his eyes again, and seeing something more than a teasing spark in the gray-blue pools this time. Something warmer, deeper. A longing. She feared her eyes welled with a similar ache. "I'm going to miss your company."

"I'm going to miss coming over here." He leaned back against the counter, his eyes even with hers. "It's been nice getting to know you, Cora."

And he had, she realized. In their few weeks together, Max Dempsey may have learned more about her than Harry had in two years. Or maybe she had simply shared more of her heart with him. Was that a betrayal of her marriage? Cora felt a pang of guilt at the possibility, but another wave of longing swept it quickly away.

The room hushed. Even the breeze through the screens seemed to hold its breath.

Max broke the heated silence first. "I should let you get those back to the beach," he said, nodding to the bottles.

"Right," Cora said, flushing at the reminder. Everyone waiting for her down on the beach, thirsty and impatient. Gone this long, Harry might have grown concerned.

Bottles in each hand, Cora crossed for the door, slowing briefly at the screen, as if she had remembered something, something crucial, but she stopped herself from turning and, pulling in a sharp breath, pressed through instead.

* * *

For the rest of the day, Cora couldn't bring herself to leave the kitchen. Even when night came and Harry went to bed first, she had volunteered to turn off the downstairs lights just so she had an excuse to linger in the space.

When she entered their bedroom, Harry sat at the edge of the bed, his pajama top undone.

"I was worried you might have started cooking something down there," he said.

"I was tempted," she admitted.

Her husband stood and came toward her. "So much for hoping the thought of me waiting for you in bed might be equally tempting," he said, cupping her cheek.

Cora smiled against his palm. "You know it is."

"Then how about this?" Harry pulled his hand from where it rested behind his back and revealed a small jewelry box. She took it carefully, marveling at the intricate nest of curling ribbon that nearly covered the top.

"I was saving it for your birthday," he said as Cora worked to find the seam in the bow. "But I just thought . . ."

"Oh, Harry . . ." She lifted the bracelet out of the box, a four-leaf clover charm dangling from the gold chain, and recognition sparked: It looked exactly like the one Lois had worn to the club. Cora even swore Lois's bracelet carried the same clover charm.

"Let me put it on you," Harry said, taking the chain from her.

Cora raised her hand. His fingers shook slightly as he worked to open the clasp. "The idea is that you can make it your own," Harry said as he laid it over her wrist. "Personalize it with whatever charms you like. I just got you that one to start. You can take a look at Lois's, give you an idea of what other charms are popular."

Cora watched him struggle to close the clasp, his tongue poking through his teeth, and she couldn't help wondering: If this was supposed to show her own personality, then why would she just want to copy what everyone else has?

"There you are," Harry said, wearing a pleased smile.

Turning her wrist, Cora tapped the clover, ringing it like a bell. "Maybe I could find a charm of a little saucepan," she said. "Or maybe a whisk. Something for the kitchen."

"You love it, don't you?"

"You really have to ask?" Cora sighed. "It's the most beautiful kitchen anyone has ever had, Harry."

His smile tipped slightly. "I meant the bracelet, darling."

"Oh. Of course." A twinge of regret sparked in her stomach. "I love it terribly."

"Good." Harry drew her into his arms and dropped a

kiss on her head. "I'm sorry if I was harsh the other night." He pushed out a weary breath against her temple. "I have nothing against that girl at the club. Or any of them. They work hard. I know that," he said patiently. "But my father worked hard, too. And his father, and his father. Just so we could belong here—and we earned that."

Drawing back, Cora stared up at him, dumbfounded at his claim. "Harry, your family has been on this island almost as long as it's been poking out of the sea. You were born into it. That's not the same as earning it. Someone like me, or Betty—or Max, for that matter—we have to earn it," she said. "Don't you see that?"

"Now hold on a minute." Her husband's smile sank. His hands moved up, closing around her upper arms. "You're my wife, and I won't have you lumping yourself in with those people. Especially not Dempsey. I know how men like him operate, Cora," he said gravely. "The island is full of them. Transients who have no problem taking our money with a smile, then in the next breath they're passing the buck, griping about how we're the reason they can't keep a job or are always broke because they spend too much time at the bar or the racetrack."

"He didn't say anything of the sort, Harry."

"You don't have to defend him, darling. You have a good heart—that's part of what I love about you—but you can also be too soft. You can't let these people and their sob stories get to you. You're not pouring coffee to those sad sacks at the restaurant anymore."

When Harry pulled her to him again, Cora bristled against his chest, swallowing the urge to remind her husband that he had been one of those sad sacks once.

"I just know how things are here, darling," he said, "You have to trust me."

"But I need friends, Harry. Surely you can understand that?"

"And you have them. Lois, Irene . . ."

"Those are your friends."

"They were, at first, yes," he said. "But now they get to be yours, too. Isn't it wonderful?" He swept her hair behind her ears, palming it smooth as if she were being styled for a portrait. "It's all set for you here, darling. Like a pair of shoes. All you have to do is step in and start walking."

The analogy, meant to comfort her, Cora suspected, filled her instead with a strange ache, but she kept her smile intact, determined to make her point.

"And I'm grateful, Harry. But I'm talking about the friends I'll make on my own."

Her husband looked down at her blankly, as if she were speaking in another language. She searched his eyes, seeking confirmation, even as a thread of unease begin to stitch itself up her spine, but he didn't answer, just leaned forward and pressed his mouth over hers again, kissing her so hard that Cora believed he was trying to rub the stain of something off her lips.

24

1999

Long after the coals have burned down and the bowls of shells have been emptied, the briny fragrance of the clambake lingers inside. Cleaning up in the kitchen, Cora can still smell the salty smoke in the air. It was a wonderful bake, despite its rocky start. Wes, not surprisingly, folded himself into the crew almost immediately, Michelle's darling boyfriend volunteering for pit duty and then, when the fire had burned down enough and the coals were hot, circling the fire with Tom, both of them slinging seaweed hissing over the hot rocks while Michelle and Tiffany made trips from the house with the food. After feasting on mussels and littlenecks, corn and baby red potatoes—Cora's favorite part; how she loves the way the skins snap when you bite into the tiny jewels—they all lingered on the beach until dusk, then on the porch until full dark. Even sweet Tiffany, who had vowed not to stay past six, finally forced herself from her deck chair at eight thirty.

Now it's almost ten. As much as she treasures the energy and excitement of a busy kitchen, Cora loves the contemplative beauty in a quiet one, too. Always has. When she worked at Marigold's, she often made sure to arrive before the rest of the staff, just so she could savor the peace of the space, scrubbed clean and ready for a new day of dishes. The pans stacked beside the stove, each one a gleaming, fresh canvas. The possibility of flavors stretched out ahead of her.

Cora suspects Michelle enjoys the early morning hours in her restaurant, too; then the thought sends a spark of unease through her, reminded of the tenuous state of her granddaughter's restaurant and her relationship with Wes. Calling him without Michelle knowing had been a bold move on Cora's part, but the look of relief on her granddaughter's face when she walked in to find Wes standing there had been all the assurance Cora needed that she'd done the right thing. Now it would be up to them to fix whatever was broken— but at least they could start. And what better place to do it than here, in the healing embrace of Beech House? Even if it is the last time they will all enjoy its warmth.

On the counter, a few little potatoes remain in a Tupperware container. Cora plucks one out before carrying it to the fridge, memories floating back again as she searches for a free spot on the shelves. How many times tonight did she look around at her family and friends, the joy and gratitude swelling so quickly in her chest that she almost couldn't breathe? She felt Harry there, too; she had wanted to tell Hedy but held back, too pleased to see her daughter looking relaxed for the first time since she arrived to spoil it with a comment that might have chafed. Fifty years of being a mother, and Cora still can't seem to know the right thing to say to her daughter when it counts the most. Why is that? And how is it that she can have the opposite experience with her granddaughter? From the time Michelle was tiny, they seemed to speak the same language, seemed to know how to read the others' thoughts. When Cora talks to Michelle, the words come out effortlessly, never construed as baiting or criticism. Is that from being a grandmother or because Michelle is so much like her?

Closing the refrigerator door, Cora slows, her gaze catching on the photograph of Harry, and it feels as if someone has reached into her chest and given her heart a sharp twist.

Her eyes well up.

"You always knew how to talk to her, darling," she whispers, running her fingertips affectionately over the photograph. "Tell me what to say now. Tell me how to get it right this time to make our daughter understand."

She closes her eyes and lets the tears spill.

Was love so complicated for everyone? Cora had certainly never expected it to be. From the first time Harry Campbell walked—*darted*—into Marigold's that stormy afternoon, desperate for shelter and, then, *Oh, a piece of that beautiful lemon meringue pie?* How she'd felt a little lighter after he'd gone, how that lightness returned when he did, the very next day, looking decidedly drier, his hair slicked back not with rain this time, but pomade. How he hefted a pile of ledgers beside him on the counter, claiming to need to work, but never even cracked one open. Instead, he chatted with her, staying so long that he had to bolt from his stool, realizing he was going to be late to his meeting. Each visit after that, he arrived earlier and stayed later, lingering over whatever dish Cora made for him, telling her of all the places he had been—England, France, India—and places much closer, his family's summer house on Martha's Vineyard. Surely she had been? Cora had shaken her head, her stomach flipping when he said he would make it his mission to see her there someday—a promise Cora never dared believe he meant. So when Harry arrived on her parents' doorstep, offering to take her away to all the places he'd been, to simply take her away, how could Cora say no? With Theo back from the war, she was no longer needed to pitch in at the restaurant—and the question of *What now?* weighed heavily on her heart. Just as it did on many of her friends, women like her who had been thrust into various jobs to fill in for all the men gone to fight and found themselves with an unexpected sense of purpose—*passion!*—only to have that passion yanked from them as quickly as it had been delivered. Of course, there had been fraught moments when Cora had worried that blending into Harry's rarefied world on the Vineyard would be a challenge, but she'd successfully carved out her place in the unfamiliar world of the restaurant, hadn't she? How much harder could it be to find her place among Harry's friends?

All these years later, her naivete both outrages and impresses her.

But would she have turned down his proposal if she'd known the difficulties?

When the doctor explained how far Harry's cancer had spread, how quickly it would progress, Cora's promise to stay in Beech House after he was gone had been unnecessary, as unspoken as her promise to love him unconditionally.

Cora kisses her fingertips, then presses them to Harry's photograph, gratitude blooming as her eyes flood again. He kept his promise to bring her here and she kept hers—not just to stay, but, eventually, to thrive. Beech House became more than just her island on an island. It became her home.

And now, before she could start a new beginning with Max, she would have to face a second impossible goodbye.

The slap of the screen door jolts Cora from her thoughts. She turns to find Max carrying in a bowl and gives her eyes a quick wipe with the heel of her hand.

"Found more potatoes hiding," he says, setting the bowl on the island.

"We made too much food," she says, crossing to join him. "I put away two containers of corn—and another one of clams! What in the world are we going to do with it all?"

Max shrugs as he draws her into his arms. The wind off the water has left his thick white hair a fetching mess. She smiles.

"We could hand out the leftovers as wedding favors," he suggests.

Cora laughs. "Because what's more romantic than a cold clam."

"Better a cold clam in the hand than in the bed—isn't that how the saying goes?"

"Hmm. I'm not familiar with that one," she says, reaching up to brush the curtain of silver waves off his forehead. "Lucky me."

"Lucky us," Max murmurs as he dips his mouth down to hers for a kiss, the weight of his lips causing longing to coil deep in her stomach. Never in her life would Cora have imagined that a satisfying sexual life awaited her in her seventies. Throughout her marriage, her desire for Harry had been constant but soft, comforting and warm. As dependable as her sheet cake recipe, and always as sweet. For Max, from the start, it had been something different. An attraction that had startled her, that was always both complicated and yet worrisomely simple in its purity. And no matter how many years passed between when they would cross paths on the island—and sometimes there were many, many years—that fierce attraction was still there, immediate like a gas range lit, the click of the spark, then the rush of those beautiful blue dancing flames.

As a cook, Cora has always understood that the key to well-done food is flavor and heat, and the ability to know how much to put into each dish. At seventy-two, she understands the same can be said of love.

His arms still looped around her waist, Max leans back to search her eyes. "You haven't told Michelle yet, have you?" he asks, his voice as tender as his gaze.

Cora drops her head against his chest, drawing in a deep breath of his smoke-soaked shirt, the worn cotton slightly damp with perspiration against her forehead.

She rolls her cheek against the heat of him and sighs.

"I need to," she says. "I know I do—"

"Oh! Sorry!"

Still embracing, they turn to see Cora's granddaughter frozen in the doorway, a startled flush on her cheeks.

Max's eyes flash down at Cora's. His mouth curves into a knowing smile. *Timing.*

"Don't mind me," Michelle says, heading past them for the utensil drawer.

"You look like a woman on a mission," Cora says as Max releases her.

"A very important one," Michelle says, pulling out the corkscrew and holding it up. "I think the other one got left down on the beach."

Max glances at Cora then turns to Michelle, his hand extended. "I can bring that out for you," he says. "I still need to give the coals a last splash."

Cora catches Max's attention and mouths *Thank you* as he rounds the island, slowing to give Cora's hand a reassuring squeeze on his way out.

When Max is gone, Cora turns to find Michelle has

watched him leave, her granddaughter's gaze still lingering thoughtfully on the doorway.

"I like him, Grams."

"Me, too." Cora crosses to the island. "I saw the two of you earlier. You looked deep in conversation."

"He was asking me about Piquant. He seems to think everything's going to work out. Like someone else I know . . ." Michelle casts her a teasing grin. "I'm not sure the world can handle two insufferable optimists under one roof, Grams."

"Not only can it handle us, it needs us." Cora looks in the direction of the porch. "Did your mom already go up?"

"She's still outside talking with Wes and Tom."

When Michelle squares her with a wary look, guilt flares.

"I know you're not happy with me for calling him, Michelle—and you have every right to be mad. It was a pretty sneaky move."

Her granddaughter's chastising pout is short-lived. In the next instant, Michelle's pursed lips soften into a grin. "Mostly I'm just so relieved he agreed to come, I can't feel anything else."

"He adores you, darling. It's obvious."

Now her granddaughter's appreciative smile thins. Lines of doubt appear across her forehead. "I'm not sure it's so obvious anymore, Grams."

"He's here, isn't he?" Cora says, tilting her head to try to catch Michelle's downcast eyes. And as she waits for her answer, resolve swells. Cora has done everything she can to soften the blow for her beloved granddaughter. It's time.

"Darling . . ." she begins carefully.

Michelle's eyes rise, flicking over Cora's face.

"I have something to tell you."

25

Harry set down his suitcase in the kitchen doorway and shook his arms into his suit coat.

"Darling, you know if I thought there was any way they could have this board meeting without me, I wouldn't go," he said, picking his hat off the rack and tapping it onto his head.

Cora handed him his coffee, her charm bracelet clinking against the mug like a miniature wind chime. "You promised no more trips for the rest of the summer."

"It's just one night, darling. And I'll take the car so I can come back and forth that much quicker, all right?"

She offered a stoic smile, even as the prickles of loneliness began to pulse in her chest. Unlike the last time Harry had left her, the house was now bereft of the constant flow of repairmen and builders. The lawn was visible again, cleared of the weeks of materials and equipment, the driveway no longer a crowded maze of trucks and wagons. The symphony of hammering and pounding and footsteps that had been a constant from the day they'd arrived vanished. After weeks of nonstop noise and commotion, the whole of Beech House was quiet.

But it was, of course, in the kitchen where Cora felt the silence most keenly. It had been over two weeks since Max had left, taking the last of his tools with him, and Cora still found herself expecting him every morning when she came downstairs to make coffee, still felt an unwelcome flicker of disappointment when she remembered he wouldn't be coming by anymore. Their cohabitation had become routine, their conversations while he worked and she cooked as core an ingredient in her recipes as eggs or herbs. Even when he was home, Harry's work kept him in the study for hours, and when he wasn't making phone calls or balancing ledgers, her husband was at the Welches' or the Middletons', practicing his swing for the upcoming tournament.

In just a month, Max Dempsey's company had become sewn into her days, and the kitchen, for all its beauty and function, felt too quiet. It seemed that every day in the space, she found reasons to thank him. How she wished he might find an excuse for one more visit so she could tell him how marvelously things worked. How ingenious the smallest details had revealed themselves to be. The drawers for flour and sugar always within reach. The knife slots. The rotating shelves. The dividers for her spice jars and dried herbs. How she wished she could tell Max Dempsey other things, too. Although she could never be certain what those things might be. Only that longing rose up in her now and again, and at the strangest times. When she was whisking a marinade, or lying in bed, feeling the night's breeze feather her bare shoulders. When she rode with Harry, Cora found herself scanning the road and driveways for a glimpse of Max's truck, wondering if he'd moved on to another kitchen somewhere on the Point, or maybe even off island . . .

Harry brushed at his coat sleeves. "Just like always, you can call Lois or Irene if anything should come up," he said. "Phil knows I'll be gone. He's frantic, of course, what with the tournament being this weekend, that I'll get soft before we compete."

At long last, the famous Half Shell tournament was nearly upon them. Between the committee meetings to plan the event and the constant retelling of previous tournament wins at every party, Cora was looking forward to watching her husband play, even if her nerves frayed at the prospect of being thrust into the company of nearly the whole Point. Harry assured her daily that she was becoming more and more an islander, but Cora didn't always believe him. And even though she knew he meant it as a compliment, a part of her worried about what was happening to the parts of her that weren't an islander. Would they remain detectable, or were those qualities of herself like herbs, that if a cook added too much its flavor would overwhelm a dish, disguising all others, tasting of only one.

* * *

"You sure you don't want Jerry to run this over to you when he makes his deliveries in the morning, Mrs. Campbell? It's awfully late to be walking home."

The Point's postmistress spread her chapped hands over the wide package she had just hefted onto the gatehouse's mail counter and gave Cora a quizzical look over the top of her glasses.

Cora considered the offer, torn. Dusk was falling and the box was indeed cumbersome, not to mention early—she hadn't expected the new coverlet and shams she'd ordered to arrive for another week—but they would make a delightful surprise when her husband returned. Fresh linens for a fresh start, she'd thought, and she was anxious to get them home as soon as possible.

"Thank you, Mrs. Peabody, but I can carry it myself," Cora said, grateful to find that the package wasn't nearly as heavy as its size might have suggested as she drew it down from the counter. Stepping back out into the low light of evening, she enjoyed a flicker of comfort at the ease of the transaction, how even something as small as the postmistress knowing her name made her feel as if she was truly part of life here in Oyster Point. Just as Harry had promised that first night on Lois and Ned's porch.

After trying out a few different positions, she had the box settled comfortably against her side by the time she was several yards from the gatehouse. She only hoped she didn't twist her ankle, the telltale shadows of the road's rutted dirt muted in the milky light. The length of the box made it difficult to see the shoulder as she walked, though she wasn't in danger of being run over, since there was no way a driver would miss the sight of her even if Cora couldn't clearly see them. Still, when she heard the faraway rattle of an approaching car, she slowed to make certain to be out of reach. Lowering the package, she saw the front end of a truck, its faded blue paint looking more like silver in the rosy light of dusk, but Cora recognized it.

She slowed reflexively, a smile lifting her lips as excitement fluttered helplessly in her stomach.

"Well, hello, stranger," Max said as he brought the truck to a sputtering stop alongside her.

"Hello, yourself," she said. "How are you?"

"Never mind me." His bent arm rested on the window as he appraised her package. "Are you carrying that box or is it carrying you?"

Cora laughed, enough to jostle the package and gave it another heft to steady it. "Harry took the car over on the ferry."

"Then let me give you a ride home."

"That's silly," she said, tipping her head toward the road. "You're on your way out."

"So I'll turn around."

Before she could contest again, Max shoved the door open and climbed out, easing the box from her hands and hoisting it easily into the bed. On the passenger side, he swung open the door for her, and she hesitated a moment, suddenly aware of a fine layer of perspiration under her snood, warmth that couldn't be blamed on the temperature, since the late hour had brought cooler air. It was, Cora couldn't help thinking, as if Max was offering her something greater than a ride, as if he'd opened a door that might, if she stepped through, even take her somewhere else than just the inside of his truck. A pang of apprehension fired.

"It's a mess, I know," he said with a sheepish grin, as if he thought that might be the reason she hesitated.

Cora offered him an absolving smile. "It's fine," she said, climbing in at last.

When he shut the door behind her, the coppery smell of warm metal filled her nose. A nest of loose papers sat in the middle of the bench. Gathering them into a rough pile, Max shoved them through the narrow gap behind the seat and sent the truck chattering forward.

"Are you here on another job?" Even as Cora asked the question, a flutter of envy rose. What lucky person would be next in line to enjoy his building talents, and, of course, his charming company, too?

"Not me," said Max. "My brothers. They're rebuilding a porch. I've been dropping off lumber for them this week."

She regarded him fondly as he swung them around in

the gatehouse horseshoe. He looked different to her somehow. More put together. His shirt tucked in all the way. And
he appeared to have brushed his hair, maybe even recently
shaved. She didn't think it was possible he could look more
handsome, and yet . . .

The truck hit a bump, shaking her from her study.

She directed her gaze back to the road and pressed her
hands into her lap, aware that her pulse had picked up speed
with the truck.

"Everything working all right?" Max asked.

"You mean, in the kitchen?" she asked, then flushed with
annoyance at herself—*What else would he mean, silly?*—and
answered quickly. "Oh, it's brilliant. Every part of it."

The road straight now, Max let his hand hang over the
wheel, the hard knots of his knuckles catching the light, and
her thoughts drifted back to the day they'd compared scars.
How he'd scanned her fingers, his thumb absently tracing
circles over her skin. How quickly she'd tugged free when
the phone had chimed, as if she had accidentally grabbed a
hot pan handle.

She worried a loose thread on the hem of her blouse.
"Do you think you'll take another job here on the Point?"

He shrugged. "I've had inquiries, but right now I'm
cooling my heels. Trying to figure out my next move."

Something in the way he said the word made Cora think
he meant more of a geographical move than a professional
one, and the possibility sent an uneasy tremor across her chest.

"Do you think you might leave the Vineyard?" she asked,
hoping her voice sounded casual, maybe even indifferent.

"I might have to. I think my sister-in-law is getting tired
of me sleeping on the couch."

When he laughed, Cora joined him, grateful for the burst of sound in the silence. A car passed, and she felt a strange flicker of worry when they were near enough to see the driver, then a rush of relief when she didn't recognize him. It hadn't occurred to her to worry that someone might see her riding with Max. Why should it? Harry certainly wouldn't have objected to her accepting a ride to avoid breaking her neck getting his bedcover home, would he?

"If I do leave," Max said, "it'll only be for a little while. I always seem to find my way back here."

He glanced over at her and another memory flashed, his words from the first time they met, in evening light not so different than this: *That's the great thing about an island. You can't really get lost. Eventually you come back to the same spot . . .*

The sign for Beech House appeared and Cora's heart fluttered with what should have been relief but felt to her much more like disappointment. She wished foolishly for more time.

Max pulled the truck under the weeping beech, where he always parked it, as if this were any other day.

"I'll carry it inside for you," he said, already climbing out, once again too swiftly for her to contest and filling her with a rush of gratitude that she didn't have to. Because she didn't want to.

As she followed him across the driveway, she smoothed down the front of her wrap dress, wishing that she was wearing a more flattering style and scolding herself for the thought.

Through the screen, Max set the box against the wall just inside the door and stepped back.

"I should let you get on with your dinner." He raked a hand through his hair, but still the tumble of waves refused to fall evenly to one side. "I'm sure you have some great feast waiting for you and your husband."

"Harry's in Boston until tomorrow. It's just me tonight," she admitted, then glanced up to find Max's gaze there. Heat danced across her forehead. Why had she told him that?

She reached back and touched her snood, suddenly desperate for something to do with her hands. "It won't be anything fancy."

Leaning against the door, Max chuckled low, and her heart lifted. How she'd missed that deep, warm sound in this room. "Your idea of not fancy is what most people wait all year to make for Christmas dinner."

"I hope most people don't celebrate Christmas with meatloaf sandwiches."

"I happen to love meatloaf sandwiches," he said.

"You're welcome to join me."

Max blinked at her as if he wasn't sure he'd heard her right, and Cora suspected she wore a similar look of surprise on her face. The invitation had startled her equally. And yet why should it? How would this be any different from the dozens of times they were alone together while Harry was traveling, or just up the beach playing tennis with Ned and Phil?

"If you think your husband won't mind," Max said.

"Harry hates meatloaf sandwiches."

But that wasn't what he had meant and Cora knew it.

Still, as she searched Max's eyes in the expectant silence, her heart raced, unsure of what worried her more—that he might accept her offer or that he might decline it—until his lips stretched into a grateful smile, and her chest expanded with relief.

Max wiped his palms over his smooth jaw and smiled at her, so long that Cora felt her face grow warm.

"Good thing I shaved, then, isn't it?" he said.

26

1999

Mickey remembers little about the last time she visited Beech House before her grandfather died, only that in the hours after she had returned from hospice, she had wandered through Beech House in a fog, aware of the invisible knife of death that would, at any minute, slice through their world. Everywhere she looked, she reminded herself that it might be the last time she would look upon that stretch of room, or that book spine on the shelf, or that frayed corner of the rug, while Harry Campbell was still alive. Looking back, Mickey realized the exercise had been done in the hope of making the unthinkable loss of her grandfather somehow manageable, quantifiable, controlled. But she would quickly learn there was a world of difference between going and gone.

Now, as Mickey walks through the great room, the urge to begin calculating final things overwhelms her again. She can barely get across the worn sisal rug to the porch door without tearing up. Everywhere her gaze lands, longing lands with it.

Stepping out onto the veranda, she sees Wes has wandered down to the lawn. His back to her, he scans the sky, and her heart pounds with affection.

She understands now why he really came.

The last step creaks under her weight. Wes turns, a beer bottle held against his chest.

"I wasn't sure if you'd gone up," he says, starting toward her. "Stars are incredible tonight."

"They are, aren't they?" She looks up, but all she sees is a blur of black.

She points to his beer. "I don't suppose you have any of that left?"

He holds out the bottle. "Help yourself."

She takes a long swig, the prickle of carbonation a welcomed distraction, the flush of a buzz too brief.

Wes steps into the cone of light from the porch bulbs, his eyes narrow with apprehension then understanding.

"She told you, didn't she?" he asks in a low voice.

Mickey bobs her head slowly, still numb with the news.

"It's why you came, isn't it?" she says.

"Your grandmother was worried about telling you. I couldn't stand thinking about you here, hurting . . ." Wes's dark eyes flick over her face, his brow knotting. "Why do you look so surprised?"

"I guess, I don't know . . . I figured after what I'd done . . ."

"That, what?" he asks, his voice hoarse with frustration. "That I didn't care if you were in pain?" He sets the bottle down on the wicker table and takes another step closer. "Just because I'm mad as hell at you doesn't mean I want to see you hurting. I love you. I knew this wasn't going to be easy for you to hear."

Mickey inhales, gratitude and affection swelling so swiftly in her lungs that when Wes draws her against him, she gasps with relief.

His arms close tighter around her. "I'm sorry, babe," he whispers. "I really am." He presses a hard kiss against her forehead, the weight and heat of his mouth the anchor she's craved for days now.

"I'm sorry, too." She leans back to search his dark eyes, hoping he understands that she isn't just talking about losing Beech House. But as grateful as she is, she knows this doesn't solve everything. She's broken something big. They still have work to do. Trust to repair.

But it's a start, Mickey thinks.

"What room is mine again?" Wes asks as he glances up at the second floor.

"The Espagnole Room."

He sucks air between his teeth. "That's not a particularly sexy sauce, you know. Pretty basic, as sauces go."

"Yes, but it has a strong taste," she points out. "And it's the basis for some other very beefy sauces."

"That is true." Wes squints thoughtfully. "Beefy . . ." A smile starts at one corner of his mouth, spreading slowly, and for the first time since he's arrived, Mickey feels the delicious swell of hope. "I can live with that," he says.

27

1948

"Lemonade?"

Max slid into the banquette and laced his hands over the table. "Love some."

As Cora moved around the kitchen—her kitchen, as frequent glances up to the sign Max carved reminded her—she couldn't ignore a strange flutter of nerves. Her actions— fixing him something to eat, or pouring him a glass of cold lemonade—were no different from those she might have performed with him in her kitchen before, and yet a newness floated around her stomach, butterflies taking flight as she spread seasoned mayonnaise over the bread and laid fat slices of cold meatloaf over it.

But it was only when she plated the finished sandwiches, carried them to the banquette, where he waited, and set them down that she understood the reason her heartbeat hastened: All the times she served Max something while he was here, it was always while he worked. Tonight, they would sit down to eat together. Like they were—

She stopped the word before it could flash through her thoughts.

Max stood as she slid into her side of the banquette. She offered him an appreciative smile even as a blush crept up her neck for the gesture, then thought wistfully of how Harry had always done the same when they'd been courting. How he'd ceased to stand for her once they were married, because of course he would. Still, Cora wondered as Max sat back down: Would he be the sort of husband who might continue to stand for his wife long into a marriage?

"Seems like you're really settled here," Max said, looking around.

The thought she had had while leaving the gatehouse earlier returned, and yet when Cora met his gaze across the table, she felt her resolve soften, her confidence dim.

She shook out her napkin and smiled. "It helps to have the perfect kitchen."

He took big bites and chewed vigorously.

"This might be the best meatloaf sandwich I've ever had," he said.

"Thank you. I put basil in the mayonnaise."

"That, but . . ." Max shook his head. "It's juicy, too. I can't tell you how many times I've had meatloaf and it was like biting into a two-by-four."

Cora let out a little laugh. "The key to keeping things tender is slow heat. Otherwise, things cook too fast, and become dry and tough."

"Makes sense."

Max nodded thoughtfully, and Cora had to remind herself that she was talking about cooking. She reached for her lemonade and downed a long sip, grateful for the burst of chill down her throat.

"I noticed your herb garden is going gangbusters," he said, tipping his lemonade at the screen.

"It's coming along." Cora set down her glass. "Do you like gardening?"

He considered the question as he picked up the other half of his sandwich. "I've never stayed in one place long enough to find out."

"Would you like to try?"

He grinned at her. "Staying put?"

"No," she said, returning his smile. "Gardening."

"I'm not sure I have the patience for it."

Cora arched her eyebrow at him, recalling the way he pored over certain joints, always making sure things were plumb, or sanded smooth.

"I've seen how fastidious you are with your cabinet-work," she said. "I find that hard to believe."

Now it was his turn to wear a bloom of color from her compliment.

Max dragged his napkin across his mouth, his lips turned up in a crooked grin when he took the napkin away. "Or maybe I'll just marry a woman who likes to garden."

Their eyes met as they laughed, and for a second, Cora let the impossible thought come: *This is what it would be like if we were married, Max and I. I'd make him meatloaf sandwiches and we'd talk about why we are the way we are, and we'd give each other permission to be that way.*

"I have a confession," Max said.

Cora looked across the table to find his eyes waiting. The gray-blue pools sparkled.

"I've been hoping I'd run into you on the road one of these trips."

The swiftness with which her heart fluttered with his admission startled her. Her stomach dropped, as if she'd dared to hold her breath under water dangerously long, surfacing just in time.

Her own confession waited in her throat.

"When we drive around the Point," Cora said softly, "I find myself looking for your truck."

Max considered his sandwich for a second, then set it down, letting his elbows rest beside his plate. "You asked me why I haven't taken a new job around here yet . . . I think it's because you ruined me."

Cora fussed with her napkin. "I don't believe that. There are plenty of other good cooks on the Point who would gladly offer you homemade meals while you worked—"

"I'm not talking about free food, Cora."

She felt her face warm again. Of course he wasn't. They both understood that.

Silence fell over the table, swallowed the whole room like the seconds before a lightning strike, the air sizzling with anticipation.

She let her hands fall to the sides of her plate as he had. "I've missed our talks, Max."

"I've missed you, too."

Her heart pounded. The knowledge that she should contest his claim floating in her throat like an idling car, that she hadn't meant that she had missed him, but the clarification refused to leave her lips. That was, of course, exactly what she had meant.

Looking down, she saw that his left hand was now directly across from her right one. Barely a few inches of table separated their fingertips.

Years later, Cora would never be sure who moved their hand first, or whose fingers stretched farther, only that in the next moment, the tip of his index finger reached hers, a connection that might have been accidental if one of them drew back, but neither did.

"I'm married, Max," she said, not sure if the reminder

was meant for him, or herself, only that she felt suddenly as if she couldn't breathe while she waited for him to say something.

His brow wrinkled under the awning of tousled hair. He looked at her another long moment, his eyes flicking over her face, then his mouth settled into a resigned smile.

"I know."

Cora drew her hand down, sinking it into her lap as if it were a slippery fish, and the rumble of tires sailed in through the window, the crackling noise as loud as firecrackers in the impossibly heavy silence, startling them from the daze they'd allowed themselves to drift into.

Max climbed from his seat and crossed to look out the screen. "Are you expecting someone?"

"Not that I know of," Cora said.

"Never mind." He stepped back. "Whoever it was turned around. Must have picked the wrong driveway."

It did happen from time to time. Already this summer they'd had to redirect several strange cars back out to the road.

Still, when Max returned to the table, he remained standing, and disappointment swelled in Cora's lungs. Whatever spell they'd allowed to be cast over them tonight, the stranger had swiftly, and perhaps fortunately, broken.

Cora stood, too.

"Thanks for dinner—it was delicious," Max said, reaching to clear his plate.

"You really don't have to do that." But in trying to stop him, Cora leaned forward too quickly and suddenly they were tipped together, nearly nose to nose, his hand still holding the plate, her hand resting over his. They didn't move, like players in a child's game of freeze tag. This close, Cora could count every speck of steel in his eyes. But it was on her lips that Max's gaze lingered and she felt like she'd stepped in front of an opened oven door. Like the joining of their fingertips earlier, it would have taken nothing, a tilt of an inch or two, for their mouths to meet.

Cora stepped back first. Max let the plate settle on the table.

"I should go," he said, his voice rough with emotion.

She clasped her hands behind her, wringing the fabric of her skirt as she watched him cross for the door. She wasn't sad and yet she was sure she could cry.

"Why do I feel like I might never see you again?" she said.

"I don't know about that." Max's heavy brow was strained, but his eyes pooled with affection. "I'm sure we'll run into each other somewhere down the road."

Even as her heart continued to pound with doubt, Cora managed a hopeful smile.

She carried their plates to the sink, but made it only as far as the island, wanting one more chance to see him in this kitchen, one more moment before he walked out of her life surely for the last time, despite what he believed. Even as she turned, Cora gripped the edge of the butcher block, certain that if she didn't hold on to something, she would allow herself to be pulled to follow him. Still the urgency that thumped behind her chest continued to bubble up in her throat.

When the screen creaked open, yearning spilled over, escaping out of her mouth like a cry.

"Max?"

He slowed, pivoting to face her.

"Can I thank you now?" she asked.

He blinked at her.

Cora smiled, whatever hope she had of stemming her tears lost now. Already, the outline of him against the door was beginning to blur.

"When you first came with your sketches and I said thank you, you said you hadn't done anything yet . . ." She swallowed. "What about now?"

As Max's eyes traveled her face, they flashed with longing.

"You're welcome, Cora."

28

1999

When they climb into Wes's car the next morning, there's no question where Mickey will take him first on their island tour. At ten, an hour from opening, Chowder's Clam Shack is still quiet, its cracked paved parking lot empty except for the red delivery van and a tan Jeep. The squat shack's red shingles are still in need of a fresh coat, and the picnic tables that overlook the harbor could stand new umbrellas. Even the plastic letters pressed into the slotted sign above the order window are the same ones she and Tiffany had popped off and on dozens of times each summer. At the closed sliding door, Mickey peers in and sees Danny in the back scooping fry out of the bucket. Tiffany is beside him, rocking back and forth to whatever song is on the shack's ancient boom box. The two fans that flank the workstation roar. Mickey can practically smell the wet grease through the glass. It takes several hard raps before Tiffany turns, her face lighting up with a smile. She waves them to the side door and Mickey leads Wes around the back.

Tiffany throws open the screen. "You came!"

"Of course we came," Mickey says as they step inside, the air not yet soaked with the scent of fry oil as it will be at day's end, but still misty with the warm smell of cornmeal and salt. She looks down to see the milk crate where Buzz always stored the clean aprons and has to keep herself from grabbing one out of habit.

"Hey, superstar!" Danny appears, his meaty arms spread, his apron already spotted with islands of grease.

"Hardly," Mickey says as he pulls her into a hard squeeze. "Danny, this is Wes Isaac. Wes, Danny Bartlett."

The men shake. "Good to meet you," Danny says. "You two seeing all the old haunts?"

"This is our first stop," Mickey says. "Tiff told me about the sale, Danny. I'm just so angry for you guys."

"Yeah, well." Danny waves his hand dismissively. "Our backup plan was always to come work for you, so we're not too worried."

"You might need a backup plan to that backup plan." Mickey glances warily at Wes, but his dark eyes are tender, proof that the path to forgiveness might be closer than she's dared to hope.

"You guys want something to drink?" Tiffany frees a pair of cups from the tower by the dispenser. "Refills come free with the tour."

Wes smiles. "I'll take a Dr Pepper, if you have it."

Mickey knows she doesn't have to give her order— Tiffany has already sent a stream of Sprite fizzing down.

"I bet you guys ran a pretty tight ship here," Wes says, looking around.

Danny snorts. "About as tight as the Titanic after the iceberg," he teases, shaking his fountain drink.

"Not true," Tiffany defends. "Mick and I made a dyna-mite team at the order window."

"When she was actually at the window," Danny says,

"and not pestering Buzz at the fryer to let her cook instead of take orders."

"It's true," Mickey admits but Tiffany gives her an absolving smile.

"So you were better at making food than making change. So what?"

Mickey grimaces. "Which was always especially embarrassing, considering everyone knew my grandfather was a banker."

"But Shell could be fierce when she had to be," Danny says to Wes. "She ever tell you about the time she read some poor kid the riot act because she saw him put ketchup on his crab cakes?"

"It was Howie Jackson," Mickey clarifies. "And he was twenty. And he should have known better. He's lucky we ever served him again, frankly."

"Just what every clam shack needs," says Danny. "A food purist."

"Damn straight." Mickey loops her arm through Tiffany's and tugs her close. "Danny, you mind if Tiff and I take a soda break?"

Tiffany's husband snickers and rolls his eyes at Wes. "As if they ever cared if I did."

* * *

"Don't tell me this is the same picnic table!" Mickey cries when they push through the kitchen screen and step outside to the break area.

"How could we get rid of it?" Tiffany asks as they climb up with their fountain drinks and settle on the top. "It's a historic artifact. Look." She shuffles over to point to a faded scrawl carved into the weathered wood: *Tiffany and Danny, 4EVER.*

"I remember when you wrote that," Mickey says, twisting to scan the tabletop. "I think I wrote something somewhere, too . . ."

"Here." Tiff leans back.

MC x JC. Jason Carlisle. A friend of Danny's, he'd worked here the summer they were seventeen. He looked like Rob Lowe. Mickey's crush had been epic.

"Does anyone ever actually use this for eating?" Mickey asks.

"After all those summers of us putting our asses on here? God, I hope not."

Mickey snorts and they fall against each other laughing. Wes and Danny's voices sail out through the screen.

"I thought you said he wasn't coming."

"Cora called him. She told him I might need him here . . ." Mickey feels her lighthearted smile fade. She plays with her straw, jabbing it into the mountain of ice. "Beech House is going on the market."

"What?" Tiffany leans back. "When?"

"This fall." Mickey glances up at Tiffany. "You don't look surprised. Did you know?"

"No, but . . ." Her friend offers a weak shrug. "It's one hell of a great house, Mick, but it's not exactly retirement-friendly."

"I just wish there was a way to keep it, that's all."

"Of course you do." Tiffany leans against Mickey's shoulder. "So he came to help cushion the blow. He's a keeper, Mick."

Mickey bobs her head, warmth blooming again at the reminder. "Tell me about it," she says, hearing the men's combined laughter grow louder. She never had any doubt that Wes would fold easily into her world here, that her friends would love him as much—well, almost as much—as she does.

"He's so much hotter than Jason Carlisle, by the way." Tiffany pulls the pen from her apron pocket and holds it out. "Want to edit your work?"

"And deface a historic artifact? No way." Mickey turns to square Tiffany with a hard look. "Now what about you? And don't blow me off, Tiff. I want the truth. What are you guys going to do?"

Tiffany stabs her straw into the crushed ice and sighs. "Danny and I want to start over—we've saved enough—and we want to stay on the island, but everything's gotten so expensive. We'd even be willing to build something ourselves, but who can afford land?"

Mickey scans their feet on the bench, hers in espadrilles, Tiffany's in plain sneakers, and smiles wistfully, remembering the matching Keds they always wore to work. How they'd doodle on the canvas with the counter Sharpie when they'd hit the midafternoon lull.

"Do you ever wish we made a go of something here on the island together?" Mickey asks.

"Of course I do," says Tiffany. "I think about it all the time."

Mickey looks up, meeting her friend's warm smile. "You never said anything."

"Because I knew you wanted to make it big off the island. And Danny and I were in love. I wasn't going anywhere, Mick. You were."

She'd gone, all right . . . but why had she never considered coming back?

Mickey moves her foot to give the side of Tiffany's sneaker an affectionate tap. "We did make a great team, though, didn't we?"

"The best," Tiffany says, nudging Mickey's foot back. "You ever want to do it again, just say the word."

29

The last thing Hedy needs is more coffee, but when she steps into the kitchen to find someone has made a fresh pot, she can't resist a splash. While she was glad to see Michelle and Wes take off after breakfast, their departure seemed to signal some kind of shift in the house, a hastening of its heartbeat. With the wedding just a day away, everyone in the house has scattered, tucked into their roles. Her mother is outside with the event rental coordinators, showing them where to set up the chairs and tables. Max has gone into town to pick up the wedding rings from the jeweler. Tom has been holed up in the office, on and off the phone all morning. Hedy knows she should probably check her voice mail, too, but she can't bring herself to dial in. Instead, she's still doing battle with the seating chart. If her father were here, he'd tell her to leave the damn chart and set them up a game of chess on the porch. While they played, Hedy would ask him what he thinks Michelle should do about her financial troubles, what he thinks Hedy should advise her to do. He'd ask Hedy about her recent sales and she'd ask him what has gone on the market on the island. But who is she kidding? The subject she would want most to unpeel with her father is the most impossible of all. How would he feel to know his wife was starting over with someone else, someone from their shared past . . . ?

Michelle's earlier comment after seeing Lois Welch still hangs around Hedy's thoughts, prickly like the grit of left-over sand in one's shoe. Had her daughter misunderstood what Lois Welch had implied about Cora? Had the woman indeed meant that Hedy's father and mother were well matched, or had she, in fact, meant Cora and Max?

"Please tell me you're not still fighting over that seating chart?" Hedy's mother asks, stepping into the kitchen. "I don't want you wasting any more time on that. I'm sorry I ever gave you the job. It's really not that important, you know."

"It is, Mom," Hedy says. "People like being told these things. They like to know where they belong."

"It's a wedding dinner, darling. Not a cross-country move. You're making far too big a deal."

Says the woman who could have easily married quietly at a courthouse but instead invited every person who ever knew my father, Hedy thinks sourly to herself.

She slugs her coffee. "You say it's not a big deal, and then you invite half the island. Which is it?"

Cora rests a hand on her hip. "Is this because I called Wes without telling anyone?"

"Personally, I wouldn't have stepped in like that, but—"

"Then you are upset with me about it."

"No, Mom."

"What then?"

"Hello in there!" The screen rattles with a knock, inter-rupting them, and Hedy twists in her seat to see Lois Welch step inside, dressed in a striped boat top and linen slacks, the woman's black-and-silver hair swept up in its trademark, spray-sealed bouffant, a vase of carnations in her hands.

Her mother's weary expression shifts, her features bright-
ening with a welcoming smile as she crosses the kitchen to
greet Lois.

"You didn't need to bring flowers."

"I didn't," Lois says bluntly, moving the flowers to give
Cora a brief air kiss. "They were delivered to our house by
mistake. I don't know how long they'd been sitting out there
on our porch when I found them."

"They still look fresh," Cora says cheerfully, taking the
bouquet and setting it on the banquette.

"That's one thing you can say about carnations. They
may be cheap, but they're hearty. How's the blushing bride?"

"Far too old to blush anymore," Cora says, patting Lois's
arm, "but fine, otherwise."

"Oh, hello, Hedy, dear. I didn't see you there." Lois slows
at the banquette to lay a hand on Hedy's shoulder. Hedy
feels herself bristle reflexively, not sure what the source of
her agitation is. But even her smile feels tight on her face.

"Is that the seating chart?" Lois leans over for a look,
bringing a whiff of spray starch and Chanel. "I'll gladly sit
with anyone," she says. "Except the Robinsons. Oh, and
Marcia Sterling. She's been at me to join her book club and
they read absolute garbage." Lois blinks around the room.
"Is the groom here?"

"Max is picking up our rings," Cora says.

"Not long now, is it? Oh. Ned wanted me to confirm
dress. The invitation didn't specify. Coat and tie all right?"

"Coat and tie are fine," Hedy's mother says patiently. "But
Ned is welcome to wear whatever he wants."

"Oh, you know he'll love hearing that."

Hedy runs her tongue over her teeth. Poor Ned Welch.
A part of her has always felt sorry for Lois's good-natured

husband. While Hedy fantasized about what it might be like to be Lois Welch's daughter, she didn't have to imagine having Ned Welch as a father. Her own father was equally easygoing, more interested in the game of tennis than the sport of gossip that the women of Oyster Point played every summer. But could it be that Hedy's own mother had been a victim of their rumor roulette all those years ago?

Hedy returns her attention to the seating chart, her cheeks burning at the possibility. And here her mother stands, still letting Lois Welch into her kitchen? Does her mother have no self-respect?

Lois fingers her necklace, worrying the oversized white beads. "Are you sure there's nothing I can do for tomorrow, Cora?"

Haven't you done enough? The question burns at the back of Hedy's throat, her fingers itch with it. She sets down her pencil and stands abruptly. "No, thank you. We're fine."

"Oh." Lois wears a startled look. "Well, then I won't keep you all." She waves as she exits. "Call me if you change your mind."

Hedy crosses to the sink, suddenly, desperately needing a glass of water.

"It's one thing to be prickly with me, but it's not like you to be so chilly to our friends," Cora says.

"When you say your friends, do you mean yours and Dad's—or yours and Max's?" Hedy asks, shoving the tumbler under the tap.

"I'm not doing this to hurt you, Hedy. You're a grown woman, so I'm not sure why you feel the need to talk to me like a petulant teenager." Her mother comes beside her. "Do you want to tell me what this is really about?"

"I remember things, Mom," Hedy says, keeping her gaze

fixed on the advancing water. She drains half the glass, then lands it on the counter.

"What things?"

"I remember that Max came here once to fix something and Dad wouldn't let him in the house . . ." Hedy pauses, waiting to see her mother's reaction.

Cora's eyes widen, blinking quickly to suggest just enough understanding of the memory that Hedy dares to continue.

"And that night at dinner, Dad said something . . . that if I wanted to know why the step wasn't fixed that I should ask Lois Welch. And you got up from the table and walked off."

Cora tucks a few loose silver strands calmly back into her bun. "I did, yes."

While Hedy is grateful for the confirmation, it's not enough. She needs more.

She leans back against the counter and folds her arms, feeling her heart pound under her fisted hands. "Is it because you had an affair with Max that summer?"

"What?" Cora turns, her eyes blazing with alarm. "Of course not. How could you ask me that?"

"Michelle saw Lois on the beach yesterday, and Lois said something under her breath about you and Max being suited from the start. That she knew it the first time she saw the two of you together. What did she mean by that?"

Cora runs her fingertips across her throat and sighs. "It was a long time ago, Hedy. A million years."

"If it was so long ago, then why do I still remember it? And why is Lois talking about it?"

"There was a misunderstanding . . ."

"You mean a rumor?"

Her mother's lips stitch together. "Is that why you were rude to her just now?"

"*I'm* rude?" Hedy blinks. "I'm not the one who spread gossip about you, Mom. How can you be so nice to her?"

"Because she's my friend, Hedy. She's been my friend for over fifty years."

"Your friend who talked about you cheating on Dad behind your back? Who started a terrible rumor?" Hedy can feel her cheeks blazing. "I'm right, aren't I?"

Cora turns back to Hedy, whatever softness that had pooled earlier in her mother's eyes hardened.

She points Hedy to the banquette. "I think you better have a seat."

"What for?"

Her mother's voice is as steely as her gaze. "So I can tell you how quite wrong you are, my darling."

30

1948

After hearing about little else for weeks, Cora was relieved to see the day of the tournament finally arrive. Just before ten, Harry steered them through the gateposts of oaks into the club's dirt drive. He'd said little since they left Beech House fifteen minutes earlier, and his knuckles glowed white on the steering wheel.

As he pulled them into the parking lot, Cora reached across the seat to offer his leg a comforting touch. "You seem nervous, darling."

"Of course I'm nervous." Harry swung a grave look at her. "I held the Point title for five straight summers. This is the first competition in over three years."

Her husband had only told her all of this a dozen times, but Cora still nodded patiently, smiling at the irony of the moment: Just weeks ago she had voiced the same nerves at meeting all of their neighbors and it was Harry reassuring her. The symmetry filled her with a bloom of comfort.

"It's only the first day," she said.

"Yes, but the first day is hugely important, Cora. First impressions are everything."

As if he needed to tell her that. But Harry had explained to her that in previous years the competition had been a much quieter thing, played out on neighbors' courts, their only spectators often bored seagulls, but that, like so many things in this summer of renewal, the event was another excuse for a grand party. "Now I have to worry about some great big audience," he'd huffed.

"At least you'll have a nice day to start," Cora said brightly. And they would. After the threat of rain the day before, the Point had held a collective breath in hopes that the clouds would exit by the morning. Even the mist that clung to the grass and rooftops every morning like stubborn spiderwebs seemed to understand the importance of the day, evaporating so swiftly and thoroughly that the toes of Cora's pumps remained dry as they crossed the lawn to a wide crescent of chairs and blankets that had already been staged around the courts. Seeing Ned, Harry kissed her goodbye, and Cora made her way to the refreshment table to deliver her tray of canapés.

As she approached the spread of dishes and the flurry of women setting up, Cora looked to the club's veranda, where waitresses moved through the umbrella tables, wondering if she might see Betty, only because it meant a connection to Max, proof that maybe he was still on the island.

In the past few days, Cora had found her thoughts drifting often to the memory of their dinner together, guilt and pleasure dueling in her heart . . .

"We've been looking for you!" Irene appeared beside her. "We're over there," she said, pointing to the lawn, where Lois and several other women sat under striped umbrellas. "Come join us. Men's doubles are starting."

* * *

Cora may have known nothing about men's doubles, but within a few minutes of their match, she knew enough to understand that Harry and Ned were losing. Badly. Compared to the two men they were matched against, they flailed around like angry ostriches.

If Cora had any doubt, Lois's continuous heavy sighs confirmed it.

"What a disaster," she said, fanning herself with her magazine.

"If they lose this match, will they be out of the competition?" Cora asked.

"We should be so lucky," Lois said.

"Phil's up next," said Irene. "But don't hold your breath."

"Harry will be a bear," said Lois, turning to Cora. "Have you had the pleasure yet of beating him in chess?"

"I don't know how to play," Cora said.

Lois laughed. "Don't let him teach you. When we were younger, I refused to play him in any game. Chess, cards. Forget it. He's a miserable loser."

Irene blew out a curl of smoke. "As if Phil is a walk in the park."

"Harry was awfully edgy this morning," Cora admitted. "Really, he was a nervous wreck."

"See what I mean?" Lois leaned closer. "A word of advice: Men don't like to lose. Games. Jobs. Women. It's just a fact."

"Except for Ned," Irene said, wagging her cigarette at Lois. "He always seems so sunny when the boys come back from a round of golf."

Lois sighed. "It's true. My husband is a gifted loser."

The women laughed and Cora joined them, a tremor of relief sparking in her stomach. At last, something they all shared. Cora may not have summered on yachts or traipsed over Europe, but she was married to a wealthy island man who, as ridiculous as it was, moped around after a lost tennis match like the other women's husbands.

This, Cora thought. *This was what it was to belong to a group of women friends.*

All her years at the restaurant, she'd been surrounded by men, grown comfortable in their easy camaraderie, but the company of women had always seemed so much trickier to her. Her own mother had had few female friends, Cora's father having been openly possessive of her mother's attention, so Cora had struggled to navigate that world in school. But maybe now, at last, she might find her footing.

"Oh, damn, Arnie's skinned his knee or something," Irene said, rising from her chair. "Be right back."

"That boy is so accident-prone," Lois said when she'd gone. "I swear he can't even stand up without drawing blood."

"Boys can't be easy," Cora said.

"Oh, boys are fine. It's men who are hard."

"Then I'll hope for a girl."

Lois smiled. "Me, too."

The conversation stalled and Cora scanned the courts, watching Harry dart and dive.

"It took me a while, too, you know," Lois said.

When Cora looked back, she was startled to find Lois Welch squaring her with a warm smile from the other side of Irene's empty chair. Confusion flickered. Did Lois mean it had taken her a while to fit in? Surely not. Lois had been born into this world.

"To get pregnant," Lois said. "We were three years trying for Timmy."

For a moment, Cora believed she saw the sheen of tears

welling in Lois's eyes. She didn't know what to say, or if she should say anything.

Lois continued to hold her gaze urgently.

"What I'm saying is that I understand, Cora. I know how hard it can be. It may seem like I can't possibly, but I do."

Suddenly, strangely, Cora felt the prickle of tears crawling up her throat.

She nodded. "Thank you, Lois."

"I know I'm not always the easiest person to be around, but I want to be your friend, Cora. I have a feeling you and I could be that. Really, I mean. I have a feeling you're the sort of person a person would want as a friend . . ." Lois's expression shifted, turning worried. Or maybe just unsure. Even her voice wavered. "A real friend."

"Well! That was an ordeal." Irene returned, falling into her chair in a huff, filling the space between Cora and Lois, but somehow Cora felt the startling thread of their connection still intact, Lois's words still echoing.

A real friend.

The whistle sounded, signaling the end of the match. Cora looked toward the court, seeing the four men at the net, exchanging handshakes. Cora watched Ned climb the lawn toward the club, Harry beside him, her husband's racket stiff at his side as he stalked up the grass.

"We're taking the kids back to the beach," Irene said. "Let the men stew in their angry juices here alone."

Lois leaned forward to talk around Irene, drawing her lips into a smile that Cora had never seen on the woman before. Not on any of the women she'd met here in Oyster Point. A soft smile, a genuine smile.

Then, reaching across Irene, Lois laid her hand over Cora's where it rested on the arm of her lawn chair.

"Come with us, won't you?" Lois said.

Cora smiled. "Just let me tell Harry," she said, "and I'll meet you at the car."

* * *

Despite her speed, Cora wasn't able to reach the club before Harry disappeared around the side of the building, presumably to the men's changing room. While she wouldn't dare to enter through that door, she could certainly wait for him outside, couldn't she? Rounding the corner, Cora nearly collided with two men in tennis whites and stepped back, only to feel the bulk of someone behind her.

"Oops—easy there!"

She whirled to face Ned Welch, who leaned in to steady her with a broad smile, his round face still deeply flushed from exertion.

"Funny meeting you here," he said cheerfully.

"Isn't it?" Cora teased back, relieved to find a friendly face in the crowd. "I'm looking for Harry."

"He went in to get us drinks."

More men walked past and Cora stepped aside to clear the path.

"Did you see our match?" Ned asked.

"Every minute."

"Then my apologies." He clapped his free hand over his heart and tipped forward in a mock bow. "No one should have to witness that kind of carnage."

Cora laughed. "It really wasn't that bad."

Straightening, Ned laughed with her. "You really are too sweet, aren't you?"

"I wouldn't go that far."

"You wouldn't, would you?"

She laughed again but something in the slant of Ned Welch's eyes made her think he might not be kidding, and the hairs on the back of her neck prickled.

Please, no, Cora thought. *Not Ned, too.*

She motioned to the clubhouse door. "I should go find Harry."

"I wouldn't bother looking. It's a madhouse in there. He'll be out soon."

Ned stepped closer. Cora could smell his sweat, syrupy with alcohol and aftershave.

He raised his racket. "Do you know what they call this part, Cora?" he asked, flattening his fingers over the center of the webbing. "They call this the sweet spot. What do you think about that?"

She took a step back to widen the space between their bodies, but there was a wall of men behind her, allowing her only a few extra inches.

Dread pulsed at her temple. What was he doing?

Ned drummed his fingers over the racket's center, his eyes level with hers. "You and that townie cabinetmaker should be more careful in the future. Just because Harry is away doesn't mean there aren't still people to see."

Cora's breath caught, her heart racing with understanding: the car that had pulled into the driveway and then left.

"Max Dempsey gave me a ride," she said tightly. "I had picked up a package and I was walking it home. He carried it inside for me—"

"And stayed past dark, apparently."

Heat soaked her face. "I really should find Harry." She stepped forward, but Ned blocked her path. She looked up at him, seeing him as if for the first time. Vs of spittle shone in the corners of his lips.

"Now I know why you were so worried for them," Ned said quietly.

"Who?"

His nostrils expanded. "The shedders."

Gooseflesh flared down her arms. Cora held herself, trying to rub the bumps down. "I—I don't understand . . ."

"Isn't that what you are, Cora? You've come here and you've sloughed off your old shell, and now you're waiting for your new one to harden and just hoping like hell that nothing eats you before it can, right?"

Ned Welch's eyes, once offering a dependable warmth, frosted over, and Lois's words flashed through her racing thoughts: *Men don't like to lose . . .*

Her heartbeat accelerated with anger now, any worry gone. Cora pulled in a quick breath and pressed forward, around Ned and down the walkway to the front of the club, not slowing her quick steps until she was through the foyer and back outside, and even then, she wasn't sure where she meant to go, only that she needed to get far, far away.

* * *

Cora didn't mean to walk the whole way home. She only wanted to get a good distance from the club, to get through the crush of all the spectators and the lawn chairs and find herself down on the beach, near the water and its cleansing surf, but the shore stretched out so beautifully far, and when she peeled off her pumps and sank her bare feet into the sand, she felt certain she could have walked forever.

By now, she knew which dune held Beech House behind it. Unlike the first time she had to find her way home, the first time she met Ned Welch and all the other Point people who, she understood now, would define her world here always. The first time she'd met Max.

Max.

How could she explain the bond they'd forged in such a short time? Why did she have to? And if it had been something more, something wrong—not that she believed it was, no matter what ugliness Ned tried to suggest—neither of them had acted on it.

Still, as she climbed the bluff, her heart finally slowing now that the anchor of Beech House stood before her, a spark of longing flickered.

At the top of the rise, Cora stopped, seeing Harry's silhouette on the far end of the veranda, leaning against the column, staring out at the water.

Nearing the house, she waited for him to catch her in his periphery, but he didn't turn, didn't seem to see her.

"Harry?" she said carefully, then again once she'd climbed the two steps to the porch floor, firmer now. "Harry, what's wrong?"

His gaze remained forward. "Do you love me, Cora?"

She slowed. Panic washed over her skin, flushing her like a fever. Had Ned told him what he believed he'd seen?

"Why would you ask me that?" she whispered.

Her husband shifted against the column. He was still wearing his tennis whites. The hair on his calves was shiny with clay and sweat. "Are you sorry you married me?"

"Harry, please. What is this about?"

He pivoted slowly, but his eyes found hers immediately and his voice was husky with emotion. "I know it isn't easy here. It wasn't easy for my mother. She would never say so but she worked very hard to fit in here and my father loved her for it. And I promise to love you for it, too." Pushing himself off the column, Harry crossed to her and took her by the arms. His eyes flicked over her whole face, desperately, as if her features were a riddle he meant to solve. "Do you understand what I'm saying to you, Cora?"

"I'm sorry about the match, Harry. Really, I am."

His gaze continued to search hers, as if he had no idea what she was talking about. As if she wasn't even speaking English.

"Nobody can be everything to one person, Cora. But I know what I can be for you. And I need you to understand what it is you are for me. What we are for each other . . ." His grip fell from her upper arms and found her hands instead. He held them, his eyes searching hers plaintively. "Do you understand?"

Understand what? Cora wanted to ask. Understand that she would never be more than his wife here? That whatever currency that title bought her, it would never be enough to afford her the right to call herself an islander, a member of the larger club of this place, the one that existed outside of the walls of the building that overlooked the Sound? Or did he mean for her to understand that she could never speak of her past, and yet it would always be held against her somehow?

Cora wanted to ask him to clarify all of it, but the tumble of words withered in her throat. Why waste her breath asking questions she already knew the answers to?

And when Harry opened the porch door and stepped back to allow her entrance first, Cora felt her husband's fingers weave through hers and squeeze tight.

He must have been hungry after his match, she thought as they walked inside. "I could make you an omelet while you clean up," she offered. "Or one of those grilled cheeses with basil and fresh mozzarella you like so much?"

Harry touched her cheek. "A grilled cheese would hit the spot," he said.

In the kitchen, Cora took out the pan of custard she'd made them for dessert last night, hungry herself, ravenous, really, and scooped out several bites, admiring the kitchen as she ate. The polished cabinets. The island. The curved piece of wood that hid the sink light, her name on its front. When Max had carved it, had he known what he was doing? That he was making certain she would always have one place on this island that would be hers alone, that no one could dispute?

Cora liked to think he did. Because this kitchen was where she belonged. She knew that for certain.

She knew other things for certain, too. That Ned Welch would hold the secret of what he believed had happened between her and Max like one of those charms on the bracelet Harry bought for her, the bracelet that still circled her wrist. She set down her spoon and undid the clasp, letting the gold chain puddle in her hand, then she opened the spice drawer and dropped it inside.

And she knew something else, too. That in all of the activity leading up to the tournament she'd lost count of the days, and realized that her period was due two days ago, and she was never late.

Picking up the spoon again, Cora took one more bite of custard and set the pan back in the refrigerator, taking out the ball of cheese, then setting an omelet pan on the flame.

Maybe Ned Welch was right. Maybe she was a shedder, and maybe her shell would take a very long time to harden, or maybe it never would. But she would wait. And in the meantime, she would stay safe here in this house, in this kitchen, where she could always be true to her heart, true to herself. And tomorrow she would tell Harry they needed to see Dr. Fisher because he'd been right. That all she needed was a distraction, a project, and that things had fallen into place after all.

And then, later tonight, when Harry had slipped out of her and fallen asleep, one leg draped over her, the other hanging off the edge of the bed, Cora would carefully extract herself and come downstairs, turn on the kitchen light, and bake something to celebrate. Not a lemon meringue pie, because that was what she used to make to sweeten sour news, but something different. Something new. Something that was hers alone.

31

After a stop at the Vineyard Basket for a box of the bakery's famous nautilus rolls, Wes pulls them in to Beech House just before three. Mickey can hear the clatter of chairs being set up on the other side of the lawn. A cherry picker stretches into the dome of the weeping beech, bracelets of Christmas lights wound around her massive branches.

Wes pulls the key out of the ignition and sits back.

Mickey shifts in her seat to face him, wanting to kiss him. Wondering if he'd let her. Their day has been nearly perfect.

"How'd you like your tour?" she asks.

"Loved it." Wes scans the view. "I can understand what you love about this place. What I can't understand is why you left."

"Because I went to culinary school."

"No, I mean after that." He studies her a moment. "Why not come back here to open your restaurant?"

Mickey smiles wistfully. "You know, Tiffany asked me the same thing today."

"And what did you tell her?"

"I thought making it meant leaving, I guess. That it wouldn't count if I did something here on the island . . ."

She rolls her head toward him. "Did you ever think about opening something in Philly?"

Wes shakes his head.

"Never?" she asks. "But you grew up there."

"Sure, but it never felt like home to me. Not the way I can see this place feels like for you."

Wes reaches over to caress her thigh and Mickey feels her whole body soften, the relief of his touch like a hot bath. She lays her hand over his, keeping him there.

Her heart races with anticipation as his hand travels farther up her leg.

"I've missed you," she says. "I've missed you so much . . ."

She runs her fingertips over his wrist, the raised trail of veins along the back of his hand.

He palms the inside of her thigh hungrily. "I'm right here."

* * *

They can hear the kitchen phone ringing from the steps. Inside first, Wes snatches it off the receiver while Mickey walks to the island and sets down the bags of clam strips and onion rings Danny sent them home with.

"The Campbell wedding, yeah," Wes says.

Mickey moves to the sink to wash her hands, listening as the tap runs warm over her fingers, but there's only silence.

"You're not serious . . ."

She turns off the faucet. Wes looks over at her, the phone still wedged under his chin. His brow bends.

"Yeah, of course I'll tell her . . . Okay . . ."

He hangs up and turns back slowly. Alarm skitters around Mickey's scalp.

"That was the caterers," he says. "They're canceling."

* * *

"Apparently they screwed up the dates," Cora says with a heavy sigh when they are all gathered in the kitchen a few minutes later. "I called back and begged but they don't have the staff."

Mickey's mother spreads her hands over the island and sinks forward on her palms. "In less than twenty-four hours, there are going to be seventy-five hungry people expecting a seated meal," Hedy moans. "One for which I will have sacrificed a ridiculous amount of brain cells to seat them at."

"I cook for that many people every night," Wes says.

Mickey only has to meet his gaze for a second before the words are out of her mouth.

"We'll be your caterers, Grams."

Her grandmother's eyes grow big. "You would do that?"

She has to ask? If the woman asked Mickey to meet her for drinks on the moon, she'd figure out a way to get there.

"Do you have a copy of the menu?" Wes asks.

Cora reaches into a folder beside the fridge and extracts a scalloped-edged square of card stock. "We had them printed." Her forehead is still wrinkled with worry as she hands it to Wes.

"The lobster bisque might be tough this last-minute, huh?" Mickey says, reading the menu with him.

"We could serve soup shooters, instead," Wes suggests. "What about that cucumber gazpacho we did last month?"

They'll need mint. Luckily, Mickey knows where to find some nearby.

But her grandmother's hopeful expression dims again. "The caterers were supposed to handle the alcohol, too."

"I'll call Cork's," Hedy says, Mickey's mother already

plucking a pencil from the counter to start a list. "They always keep plenty of champagne in stock." Mickey remembers: The summer she graduated from culinary school, they'd been desperate for a case to celebrate with and Cork's had saved them. As if recalling the same memory, Hedy glances at her and offers a knowing smile that Mickey returns.

Wes taps the menu with his thumb. "What to do for the main course."

"It will really depend on what we can get on such short notice from the market," Mickey says.

"Or if we knew someone local we could partner with . . ."

Her gaze drifts to the island where the to-go bags from Chowder's sit, and possibility sparks.

Mickey rushes to the phone and dials the number from memory, her heart racing with excitement while she waits through two rings before Tiffany picks up.

"Tiff, remember this morning when you said if I ever wanted us to work together again to say the word . . . ?" Mickey meets Wes's eyes across the room and his crooked smiles sends a bolt of heat to her core. "Well, I'm saying it."

* * *

The first herb Mickey ever harvested from her grandmother's kitchen garden was sage, when Cora needed some leaves for a root vegetable stew they were making. Just eight years old, Mickey knew nothing about herbs—not yet—and since her grandmother believed trial and error was the best teacher, she sent Mickey off to procure a few leaves with only the hint that sage tasted earthy and peppery. Armed with her single clue and feeling prematurely victorious, Mickey pushed through the screen door, despite having no idea what "earthy" tasted like, just confident it would be evident the instant the right leaf landed on her tongue. But once inside the jungle of unlabeled plantings, Mickey had her doubts. Fifteen minutes later, after tasting every plant in the garden—and a few grasses—she returned with a handful of slightly fuzzy silver-green leaves and beamed when her grandmother clapped with delight. Mickey wore the pride of her success against her heart like a badge on a sheriff's vest. For the rest of the summer, and many afterward, the kitchen garden became her charge. Its weeding and watering, pruning and general fawning-over, Mickey's sole responsibility.

Now, as she stands with Cora at the edge of the garden—or rather, the square of earth that used to contain it—the once vibrant blooms of green now a tangled carpet of weeds, Mickey's heart sinks. The borders, once as tidy and distinctive as if they had been framed out in chalk, are now undetectable and spill out onto the lawn, or maybe it's the lawn that has absorbed the garden—Mickey can't decide which thought upsets her more. She's not surprised to see that the only herb still in attendance is a patch of spearmint, mint being the squeaky wheel of the herb world. Not unlike bamboo, once planted, it quickly takes over a garden, refusing to be overshadowed or weeded out. Knowing this, Mickey's grandmother always grew hers in containers, sinking each mint plant into the soil in its own little cage to keep it from spreading, and turning it regularly to keep the roots from escaping out of the pot's drainage holes. But mint is a survivor. It finds a way to endure even when left unattended. No wonder her grandmother loved it so much.

"Don't say it." Cora sighs. "It's a disgrace. I know."

"Come on, Grams. It's not so bad."

"Liar. I could hear your heart cracking the whole walk across the lawn."

Mickey reaches down to pluck off a spearmint leaf and rubs it between her fingers to draw out the oils, unable to resist bringing it to her nose for a fragrant whiff. She tosses it into the tangle of weeds.

Her grandmother takes her hand. "I'm sorry we waited to tell you about the house."

"It's okay," Mickey says, returning the squeeze. "I've done my share of keeping secrets lately—I'm hardly in a position to be angry." Still the reminder of the house's impending sale is like a pinch—Mickey winces at the sting. "Can you really bear to say goodbye?"

"Of course not. But it's time. This garden is painful enough," Cora says, gesturing to the nests of weeds. "Seeing it fall away because I can't take care of it wrecks me. Beech House will be next, and I couldn't bear to let it fall apart from lack of tending the way our garden has."

Mickey turns to take in the house slowly, the places of wear that may have been there for years, but which she never wanted to see. Now the constellations of age seem to be everywhere. Missing shingles; the rotting corner of a windowsill, as frayed as an old hemline. Her grandmother was right to worry. How much longer could the house withstand a gentle decline?

Quietly, they fill the basket Cora has brought with as many leaves as they can find, the fresh, grassy scent of mint filling the air as they work.

"Does this mean you and Max will leave the island?" Mickey asks. Before now, she hasn't dared think of the possibility, never mind pose the question out loud.

"We don't know yet," her grandmother says. "One of Max's brothers has a cottage in Chilmark. And Tom has made some calls for us for places on the cape. I don't know what would be harder—being away from Beech House, or staying close enough to see someone else living in her. This house has been my world for so long . . . and not just mine." Her grandmother slows her picking, a smile stretching her lips. "I know it's silly of me, but I always had this fantasy that you might come back here to open a restaurant."

"On the Vineyard?"

"At Beech House," Cora says. Her grandmother's eyes are soft as they flick over her face. As if Cora's searching for something, and determined to find it. Mickey feels her chest tighten with doubt.

Her conversation with Wes in the car floats back, how simple he made it sound. How obvious. Mickey's connection to the island was so clear to him, as clear as it was to her grandmother.

So why hadn't it been as clear to her?

Cora points to their filled basket. "Let's get moving before the weeds swallow us up, too," she says, steering them back to the house.

But even as they step back into the steady breeze, Mickey can't shake the question: Why hadn't she given the possibility of opening a restaurant here real thought before?

Not that it's worth asking now, Mickey decides as she and her grandmother climb the lawn, arm in arm. Surely it's too late.

Isn't it?

32

Shopping list in hand, Hedy is on her way to her car when Tom's black BMW swings down the driveway and slides into the square of shade under the beech.

"Caterers canceled on us," she calls to him as he emerges from the car. "But Michelle and Wes are taking over." She holds up her list and waves it. "I'm off to secure the liquor."

"Sounds dangerous," Tom says. "Want a copilot?"

Does she? She's barely had time to breathe between her mother's revelation and the cancellation news, let alone process it all. She's not sure she'd make the best company right now. But then the thought of navigating high-season traffic and downtown parking when she's this wobbly and distracted is a concern, too. She's liable to steer herself right into a tour bus of whale watchers.

Tom claps his hand on the roof. "We could take my car."

Hedy snaps open her sunglasses and jabs them over her face. "Deal."

* * *

"I keep missing all the excitement, don't I?" Tom says when they're off the dirt and onto the asphalt. "I was thinking of taking a run around the harbor later tonight but I'm afraid there might be floods or locusts if I do."

"At this rate, it's the most logical next catastrophe," Hedy says, settling in. The car's sleek black interior isn't as tidy as some other M3s she's been in (he could build a small cabin with all the coffee stirrers in his cup holder), but the leather seats, nearly pumpkin-colored, are buttery and easy to sink into and have just the right earthy smell.

He's a good driver. Calm. Focused. Not too fast but not slow, either. Stops at yellow lights, glides confidently around curves. Hedy has always believed that most everything you need to know about a man, you can discover when he's behind the wheel.

On State Road, they pick up speed, the engine humming smoothly, and her mind wanders, remembering snippets from her conversation with her mother. The news that it had been Ned Welch who had been responsible for the unfounded gossip about Cora and Max all those years ago, along with the truth that, despite her father's grumbles, there had been nothing between her mother and Max that summer, should have given her a much-needed dose of peace—so why do her limbs still feel tight with unease?

"Speaking of flooding . . . that's quite a bit of booze we're getting." Tom motions to her list. "Does this mean we need a bartender now, too?"

Hedy rolls her head in his direction. "Are you volunteering?"

"I do have some experience." He leans back, his hand relaxed over the ball of the stick. She can easily see him on the other side of a bar, flashing that smile, those gray-blue eyes. "I bartended my first few years at the architecture firm after I got out of design school," he says. "They expect you to work for free your first few years. They call it an internship. I call it a racket."

"I'm familiar with the trend." Hedy turns her gaze to the window. "I've worked with plenty of architects who are under the misimpression that we're all agreeable to working for free."

"We get a bad rap," he says. "I promise, we're not all entitled jerks."

"I'm not so sure about that right now."

Tom looks at her strangely. "I was talking about architects."

"Hm." Hedy plucks off her sunglasses and stabs them into her hair. "I was talking about men."

* * *

The inside of Cork's is frosty with air-conditioning. Hedy feels her skin prickle with cold as they wait at the register for the store manager and rubs her arms briskly to warm herself.

"At least we won't have to worry about chilling the white," Tom says.

The manager, a man their age with a white goatee and cargo shorts, arrives, scans their list, and then tells them to give him a few minutes to check the stock. Tom suggests they browse while they wait, and Hedy is grateful for movement. Initially chilled, now she feels a frustrating heat building along her hairline and across her throat. She plucks at her blouse as she follows him into the aisles, wishing her body temperature could make up its mind.

A faint Billy Joel song trails them as they explore.

"So what's your drink of choice?" Tom asks. "If we're

going to be family, we should know these things about each other."

She glances over at him, his attempt at humor somehow chafing. Is he always so cheerful? She'll admit that she's been hesitant to share her reservations at their parents marrying with him, but there's a difference between keeping something close and outright denial. Isn't he even a little rattled that his father is remarrying? Hedy wishes he'd show a little bristle, for God's sake. His smoothness is making her edges feel even sharper and she hates it.

Tom glances over at her. "Or maybe that's too personal?"

"Martini," she says flatly.

"Ah. Dry or dirty?"

"Dirty."

"Interesting." His eyes narrow on her.

"Why are you looking at me like that?" she says.

"Because you don't seem the type."

"Excuse me?"

Tom draws back as if she's coughed on him. "Is that an insult?"

"Well, it's definitely not a compliment."

They slow at a display of wine coolers, a giant cardboard cutout of a willowy young blonde in a lime-green bikini holding a bottle in each hand. Somehow Hedy doubts the photographer suggested the premium touch-up package for *her* photo shoot.

She turns to find Tom studying the display with a furrowed brow. "I've never understood the appeal," he says.

"She's a gorgeous, skinny blonde offering you a drink. What's not to understand?"

"I was talking about wine coolers," he says, and Hedy feels her cheeks pink with regret.

She clears her throat and starts walking again.

Tom follows. "So why martinis?"

That's an easy one. "My father drank them," she says. "And he'd always give me his olives."

"An olive pusher, huh? They're the worst."

Hedy lets her tight lips loosen into a smile, memory briefly slowing her racing pulse. "When I became old enough to drink, it was the only cocktail I thought to ask for. We would drink them together when I came back to the house. He taught me how to make one. The key is a chilled glass."

"I've never been a martini man but I'm open to change," Tom says. "Maybe you'll make me one?"

She thinks about the old drink cart in the great room, the one that always sat near the Wedding Wall, and feels a flush of warmth. Seeing it after her father died had broken her. The jar of vermouth he'd bought and never opened. Hedy has avoided the cart every visit since, as if by not looking too closely she can pretend her father might still be in the house, that any minute she'll hear the tinny clinks of him dropping ice cubes into the silver-plated cocktail shaker . . .

Tears prickle. Hedy swallows them and picks up her pace down the row of whiskey.

A young man in board trunks looks sheepish as he tugs down a bottle of Jack Daniel's and snakes past them.

"No way is he of age," Tom whispers when they round the end of the aisle.

"He'll be fine," she says. "I used a fake ID in here once."

"A checkered past—thank God," he says with a relieved sigh, clapping a hand against his heart. "I was beginning to feel like a very bad influence on you."

"I had my moments here, don't worry."

"In this store?"

"In this store," she says. "On the island."

"I'm intrigued." They slow at a display of vodka and Tom makes a face. "Do I get to hear about these moments or do I have to wait until you've had a few dirty martinis?"

"They're hardly scandalous."

"My bar's pretty low these days. I'm shocked when someone tells me they sample grapes at the supermarket."

"Dempsey?" The goateed clerk swings around the end of the aisle and points to them. "Your order's ready."

Back at the counter, Hedy fidgets with the strap of her purse as he rings them up. Tom stands relaxed with his hands in his pockets like they're there to pick up a few bottles for a friend's dinner. Like this could be any other day. Again, agitation taps at her chest.

"Should be quite a party," the clerk says, looking between them.

"That's the plan." Tom takes his wallet out of his back pocket and slides his credit card across the counter. "Our folks are getting married tomorrow." He gestures to Hedy. "My father's marrying her mother."

"No kidding? Good for them." The clerk trains his smile on Hedy. "Never too late for a second chance, is it?"

Hedy manages a polite smile but can't hold it. Suddenly all she wants is to get outside, to get fresh air. "Meet you at the car," she says under her breath, already headed for the exit.

Pushing through the door, she sucks in a grateful breath of the muggy air, and picks up her pace back to the car. Outside, the glare is painful after the low light of the store. She winces as she fumbles to pull down her sunglasses. Tears sting the backs of her eyes. She can't decide if she wants to throw up or bawl her eyes out. Maybe both.

After another minute, Tom emerges from the store, empty-handed.

"Where is it all?" she asks.

"I decided to get it delivered this afternoon. It's too much for one trip." Tom's heavy brow rolls forward. "Did I say something wrong in there?"

She can tell he's trying very hard to see her eyes through her shades. She's grateful for their cover.

"I don't appreciate you telling a total stranger my business," she says tightly.

Tom leans back, frowning with confusion. "It was just conversation. I wasn't aware I was spilling state secrets."

She sweeps her hand through her bob, fluffing it. "I just think it's weird, that's all."

"What is?"

"How you're so . . . calm," she says, forcefully enough that Tom takes a step back. "Your father is getting remarried and you're cracking jokes as if it's no big deal. Don't you care?"

"Of course I care. That's why I'm here."

Hedy blows out an exasperated breath. "I don't mean like that."

"What, then?"

Her heart is pounding. Does she honestly have to spell it out for him?

When Tom unlocks the car, Hedy slips inside, grateful for the escape. She's not even sure she knows what she means.

He turns on the car and waits before pulling out. "Can I tell you what I think?"

"I'd rather you didn't," she says, rummaging through her purse for a mint.

For a moment, while he silently shifts and steers them

out of the lot, Hedy thinks she's avoided his analysis, but once they are on the road, he says, "I think—and this would be entirely understandable—I think you might be jealous."

She spins in her seat and stares at him hotly. What in the world?

"Jealous of who?" she says.

"Your mother." Tom shrugs. "Maybe because she's not worried about upsetting your dad by taking another crack at marriage and you felt like you never could. At least, that's what you told me yesterday."

"I never said that." Hedy feels her face burning again. "I said I never met anyone who was worth taking that risk for again." She gives up her hunt for mints and snaps her purse closed, turning back to face the dashboard.

She can feel Tom's gaze sliding her way, hoping to connect, but she refuses to look at him.

He shifts up.

"My mistake," he says.

33

By ten thirty, there is nothing left to do but sleep. The fridge is packed. Boxes of stemware are stacked on the banquette. Cases of champagne line the hallway, ready to be chilled. Empty coffee urns and chafing dishes cover the dining table. On the counter, a few pages of notes wait, scrawls and plating sketches recognizable only to Wes and Mickey, a culinary instruction manual to tomorrow's meal.

Upstairs in her room, Mickey stands at the window, wanting to soak in the soothing rumble of the surf blowing in through the screens while Wes finishes his shower. In all the activity of the day, there hadn't been time to mull over her tangled emotions. But now, everything finished, all distractions gone, her grandmother's suggestion in the herb garden drifts back, anchoring this time, refusing to be brushed away.

What if she could try to make a go of a restaurant here at Beech House?

Sure, it would be complicated—assuming they could even get the proper permits and zoning waivers—but complicated wasn't the same as impossible.

Mickey sinks forward against the sash, savoring the freshness of the night air, the faint taste of brine in it. It had been wonderful working with Wes again, going over ingredients and recipes, troubleshooting and brainstorming like they used to do together in the early days of the restaurant, before she had to give all of her time to the books and schedules and promotion. How easy it had been to imagine them in Cora's kitchen every day.

How many times did Mickey look up from their planning work at the island and flash to a picture of tables on the wide veranda, customers eating their food as they looked out onto the water?

"All yours, Beautiful."

Wes appears in the doorway, shirtless and damp, and desire circles in her stomach, possibility rushing in with it. Mickey pulls in a deep breath, remembering the last time she kept something from him, the last time she waited to share, and resignation settles in her chest.

After all, the worst he can say is no.

"Good shower?" she asks.

"Would have been better with you in it," he says, draping his towel over the wrought-iron footboard. "Interesting collection of mattresses in this house."

"Meaning . . . ?"

He grins. "Just that it's nothing short of a miracle that so many Campbells were born with all these twin beds."

Mickey laughs. "Where's your inventiveness, chef? Who's the one always telling me you make a meal with whatever you've got in the fridge."

"Is that a challenge?" Wes grabs her around the waist and pulls her into his arms, tipping her head back to bury his mouth against her neck, the chill of his wet hair tickling her throat. When he finds her mouth, Mickey tastes the lingering sweetness of the rum he and Tom sipped at the end of the evening.

She drops a kiss on his bare chest, brushing her lips over his damp, hot skin.

"Thank you for being here," she whispers. "Not just for me, but for Cora. For pitching in to make tomorrow so special."

"There's nowhere else I'd rather be," he says.

Still in his arms, Mickey twists back to face the window, listening to the faraway pounding of the surf. Wes hooks his arms over her shoulders, crossing them over her breasts. She leans back and lets her head rest against his chin.

"When I was little, my grandparents would have parties, and I'd sit at this window," she says, "waiting until I could hear everyone outside on the veranda. Then I'd sneak downstairs and raid the abandoned hors d'oeuvres table. I'd make myself this obscenely huge plate of snacks to bring back to my bed. The Brie would have been left out for hours at that point and I remember it was like thick whipped cream. People used to bring over brownies and fudge, but I always rushed for the cheese plate and the charcuterie board . . ." Mickey wrinkles her lips sheepishly and shakes her head. "What eight-year-old picks blue-cheese-stuffed mushrooms over brownies?"

Wes presses his mouth against her temple and smiles. "An eight-year-old with great taste."

The breeze picks up, sending the sheers dancing up toward them. In the hush, the pulse of the surf grows louder.

The universe is giving Mickey her cue.

"What if we bought Beech House and opened a restaurant here?"

The question out, she waits in the silence, not daring to move or even breathe, her heart pounding in her ears with anticipation.

In the next moment, she feels Wes draw back, his hands drop from her shoulders, but only to ease her around to face him.

His eyes float over her face. "Are you serious?"

"You said yourself you never understood why I didn't open my restaurant here. And today Cora admitted to me that it had always been a dream of hers that I would . . ." Mickey pauses to gauge his reaction before she continues, relieved to see his eyes continue to flash with interest. "Being back in the kitchen with you today, working, cooking side by side . . . it's where I belong. I want to be back there. With you. Not down the road. Now."

Body to body, she's sure he can feel her heart thumping through her chest, and she dares to go on.

"Tiff and Danny could even partner with us. Tiff is a dynamite manager and she said they have enough to start over somewhere on the island. They just need a place they can afford."

Wes's eyes flit over her face, swimming suddenly with concern. "So we'd close Piquant?"

And there it is. The biggest question of all.

Mickey slips from his arms and walks toward the window, holding herself. Her heart, as usual, took the wheel before her head. She will admit she hasn't exactly thought all of this through.

"Or . . ." Wes whistles through his teeth. "Maybe we wouldn't have to."

Mickey whirls around.

"I didn't want to say anything before, but . . ." He pushes his fingers through his wet hair. "Lucas came to me asking if you'd be open to him signing on as a partner."

"Really?" The news isn't entirely a shock. Mickey knows how long their head bartender has been in the business.

She's had several conversations with him about his dreams of opening his own place someday.

"He said he could find other investors if we were ever interested in selling."

It's hardly a guarantee—but it's enough to smooth out the wrinkles of unease in Mickey's stomach for now, at least.

The room hushes with possibility again.

Wes comes beside her at the window and Mickey scans his bent profile for clues to his reaction, nibbling on her lip as she waits.

"Have you brought this up with Tiffany and Danny yet?" he asks.

"Of course not," she says. "I wanted to ask you first. I won't do this—I can't do this—if you're not on board."

He drags a hand around his jaw, studying the view another long moment before he turns to her. "It was pretty amazing today, wasn't it? Both of us back in the kitchen . . ."

She bobs her head quickly, hope soaring. It's as close to a yes from him as she dares to imagine.

"Ever since we talked in the car, I couldn't stop thinking about it," she says. "I knew I couldn't wait to tell you."

"Good. Don't." Wes tugs her against him, his arms circling her tight. "If we're really a team—"

"We are," she says emphatically.

"Then don't ever keep me in the dark again, Mick." His voice is hard but his eyes burn with warm heat.

She frees her arm enough to reach back toward the night table. "Not even when we make love?" she whispers, her fingers seeking the lamp's dangling chain switch.

Wes grins against her mouth, drawing her hand back and trapping her arm behind her.

"Especially not then," he says.

You're Invited

Coraline Campbell and Max Dempsey
request the honor of your presence
as they begin a new chapter together

On Saturday, the twenty-sixth of June at four o'clock
Beech House

Oyster Point
West Tisbury, Massachusetts

Dinner to follow the ceremony

In lieu of gifts, the couple asks that guests make
donations to the Vineyard Food Pantry

34

There's already a steady breeze whipping across the lawn—
the flaps of the tent dance with it—and Mickey decides it
is the best of all signs as she comes downstairs. The universe is
breathing in and out, new beginnings. If not for the evidence
of an impending party in nearly every room, it could be any
other lazy summer morning at Beech House. The song of a
passing osprey breaking the hush. A gossamer cloud of mist
floating over the lawn and the tangy, slightly spoiled smell of
low tide coming in through the screens.

Sunlight climbs the Wedding Wall, piercing faces and
clasped hands and lace hems, depending on where in the
gallery of squares the beam falls. Despite all the prep work
they have to cram into the scant hours before the ceremony, and even though she can already hear activity in the
kitchen, Mickey slows reflexively when she reaches the collection of portraits this morning, certain the universe won't
look fondly on someone not allowing even a few seconds of
reverence in front of wedding pictures on a wedding day.
She scans the outermost frames, trying to decide where
Cora and Max's will go, or if they will be forced to demote
someone for their spot. They might have to, Mickey thinks

with a strange twinge of sadness, since the gallery is even on all sides.

Tiffany and Danny are already in the kitchen, pointing the group of summer workers to different stations in the room, college kids not much older than they all were when they worked at Chowder's, but it's Wes's gaze that Mickey wants to find. He glances up at her from where he stands at the island, looking over their notes, coffee at his side, and delivers her a look that is both longing and affirming.

Does she dare to think this scene could be their future?

"Just like old times, isn't it?" Tiffany asks, handing her a mug of coffee.

"Except this would be Sprite," Mickey says.

"Enough chitchat, ladies," Danny calls from the banquette where he's unloading a cooler. "Let's get to work."

They laugh even as they roll their eyes and Mickey groans playfully, "Like old times, all right."

* * *

After searching the upstairs, Cora finds her husband-to-be (the word still causes her to smile) at the far end of the great room, admiring the Wedding Wall.

She crosses to Max slowly, wanting to take her time. After all the years they waited (too busy living their lives to realize, of course, that that was what they were doing), they have a bit more of it now. The last rope of string lights has been wound around the weeping beech. Under the tent, chairs have been unfolded and lined up. The wooden dance floor has been laid down. All that's left to do is get dressed and, well, married.

Coming around to his side, Cora looks up to find that

282

282

Max's study of the photographs isn't wistful but perplexed, almost concerned. He squints, his lips set in a resigned line.

"I don't think we should do this, Cora."

Heat flares across her face, blooming so fast she sees stars. "What?" She looks up at him, frantic. "Are you saying we shouldn't get married?"

"Am I—?" Max turns, his eyes flicking over her face, flashing with confusion as the corners of his mouth rise into a startled smile. "Sweetheart, I'm talking about the wall," he says. "I don't think we should put our wedding picture on it."

"Oh, that!" She claps a hand against her heart and exhales, releasing a relieved laugh with her breath. "You can't say things like that to a bride on her wedding day. It's unkind. She's prone to wild thoughts."

Max draws her into his arms and drops a kiss on her upturned forehead. "A bride should have wild thoughts on her wedding day. Her wedding night, especially."

A sudden thought grips her. "I don't think we're supposed to see each other yet."

Max shrugs. "I guess we couldn't wait."

But they had, Cora wants to say, but knows she doesn't need to.

He turns her around in his arms so they are both facing the gallery of wedding portraits, and she scans the collection.

"You're right," she says. "We'd just have to take it down with all the others when we leave."

"To say nothing of there's no room," Max points out.

"True," she says. "But we could make room if we wanted to."

"It doesn't seem right to bump someone off the wall so we could have a few days up there."

A few days. Tears prickle, buoyed by the knot that forms

in her throat. When Max pulls her closer, Cora leans in to him, grateful for the sponge of his shirt to soak up those that brim before she can swallow them back.

The clock sounds. They count the chimes. Twelve.

Time to go.

35

At a quarter to two, Hedy stands in the bedroom doorway and meets her mother's eyes in the vanity mirror where Cora sits in her beaded, blush-colored dress. Her mother's hair is gathered in a low bun. An antique comb, decorated with sprays of baby's breath, sits snugly in the soft whorl of silver-red.

"How do I look?" Cora asks.

"Beautiful," Hedy says, and means it. What they say about brides is true. Her mother glows.

"I've been fighting with this comb . . ." Cora taps at her bun. "I can't tell if I've got it in straight or not."

"Here," Hedy says, stepping inside the room. "Let me."

She comes behind her mother and carefully shifts the comb's delicate teeth, not wanting to disturb the tiny flowers that are wound around the comb's top. Her mother's hair has become so thin, as soft and wispy as milkweed silk, and it startles her.

"I remember how much you used to love styling my hair when you were a little girl."

Hedy glances up to see Cora regarding her in the reflection, her mother's eyes wistful, and she feels an appreciative smile pull at her lips. "Styling is a generous word, Mom."

"Not true. You saved me a fortune at the salon."

Hedy arches a brow. As if her mother would have gone otherwise?

But she can't forget how patient her mother was, how she always kept in whatever outrageous hairdo Hedy had dreamed up, however many pins or bows, even agreeing to wear it out of the house. Hedy didn't know many mothers—especially mothers on the Point—who would have forsaken their vanity to avoid hurting their daughters' feelings. Herself included.

She chuckles. "I still can't believe you let me cut your bangs to look like Audrey Hepburn after we saw *Funny Face*."

"And you did a beautiful job."

"Dad didn't think so."

Cora smiles, shrugs. "It grew back."

A few escaped tendrils float down her mother's neck. Hedy tucks them gently into the comb.

"You were going to pin those silk chiffon flowers for your wedding, remember?"

Hedy nods slowly, recalling the quick, plain updo she ended up with instead. So many plans for her wedding that had been altered when Hedy learned she was pregnant. Everything sped up and whittled down. The service at the church, the reception at the club. Standing up there in front of Father Ellison, Hedy had been so nervous, keeping her eyes on the deep indent above Grant's lip, the way dancers are trained to find a spot on the wall when they spin to avoid getting dizzy. Two wrongs surely had to make a right, she kept telling herself as they repeated their vows, her heart pounding with doubt. How someone so good at math could get it so wrong.

Was it any wonder she hadn't dared to try again?

Her mother's comment days before flashes back, that Hedy had never introduced her father to any of her boyfriends after her divorce. Then Tom's suggestion that she was jealous, a possibility Hedy didn't dare linger on, but now can't seem to do anything but.

She lowers her hands from her mother's hair, the rash of remorse flaring down her limbs, and walks to the window. Across the lawn, the tent is a flawless white against the blue sky.

"Dad loved Grant so much, Mom," Hedy says. "He was practically his son-in-law when we were both in diapers. It's like I broke something predestined. No wonder Dad took it so hard when we broke up."

"He took it hard because he loved you," her mother says calmly. "Not because he loved Grant. Your father hurt because you hurt."

"But there was disappointment. Don't pretend there wasn't."

"There was, of course. But you weren't suited, Hedy."

The recently revealed details of her mother's fraught introduction to life on the island return to her, the early chapter of her parents' marriage that Hedy had been spared.

"I always believed you and Dad were suited," Hedy whispers.

"And we were." Cora rises slowly. "No one can really see a marriage except for the two people in it," her mother says as she crosses to the window. "Especially not their child. Your father and I loved each other, Hedy. But there were compromises. There always are. No one person can be everything to someone. I could no more be everything to your father than he could be to me."

"But Max could?" Hedy hears the bite in her tone.

"Of course not," her mother says patiently. "Max is different than your father. I love him for his differences."

Hedy keeps her eyes on the lawn, feeling tears threaten, the need to protect her memories of her father, their life together in this house, so strong her head spins. "When you told me about that summer, about how you and Max met, how hard it was for you here at first . . ." She needs a moment, an extra breath. This next part will be especially hard. "I worried you had been just . . . white-knuckling it all these years with Dad. That you were waiting until you and Max could . . ." Hedy stops, hearing herself and hating how foolish she sounds. She's nearly fifty—so why does she sound like she's fifteen? Her mother accused her of acting like a petulant teenager. Maybe because she has been.

"Never, darling. There was no pining," Cora says. "There was only living."

Hedy nods slowly. "I want to be like Tom, Mom. I want to tell total strangers that my mother is getting remarried and that it's no big deal and I'm so cool about it, but . . ." A tear escapes, landing on her hand where it rests against the sash. Her mother reaches over to dry the spot with her fingertips. "But I'm not ready to see you with someone else, Mom. And I'm afraid it will be a long time before I am."

"Then it will be a long time, sweetheart. All I know is that I don't want to start this new chapter with Max until we're clear with each other."

"We're never clear with each other, Mom." Hedy extracts her hand from under her mother's and walks to the other side of the room. "That's how you and Michelle are. You have that with her. You have it with each other. It's just not who we are."

"Why can't it be?" Cora asks, trailing her. "Because only your father got to have that?"

"I don't know that I knew him as well as I thought," Hedy says, throwing her head back to scan the ceiling.

"I didn't tell you all of that to change your opinion of him, Hedy. They were different times. Uniquely painful, maybe, for us women. When the war came, we were sent to work, appreciated for our efforts, and some of us thrived. But then the war ended and suddenly we were supposed to turn that love off, to trade our ration-free shoes for sling-backs. A real bait and switch. But for you and Michelle, it's not that same world. It's so much easier for you to make your mark on your own terms."

Hedy blows out a sour chuckle. "Don't be so sure." When she turns back to her mother, Cora's face is blank. "Do you know that when I got my most recent headshot, the photographer sent me the estimate for how much the retouching would cost? Not could cost but would—because looking younger isn't an option, it's a requirement. I'm sure that seems like a shallow complaint to you, but it's real for me. You wouldn't understand the pressure I have to stay looking young in this business."

Her mother's face falls.

"Why do you do that?"

"Do what?"

"Assume I can't understand what you're feeling, that I can't possibly relate?" Hedy's mother studies her for a long moment, her pale eyes pooling with confusion, before she pushes out a weary sigh. "Starting this new chapter with Max doesn't mean erasing all the ones that came before it. Doesn't mean they weren't the right paths at the right time . . ." Her mother's eyes hold hers. "He's a good man, Hedy. I hope you'll give him a chance."

"I want to, Mom. Especially now that I know . . ."

"Know what?" her mother presses gently.

"For so many years, I blamed you for not doing more to be like everyone else here. And I feel terrible for that. Because it's so late now."

"Not so late . . ."

Her mother takes her hands. Hedy never realized how similar their fingers are. The same long thumbs. The same small nails.

"I think . . ." Her mother's eyes are welling, too. "Maybe we're only getting started."

* * *

Passing through the great room a few minutes later, Hedy sees movement through the window. Max, dressed in an oatmeal sports jacket and khakis, paces the veranda. While she's been upstairs, someone has opened the double doors and brought out the piano—two of the nice young people who've come from Chowder's to help serve, Hedy suspects. Max stands behind the baby grand, one hand in his pocket, the other tapping at the keys. He hasn't seen her and it would be easy enough to walk past, Hedy thinks, pretend she hasn't seen him either, but something causes her to slow.

What's her rush, anyway?

She feels strangely nervous as she crosses to the door, as if she were the one getting married today.

"Do you play?" she asks.

Max looks up, surprise washing his weathered features for a moment, and then his hooded eyes settle with warmth.

"Nope. Not even 'Chopsticks,'" he says, gently lowering the fall board over the keys. "Nothing more useless than a nervous groom." He chuckles. "I'm just trying to stay out of the way, at this point."

"I'm sorry we haven't had more time to get to know each other, Max. It's been hard getting back here."

"I'm sure. Real estate is round-the-clock."

"I don't just mean because of my work," she says and his eyes light with understanding.

"I'm glad you and Tom have had a chance to get to know each other a little."

Tom. Hedy smiles reflexively, then feels a twinge of remorse, remembering their heated conversation in the liquor store parking lot, their near-silent ride home afterward. Why has she been so determined to find fault in him, to push him away? She can't remember the last time she's ever felt such ease in the company of a man.

Max hitches his chin toward the house. "How's she doing up there?"

"She's almost ready," Hedy says.

"And what about you?"

Max tries to catch her gaze again, and this time Hedy lets him, even as her eyes fill.

"I'm not sure," she says softly, the words coming out like a breath held too long underwater. The relief is so much greater than the fear.

"I understand." And Hedy believes he does. So she lets Max Dempsey hold her gaze an extra moment and something warm shifts against her chest. Something grounding. Something almost familiar.

Her mother is right. His eyes smile even when his mouth doesn't.

* * *

The guests seem to arrive all at once. Hedy is pointing her mother's friend Vincent, the pianist, in the direction of the veranda when Tom recruits her to help with parking. He looks handsome in a crisp white button-down and sky-blue tie. She is inclined to tell him so. She's inclined to tell him other things, too. Like that she's sorry for being so short with him, that he has as much right to be comfortable with this marriage as she has to be uncomfortable with it, and that she can be a hell of a lot of fun when she isn't feeling sorry for herself. But there isn't time. As soon as she steps outside, she nearly collides with Ned Welch coming up the lawn from the driveway.

"Well, look at you." Ned grabs for her before Hedy can respond, clapping both of his damp hands around hers and tugging her in for a kiss on the cheek. "How are you, sweetheart?"

"Fine, Ned," she says tightly. She draws back, but his hands hold on. White whirls of hair sprout from just below his knuckles and continue, undisturbed, over his wrist, shrouding his watch like a stone path buried under weeds.

Her mother's admission floods her.

Ned steps forward, his voice dropping as if he has some great secret to tell her. His breath is hot and edged with wintergreen. "I want to say from the start, I understand this is hard, Hedy. And I'm here for you, all right? We both know this whole thing would absolutely crush your father. And here," Ned says, shaking his head. "At his house."

His words are biting, like an insect sting, and Hedy jerks, tugging her hands free.

"This is my mother's house," she says calmly.

"Well, yes, now that he's gone, but—"

"The daughter of the bride!" Irene Middleton appears beside them with a laugh. "Now there's something you don't hear every day."

Somehow Hedy manages a polite smile in return.

"Lovely day for a wedding, isn't it?" Irene's hair is still bleached but short, swept across her forehead in careful points. She lowers her sunglasses and scans the lawn. "I seem to have lost Phil. I'm sure he'll turn up in time for the meal," she says, testing the backs of her earrings. She tilts her head at Hedy. "Cora said something about lobster?"

Hedy feels the words rush up her throat, too fast to be held back, and why should she?

She only hopes her mother can forgive her.

"Yes," Hedy says, then looks directly at Ned. "Shedders. I understand you're a big fan."

Ned Welch squints at her, blinking rapidly, as if Hedy has startled him with a flashbulb.

Hedy leans in, unable to resist.

"And this has always been my mother's house, too," she whispers low. "Always."

Marching past them and in the direction of the slow stream of cars, Hedy's heart is still pounding so fiercely from the exchange that she doesn't see Tom come beside her.

He touches her elbow. "Everything okay?"

"Everything's great," she says, maybe a little too enthusiastically. "Why?"

"Because you have kind of a wild look in your eyes."

She grins up at him. "Is that a compliment?"

He laughs, taking her cue. "Well, it's not an insult."

36

The four of them are a well-oiled machine.

And why wouldn't they be, Mickey thinks, as she looks up from the sea of shot glasses she is filling with cold cucumber mint soup to scan the busy kitchen: Wes at the stove, shaking a pan of scallops in each hand, his dark hair curling in a cloud of salted steam. Danny pointing the constant stream of servers—Chowder's beloved staff—from one station of dishes to the next. Tiffany at the banquette spooning whitefish ceviche into ramekins almost as fast as the servers can sweep them up and take them out to the tent. Never mind that they've never partnered to feed a dinner of seventy-five before today. Mickey is fairly certain that Beech House's kitchen—*Cora's Kitchen*, she reminds herself with a quick look up at the sign above the sink—has never known so much activity, such a tapestry of fragrances and flavors.

Rounding the island as she pours, Mickey reaches the side closest to Wes at the stove and can't resist leaning back just enough to brush his shoulder with hers. In the glorious, grease-soaked crush of prep, whatever last, loose threads of their challenges back in Baltimore have been absorbed, folded into the crème fraîche, baked into the popovers.

They are, once again, partners.

She spins to the side for a peek at his work. The scallops sizzle in their buttery beer bath, the rising heat mirroring her own racing heart. It's nonstop now, but when the rush is over, she and Wes will pull Tiffany and Danny aside and deliver their proposal with crossed fingers and open hearts.

Mickey's squirreled away a bottle of wedding champagne. Just in case.

"Hi, chef," she whispers, pressing her back against his.

Over his shoulder, he says, "Hi yourself, chef." And she smiles.

"God, I love when you call me that."

* * *

Two hours later, the last of the plates and bowls have been removed from the tables, the cake is cut, and the temporary redwood floor in the middle of the tent is cleared for dancing. Mickey is touring the veranda, picking up abandoned wineglasses and champagne flutes when her mother finds her.

"Dinner was perfection, sweetheart. People are raving."

"You and Tom looked like you were enjoying your meal together," Mickey says.

"He's easy to talk to," is Hedy's short reply, but Mickey sees a pleasurable grin dance at her mother's lips before she turns away. No wonder she seems more relaxed.

Mickey smiles. "Grams looks beautiful, doesn't she?"

"Radiant." Her mother turns to her. "Do you ever wish that I'd gotten remarried?"

Mickey blinks at the question. "What? No," she says. "I mean, of course I worry about you being alone sometimes, but I never wished for it. Never felt like you were missing something. You've always provided for me on your own, always made your own money . . ." She searches her mother's face, her eyes pooling with something that Mickey can only describe as longing. "Is this because of today, or is this about something else?"

Her mother takes both of her hands and grips them as if Mickey's an untethered balloon almost lost to the ceiling. "You know you could never disappoint me, right?"

"Mom, if this is about the restaurant . . ."

"I'm not just talking about the restaurant, sweetheart." Her mother's face is soft, the tight lines that she has worn at the corners of her eyes since she picked Mickey up at the ferry are no longer etched as deeply. She can't remember the last time she saw her mother's face so soft.

They each collect more glasses and step inside. Across the room, a few guests mill around the Wedding Wall, pointing. The object of their interest is a black-and-white photograph of a man and a woman, dwarfed in front of a massive stone fireplace, not so unlike the one where the portrait has lived for all the summers Mickey has been coming back to Beech House. Which is how she recognizes it from so far away.

"Mom? Is that . . . ?"

Her mother nods. "It was Max's idea."

"But I thought the rule was—"

"No more rules," Hedy says. "That, apparently, is the new rule."

They cross to a pair of wing chairs to collect an abandoned highball glass.

"You know, when your grandmother said she and Max wanted to sell, I was actually relieved that I wouldn't have to get used to seeing her with someone other than your grandfather in here, but now . . ." Mickey watches her mother scan the room, waiting. A relaxed smile pulls at her glossed lips. "I think I could have figured it out," Hedy says.

Lately Mickey has thought the same thing.

"Do you think they'll leave the island?" she asks carefully.

Her mother shrugs. "Maybe. But even if they do . . ." She pushes a loose tendril behind Mickey's ear. "You'll always come back here. You belong here, Michelle." A small laugh penetrates her mother's grin. "In fact, don't be surprised after tonight's gorgeous meal if you and Wes get asked to open up a restaurant right here."

"Funny you should say that."

Now it's her mother's turn to wear a quizzical look.

From outside comes the click and sizzle of a PA system being turned on, tested.

"You'll come out for their first dance, won't you?" Hedy asks.

Mickey threads her arm through her mother's. "I didn't know Grams liked to dance."

"I'm realizing I didn't know a lot of things about her."

The confession is quiet, so low that Mickey can't decide if her mother means for Mickey to hear it or not, but she nods in agreement all the same.

37

Despite her mother's theory that most of the guests would make quick exits once the food and cake were gone, Hedy is pleased to see there are still deep clusters of neighbors and friends circling the dance floor when Max leads Cora onto the floor for the first dance. The DJ, a great-nephew of Max's, stands behind his equipment and warm laughter rumbles through the crowd as the poor young man struggles to find the right recording. Another young man bolts out of the crowd to help and soon the familiar strings of "Someone to Watch Over Me" hum loudly. Hedy has no idea why her mother and Max chose it as their wedding song, but not knowing doesn't bother her. She thinks fleetingly of her question to Michelle minutes earlier, how her daughter had looked at her with surprise, but how good it felt to say the words, to put them out into the air. So many conversations she has avoided over the years.

Maybe Hedy's mother isn't the only one starting a new chapter. Maybe they are all just getting started.

Like Cora assured her: Maybe it's not so late.

Hedy returns her attention to the dance floor. She has seen her share of wedding dances and it's usually obvious who is leading and who is following, but watching her mother in Max's arms, Hedy can't tell this time. They move with equal ease, equal purpose, and she wonders fleetingly if it would have been so for her father and her mother if they'd had a proper wedding, instead of the cursory ceremony. An abbreviated celebration much like the one Hedy had with Grant—a symmetry that occurs to her only now. Hedy suspects her father would have led as a dance partner, the way he tried to lead her mother her whole life here on the island, and Hedy feels a pang of grief, not quite sure for who. So instead, she keeps her gaze on the new couple, who are not so new, she reminds herself, as they are joined by others, and decides that's okay, too.

"Want to dance?" Tom arrives, his shirt sleeves rolled up now, the knot of his tie loose and tired, but his gray-blue eyes sparkle playfully.

"Love to."

"We should stick to the edges," he says as she follows him in to the crowd. "I need a lot of space when I dance."

"Should I be scared?"

"With those heels," he says, motioning down to her high pumps. "I'm the one who should be scared."

"I thought architects wore steel-toed shoes," Hedy teases as he circles her waist with one arm and sweeps up her hand with the other.

"Only on job sites."

They sway. She catches a whiff of his aftershave. A little leathery but fresh.

"You're not so bad," she says.

"I'm terrible. My strategy is to keep you moving so much you can't tell."

She leans back into a laugh. He spins her into him, whirls her back out.

"I think everyone pulled together pretty well," he says.

"A team effort, to be sure." She feels the tug of regret. "I'm sorry about earlier, Tom. How rude I was in the car."

"You weren't rude. You were hurt."

His absolution is generous. She feels her fingers relax inside of his. "Yes, but it isn't fair of me to expect you to share my feelings about this marriage and then be cross with you because you don't."

"Just because I'm cracking jokes doesn't mean I don't have mixed feelings, too, Hedy." His eyes hold hers.

"What you said about me feeling jealous—"

"It wasn't my business, or my place."

She shakes her head. "I think I do envy that my mother has taken this second chance and I can't seem to do the same. You were right."

"Well, don't get used to it—it rarely happens." Again he spins her out and draws her back in. "How are you feeling now?"

"Oh, you know. A little old, a little new . . ."

"Borrowed and blue?"

She smiles. "Not so blue, actually."

"Good." Tom glances down. "That's a knockout dress on you, by the way."

"I'm fine, really. You don't have to flatter me," she says even as she feels delighted heat bloom on her neck.

"That wasn't flattery. That was flirting."

"Flirting?" She leans back and blinks at him. "Are you honestly making a pass at me?"

"Only if it's working. Then I absolutely am."

"As of two hours ago, we became related."

"Not by blood."

"You're insane," she says, whirling away from him and returning when he tugs her back.

"I heard the craziest gossip just now. Apparently, some very talented young chefs want to buy Beech House and turn it into a restaurant," he says.

"This island runs on gossip. You can't believe most of it."

"You shouldn't." Tom swings her around.

"Agreed. God knows what they'll be saying about us tomorrow morning. Dancing like this."

"Imagine what they'd say if I kissed you."

Heat flutters in her stomach. Her gaze drops reflexively to his mouth and he smiles.

"They'd probably drop dead," she says, wondering what happened to the sea breeze they were enjoying earlier.

"Good point." His arm tightens around her waist and brings her closer. "Maybe we should break them in easy with a little dirty dancing first."

Before she can contest, he's dipped her backward, so far that she lets go a delighted cry and is still laughing when Tom brings her up again, close enough this time that she can see flecks of brown floating in the gray-blue pools of his eyes. His hand spreads out against her back, a wall of heat across her spine. She leans into it.

"Think you might start coming back here more often again?" he asks.

"Why?" She smiles. "Want to sign us up for dance lessons?"

He grins. "How'd you guess?"

38

The last batch of guests leave in a coffee-colored Cadillac. By
ten thirty, Beech House is theirs alone again. In the kitchen,
Mickey scans the space as if for the first time, not one of the
last, as she feared she would have to start doing just a day
before. Sharing the news of her and Wes's plan had been its
own celebration—knowing that they would be able to keep
Beech House close for another generation, and maybe another beyond that. Tiffany and Danny's reaction had been
just as they'd hoped. Now the real work would begin.

Tomorrow, Mickey thinks as she turns to see Wes walk in
with a bottle of wine. Tonight still belongs to Cora and Max.

"I managed to find us a pinot," he says.

She smiles. The first bottle they ever shared together was
a pinot noir. Consumed at a little bar in the Inner Harbor.
It's more than fitting.

She points to the counter. "The key's in the—"

"Middle drawer," Wes says, already extracting a corkscrew with a decidedly proud grin.

"Look at you. One day and you've learned your way
around this kitchen."

"I'm quick like that." He drives the screw's point into
the cork. A few twists and it comes free with a dull pop.

"This might call for another kind of celebration tonight. Think we could both fit on that twin in your bedroom?"

Mickey opens one of the boxes of the rented stemware and pulls out two fat-bowled wine glasses. "Just warning you," she says as she sets them down in front of him. "These mattresses squeak. *A lot.*"

Wes snickers as he pours. "I went to summer camp. If anyone knows how to get off on a squeaky mattress without making a sound, it's me." He slides a glass toward her. "I got ahold of Lucas."

"What did he say?" Mickey asks carefully. Worried Lucas might say no and break the spell before they could even leave the island, she pressed Wes not to tease the subject until they were back in Baltimore, but he insisted.

"He practically dropped the phone, he was so excited."

"Really?"

"I said we'd talk more when we get back. In the meantime, he's going to reach out to the bank, circle back for a few investors who've shown interest."

It's good news, of course it is, and her amazing staff deserves it, but still Mickey feels a conflicted tug as she slides her fingers around the base of the stem and swirls her wine.

"Maybe we should stay the course, Wes. If you think we could find the resources to start over here then maybe we should just sink that money into Piquant instead of . . ."

But Wes's even, no-nonsense gaze over his glass quiets the rest of her words.

He sets down his wine and leans in. "You and I both know this isn't just about the money. If it were, we could borrow more. This is about where you belong, Mick. And it's not up in that office, pushing papers and balancing books. It's about us doing this together. Every part."

"Then you'd give me a second chance to do it right this time?" she asks. "Even if it means moving here?"

"Even if it means moving to Mars."

She laughs. "I have heard Tex-Mex is blowing up there."

He tips his glass to hers and they drink. The wine is velvety and slightly smoky. She'll definitely save the bottle. It would be perfect paired with his miso salmon. Or maybe a different dish. They'll have to come up with a new menu here. Using local ingredients, of course. Bluefish and scallops. Beach plums and summer squash. Mickey can hardly wait.

"I could get used to this sight." Cora steps into the kitchen, still in her wedding dress.

"That's the idea, Grams."

Mickey's mother is right behind her. "Can anyone join this party?" Her mother's feet are bare and Mickey smiles. Just how much dancing did she and Tom do?

"I want to be clear, Grams," Mickey says when they're all gathered around the island. "We're prepared to pay you whatever you're asking. Between all four of us, we can swing it."

"It's not about the money, sweetheart," Cora says. "Max and I have savings, we'll be comfortable no matter what. I want to be sure—I want you to be sure—that this is what you want. Because I can't let you do this for me."

"We're doing it for all of us." Mickey looks over at Wes. "Or at least we're going to try to. Tiff and Danny are pulling together what they have, and Wes and I are going back to do the same in Baltimore."

"And there's also the small matter of zoning," Wes adds.

"And if we could get permission, it might mean making some changes to the layout in the house," Mickey says carefully, hearing the uneasiness in her voice. In their excitement, the possibility of having to make major structural changes to the house has been conveniently avoided. "I know how protective we all are about keeping this place intact."

"Darling, I had to make peace with that possibility the minute I agreed to put it on the market," her grandmother says. "Knowing it could stay in the family . . . Whatever you have to do, I know it will be perfect."

Her grandmother squeezes Mickey's hands, and Mickey squeezes back. They are still many steps away from making this dream a reality, but their chances are good.

Hedy steals a sip of Mickey's wine. "Tom and Max went out to the tent with cigars and scotch if you're interested, Wes."

"What about me?" Mickey says. "I can't be interested in a cigar and some scotch?"

Her mother's brow rises. "You don't smoke, remember?"

Mickey looks at the ceiling. Grinning, Wes slows on his way past to deliver her a kiss, taking the side door to the lawn.

Just the three of them now, Mickey feels a swell of calm as she looks around the island at her mother and grandmother. At least, that's what she feels right now. Give her a minute, and she'll surely feel something else—relief or maybe longing. So much has happened in so few days, it's no wonder her heart can't keep up. But she'll gladly ride the wave of whatever emotions roll her way. There's so much ahead, she thinks. So much to look forward to.

Mickey used to believe that time stood still at Beech House. For the first time in her life, she's grateful it doesn't.

"I think this calls for a toast," her mother announces, spinning for the fridge.

"Another one?" Cora wrinkles her lips. "Surely there must be some limit on how many toasts a person can make in a day?"

"If there is," Mickey says, "I'm pretty sure wedding days are exempt from the rule."

Her mother roots around for another minute then emerges with a mason jar, three-quarters filled with a familiar watermelon-colored liquid. Mickey smiles. The last of yesterday's pitcher of lobster daiquiris.

"Seems fitting," Hedy says, giving the jar a hard shake. Mickey takes down three juice glasses and sets them on the island, savoring the fragrant cloud that floats up when her mother pours.

Mickey lifts her tumbler and Hedy and Cora do the same, their glasses uniting with a resonant *ting*. They sip slowly, reverentially.

"Not bad," her grandmother says. "Could be stronger, though. I only see one of you."

"Very funny, Mom," Hedy says, but there's a smile when she leans gently against Cora, and it's still there when Mickey's mother lets her head rest briefly on Cora's shoulder.

"Maybe you could put these on your menu," her grandmother says.

Hedy bobs her head approvingly. "Every restaurant needs a signature drink. Speaking of which . . . this restaurant of yours is going to need a name."

True, Mickey thinks. There's so much to do to open a restaurant, so many decisions to make. Having opened her own, she knows well. Some decisions are fraught—like décor and menus. Hiring staff and choosing vendors. But then there are the decisions that are easy. So obvious, such givens, that they can't even be called decisions at all . . .

Mickey lifts her gaze to the carved sign above the sink and smiles.

"I think it already has one."

Acknowledgments

I have no doubt that if writers had to give their thanks in front of a live audience, like at award shows, every one of us would barely be halfway through our list of names before they turned on the music to usher us offstage.

To Christy Fletcher, and the entire team at Fletcher and Company, my deepest and enduring thanks. To my agent and my anchor, Rebecca Gradinger, and her colleague/story wizard, Kelly Karczewski, whose insights and inspiration, constant counsel and support, helped to focus this shape-shifting novel from the very beginning in ways I can only call magic. Despite my best intentions, I know I won't ever be able to thank you both enough.

A book's journey is dependent on the support and talent of so many people on its way to readers' hands, and during every step I am reminded how very lucky I am to call St. Martin's Press my publishing home. To my editor, Alexandra Sehulster, without whose wisdom, guidance, and grace, this book would not have evolved into the novel it wanted to be all along. Thank you for your unerring faith in this story, and for loving these characters and their journeys as much as I do. I'm so proud of the worlds we have built together. My great thanks also to assistant editor, Cassidy Graham and associate publisher, Anne Marie Tallberg, for your help and counsel. To marketing rock stars Marissa Sangiacomo and Brant Janeway, publicists Rebecca Lang and Ciara Tomlinson, and to Hannah Jones, Laurie Henderson, and Janna Dokos in production—a thousand thank-yous! Once again, designer Danielle Christopher has gifted my book with a jaw-droppingly gorgeous cover that I want to transport myself into every time I look at it, and designer Meryl Levavi has made my words look so beautiful on the page. To brilliant copy editor Janine Barlow, who made sure my manuscript didn't go out into the world with spinach in its teeth (or pages)—thank you! And to the entire Macmillan sales team, who do an amazing job of getting my books into readers' hands. My gratitude is immense.

Writing may be a solitary craft but the writing community is anything but. My thanks to those whose generosity of spirit knows no bounds: Jackie Cangro, Christina Clancy, Jackie K. Cooper, Barbara Davis, Trish Doller, Melissa Crytzer Fry, David R. Gillham, Nina de Gramont, Kristy Woodson Harvey, Ann Hite, Meredith Jaeger, Marjan Kamali, Orly Konig, Sally Koslow, Kerry Lonsdale, Jane Porter, Erika Robuck, Carmen Tanner Slaughter, Wendy Wax, Tamara Welch, and Karen White.

Special love always to my very dearest PB Writing Group: Kim Wright, Marybeth Whalen, Joy Callaway, and Kim Boykin. No matter how much distance the map puts between us and our tables, may we always stay in each other's stories.

To A and M, for being so much more than family. We never forget how lucky we are to have one another.

And to I, E, and M. My home, my heart. I love our story best of all.

1. Would you have told Wes the restaurant was in trouble? Did you empathize with Mickey's situation, or do you think you would have handled it differently?

2. Explore the theme of secrets in the novel. Mickey keeps the restaurant's status from Wes and her family in the beginning. Cora has kept the feelings she experienced in the past secret for years. Are there any secrets you've held on to for a long time? Do you feel guilty for holding them, or do you feel it is the right thing to do? Are there differences between the secrets Mickey keeps and the ones Cora does?

3. Hedy is portrayed as the most pragmatic and practical of all three women, yet she is often the most rattled by small situations. How does Hedy's perception of herself clash with her behavior? How does her relationship with her father affect the relationships she has with the rest of her family?

4. Put yourself in Cora's shoes. Would you have stayed at Beech House and tried to make friends? Would you have asked to leave? Would you have felt your feelings for Max were a betrayal of your marriage, or would you have taken things further?

5. A family wedding is a big event that can bring people together, and in this case, it's a celebration for the matriarch of the family. What did you think of Cora getting the chance to experience something that is more typically reserved for those who are younger? Why do you think, as a culture, we reserve certain celebrations for younger generations, and are less inclined to support them as people grow older?

ST.
MARTIN'S
GRIFFIN

6. When Cora arrives at Beech House as a young woman, she doesn't feel at home, in the house or in the community. By the time Mickey is a grown woman, Beech House has become a generational staple for the Campbell women and is an integral part of the future. How does this illustrious, somewhat intimidating house become a home? How does Max's influence on the kitchen help make Beech House a home for Cora? What does home mean to you? Do you think it is a feeling you can grow into over time?

7. Motherhood is a prevalent theme in the novel. What do you think of Cora and Hedy's relationship? Do you attribute a sense of "failure" to either Cora or Hedy for them not being close in adulthood? How does their relationship fulfill some expectations of the mother-daughter relationship, and how does it fall short of what you expected? What suppositions and assumptions do you bring to a mother-daughter relationship, and did the book make you think about them any differently?

8. The past events in this novel very much affect the present. Has anything happened in the past that has had a big effect on your life? Why do you think the ripple effect of events is so strong in this book?

9. The book opens on Mickey with her restaurant, and perhaps relationship, in jeopardy. By the time the novel ends, her future is secure. Do you believe that everything happens for a reason, or that you can be lucky in life with timing? How does that work out for Mickey? Do you think it worked out for Cora?

About the Author

Erika Montgomery Marks

A card-carrying cinephile and native New Englander, novelist ERIKA MONTGOMERY lives with her family in the mid-Atlantic region, where she teaches creative writing and watches an unspeakable amount of old movies. She is also the author of *A Summer to Remember*.